APRONS & VEILS
BOOK TWO

The Pursuit of
Miss Parish

GRACE HITCHCOCK

VALMONT
HOUSE PUBLISHERS

The Pursuit of Miss Parish © 2023 by Grace Hitchcock

Published by Valmont House Publishers

GraceHitchcock.com

All rights reserved. No part of this publication may be reproduced or transmitted for commercial purposes, except for brief quotations in printed reviews, without written permission of the author.

Names: Hitchcock, Grace, author.

Title: The Pursuit of Miss Parish / Grace Hitchcock

Other Titles: the pursuit of miss parish

Series: Aprons and Veils ; book 2

Identifiers: ISBN 979-8-9858217-4-1 Paperback | 979-8-9858217-5-8 Hardback | 979-8-9858217-6-5 Ebook

Subjects: Christian Romantic suspense fiction

All scripture quotations, unless otherwise noted, are taken from the King James Version of the Bible.

This book is a work of fiction. Names, characters, places, and incidents are either products of the author's imagination or used fictitiously. Any similarity to actual people, living or dead, organizations, and/or events is purely coincidental.

Cover design by *Carpe Librum Book Design*

Author is represented by The Steve Laube Agency

MORE FROM GRACE HITCHCOCK:

APRONS AND VEILS SERIES:
THE FINDING OF MISS FAIRFIELD
THE PURSUIT OF MISS PARISH

AMERICAN ROYALTY SERIES:
MY DEAR MISS DUPRÉ
HER DARLING MR. DAY
HIS DELIGHTFUL LADY DELIA

TRUE COLORS SERIES:
THE WHITE CITY
THE GRAY CHAMBER

NOVELLAS:
HEARTS OF GOLD, A HISTORICAL ROMANCE COLLECTION
"THE WIDOW OF ST. CHARLES AVENUE" IN SECOND CHANCE
BRIDES COLLECTION

*For Dakota,
the Texan who stole my heart*

"He shall cover thee with His feathers,
and under His wings shalt thou trust . . .
Thou shalt not be afraid for the terror by night;
nor for the arrow that flieth by day;
Nor for the pestilence that walketh in darkness;
nor for the destruction that wasteth at noonday."

Psalm 91:4-6 KJV

CHAPTER 1

Nearing New Mexico
August 1899

With each breath, the stale air of the train and its malodorous passengers stuck in Belle Parish's lungs. *Am I doing the right thing?* She turned from the soot discolored window to Angelique, but one look at her friend's peaceful slumber, Belle knew she would only make light of their rather frightening situation. *Just remember every kind word Colt wrote in his letters. He shares your faith. How bad could a man be if he believes in the Lord?* Sighing, Belle leaned back on the stiff wooden seat and smoothed out the simple, pale pink skirt that Angelique had lent her for the journey to meet their future husbands for the first time. She tugged on the cream cuffs of her best and only shirtwaist and tried to calm herself by taking deep breaths, but the more air she gulped, the dryer her throat became.

If Angelique had not answered that advertisement in the paper on their behalf, Belle would not be here in the first place. But there was nothing left for her in Charleston. After Miss Fairfield had run away to become a Harvey Girl, life had grown unbearable, and she had been forced to quit the only position she had ever known. What else could a maid without a job do in the Wild West but follow through with the plan and marry? She shifted in her seat and tried to breathe in the air from the small opening in the train window, but the sun was melting her under her borrowed skirt, and, unlike her beloved city, there wasn't any dampness in the air to compensate for the heat. It was just plain hot.

Parched, Belle avoided the gaze of the overly chatty woman in the seat behind them and wobbled down the swaying aisle to the communal bucket of water. Using the dipper, she trickled water into one of the tin cups and slowly returned to her seat, careful not to spill her drink. She sniffed it, her nose wrinkling. Taking the tiniest sip of the musty liquid, she fought to keep from gagging, but her thirst was not satiated. She pinched her nose and gulped a mouthful. Gunshots rent the air.

The passenger car erupted in screams as the train lurched, the wheels screeching and flinging Belle onto the floor of the car, her cheek striking the edge of a seat. She lifted herself on her elbow to rush to Angelique's side, but an elderly gentleman near her pressed a hand to her shoulder.

"Stay down. They may fire into the car, Miss," he whispered, his leathery wrinkled hands shaking.

"I have to get to her!" She crawled as quickly as she could manage in her long skirts to Angelique's side, clutching her friend's hand when the sound of the car door opening accompanied by the jingling of spurs chilled her to her core.

A broad-shouldered man masked behind a scarlet bandana strode through the door, the barrel of his gun catching in the afternoon sun.

"Everyone keep your hands where I can see them. Your valuables are worth more to me than your life, so toss your jewels into my hat and we won't have no trouble."

And if one does not possess any valuables? What then? She swallowed, not wanting to know the answer as the bandit roamed down the aisle, the frightened passengers dropping the contents of their wallets and reticules into the man's hat.

"B-but my husband's—"

"I don't care. Drop in that gold locket."

The woman bent with time gripped the locket at her chest. "You would take a widow's last link to her husband?"

For his answer he reached out and snapped the chain from her neck, dropping it without ceremony into his hat before striding to the next passenger.

Angelique trembled, and Belle wrapped her arm over her shoulders, tucking her head into Angelique's as the man drew closer, praying for deliverance.

The boots paused in front of Belle. "Well, what do you have for me, ladies?" He nudged Angelique's hand with his foot. "A pretty ruby ring, perhaps?"

Belle jerked up, sitting back on her heels, glaring at the man. She couldn't tell from his mask, but from the crinkling of his eyes, she could guess he was laughing at her anger. He squatted down to them, jangling the hat before them, his stench of sweat and tobacco causing the musty water to churn in her belly.

"Put something in the hat, ladies. One can't expect to ride this train for free." He nodded to Angelique's hand.

"It's from my fiancé." Angelique whimpered.

His hand rested on his gun belt. "I'm sure he'll buy you a new one."

Belle rested her forehead against Angelique's, whispering, "Rudy cares for you more than any ring."

As Angelique drew it off, the bandit turned to Belle. "And what about you?"

"Time to go." Another masked man stood at the back of the train car, his Stetson pulled low enough to shield his eyes from her.

The bandit with the scarlet bandana shook his hat in front of Belle. "Last one."

"Let's go!" The second man shouted as a shot sounded from outside the car, the travelers wincing as the bandits bolted for the backdoor and leapt on their horses, riding away.

The travelers scrambled to their feet, mothers comforting their crying children as the men gathered, ensuring that all was safe.

"I can't believe he took my ring. Oh Belle, what will Rudy say?" Angelique sobbed as she and Belle lifted themselves to their seats.

Belle patted her friend's back. "I'm certain he will understand, and if he doesn't, you don't need to be marrying him."

A giant of a man strode into the train car, his vest pulling tight against his muscled chest as he rested his hands on the guns at his hips. His piercing gaze meeting Belle's for a moment as he strode down the aisle, asking after the bandits, the name of the gang flitting through the air. The Death Riders.

"Ladies and gentlemen, I'm Texas Ranger Reid. I have been tracking the Death Riders, which is how I managed to interrupt their robbery. The Riders wounded one of the operators, but he is stable. Please rest assured that the danger has passed, and the law will do their utmost to see your lost items returned. I need to speak with the conductor and operators, but as soon as the train gets moving, I will be in the first car, conducting interviews and taking an account of all lost. Please form a line, and I will endeavor to speak to you all before we reach your destination."

After an hour of Belle comforting Angelique, and angry storm clouds filled the sky, the train was finally underway. Belle was never happier for the burst of soot from the engine to fill the air as the wheels churned, pulling them away from the bandits and danger. The conductor lit a handful of lamps along the train car before moving to the next as rain pelted the windows. With a sigh, Belle closed their window, as did the rest of the passengers. The air would be unbearable shortly.

"I'll be back as soon as he records the loss of my ring." Angelique rose, clutching her reticule as she hurried up the aisle, muttering to herself.

To calm herself after the horrible ordeal, Belle retrieved the tin cup she had dropped under a seat in the chaos, refilled it, and retrieved the letters from her carpet bag under the seat. She unfolded Colt's second letter for the hundredth time. The black and white picture slipped into her waiting fingertips. She turned it over and stared into the dark eyes of a striking cowboy. Belle admired her future husband's chiseled jawline, her eyes skimming down to his plaid shirt that accentuated his broad, muscled shoulders. She smiled at the way his blond hair curled at the ends and bit her lip, still astonished he was so attractive. She glanced over her shoulder to find the prying woman had fallen asleep on her husband's shoulder. Belle held the letter up to the swaying lantern hanging from the baggage rack.

Dear Miss Parish,

The land here is as rich and picturesque as any English castle you read about in storybooks. I know you're probably wondering why I've requested a mail-order bride, and it's a natural question. You see, I've been in Las Vegas for about three years, but I've been too busy building my ranch and don't have much time for courting. My friend, Rudy, suggested I join him on sending in a request to the matchmaking agency. He figured that if we did our courting through letters, we'd be less likely to put our foot in our mouths.

I've got a nice ranchero, a good piece of land, and a solid head of cattle, but it's lonely out here, and what good is having a ranch if there's no one to share it with and no one to dream with me? If you are willing to live in the "Wild" West, please continue writing me. If given the chance, I will strive every day to make you the happiest woman alive.

Sincerely,
Colt Lawson

BELLE SLOWLY TUCKED the letter inside the envelope, reached for her carpetbag, and retrieved the old cigar box that had been her father's, setting the packet of letters inside. She lifted her mother's yard of lace and trailed her finger over the intricate design. It wasn't much, but Mother had always promised Belle that she could wear it on her wedding day. She wound her father's pocket watch and held it in the palm of her hand, the watch fob that ended in her mother's plain silver wedding band dangling through her fingers and swaying with the train. She closed her eyes, letting the gentle ticking take her back to sitting on her father's knee, reading her parents' small, worn Bible that she carried yet. She stroked the cover and longed to hear the sound of her father's voice reading passages of scripture. She couldn't remember much about her parents, save the absolute knowing that she had once been loved and cherished. *Perhaps with Colt, there's hope of having that again.*

The conductor strode through the car door and shouted, "Las Vegas! Next Stop!"

Angelique charged down the aisle behind the man, her green eyes flashing toward Belle. "Las Vegas? That line took an eternity. I have to freshen up for Rudolph!" She whipped out her handkerchief and dipped it into Belle's tin cup as she muttered something about first impressions and how vital they were.

"I was going to *drink* that." Belle complained. Sighing, she surrendered the cup to her friend's ministrations. "You look fine."

"Only fine? That ranger didn't even get through seven passengers' stories before the conductor began warning the car of our impending arrival, leaving me precious little time to visit the women's lavatory to freshen up." Angelique patted her neck and flushed cheeks with the damp cloth before fluffing her frizzled blonde fringe. She scowled at the smudges of dust on her handkerchief and shoved it in her reticule. Standing, she steadied herself with one hand on the seatback and retrieved her carpet bag from the baggage rack. "I hope Rudy is able to see beyond my disheveled state long enough for us to wed." She rustled to the lavatory with her bag thumping against her hip to change into the darling mint green skirt and white silk shirtwaist that she had purchased for meeting Rudolph for the first time. She had wisely chosen to wait until the last moment to change while Belle had chosen to change at the last stop . . . and then the robbery occurred.

Figuring there wasn't much she could do about her dirtied skirt with only having her serviceable navy suit to change into that Miss Fairfield had given her last year, Belle turned to the window. The rain lifted, leaving behind a fog to roam over the foothills that melted into glorious mountains beyond. It was so unlike her beloved Charleston with its enchanting breezes rolling off the bay. Being a maid to the Fairfields had been a wonderful position . . . until Miss Fairfield was forced to run away to avoid a marriage with that terrible businessman her parents thought was a suitable match for her.

She sighed, missing her city and the bay, but with no loving family desiring her presence, what was the point of enduring the snide remarks from her aunt? Aunt Suzanne had thought Belle was reaching above her station when she was promoted from a scullery maid to being the lady's maid to Miss Fairfield due to her friendship with the young lady. Aunt had never forgiven her for it. Since Miss Fairfield's departure, working under her aunt had grown unbearable. Her ribs still ached in cold weather.

"There it is! Las Vegas, New Mexico." Angelique dropped her carpetbag onto the opposite wooden bench, pressing her hand to the windowpane, her darling gown spotless.

Belle's stomach clenched. "It's so small." Catching a glimpse of her reflection in the window, she groaned—at least her cheek wasn't bruised from her fall. She adjusted her ancient chapeau. *Maybe I should have used some of my savings for a new hat. It was kind of Angelique to lend me her skirt, but what will Colt think when I have to give it back to her and I have nothing but my very worn blue dress and navy suit? Maybe I should've gotten the shirtwaist with the puffed sleeves and canary yellow skirt.*

Angelique sank onto the bench and pressed her hands against the window, squinting to make out the figures on the platform. "Oh my. This will be quite the change after the hustle and bustle of Charleston." She pulled away and seized Belle by the hand, squeezing tighter and tighter at every turn of the slowing wheels. "This is it. There's no turning back now." Angelique's freckles stood out on her nose. "What if Rudolph doesn't think I'm pretty? What if he thinks that I don't look anything like the picture I sent him, and he wants his ring back and I don't have it to give him?"

Belle patted down Angelique's wild bangs. "He'd be the fortunate one to have a wife such as yourself. You are smart, sweet, *and* beautiful. The picture didn't capture even half of your beauty because you are lovely inside and out." She swallowed, thinking how her aunt had taken one look at Belle's photograph and declared that the wide-eyed girl in the picture looked nothing like Belle and he would reject her the moment she arrived. She shook her head. *Suzanne is gone from my life. I can't let her have power over me anymore.*

Angelique pulled Belle into a quick embrace as the train came to halt at the station, steam spouting out from behind the wheels and hiding anyone waiting on the platform. "Thank you, Belle. I don't think I would've had the courage to do this without you."

"You could have fooled me." Belle laughed. "And here I was thinking I was the only one with doubts."

She released a nervous giggle. "Oh no. I'm frightened near to death. All that stuff I said in the kitchen in Charleston was just to get you to come with me to give me the courage to escape too." Angelique fanned herself with her hand, sending the pale blue feather plume on her chapeau twirling. "I can't think about it anymore or I'll start sweating, and it wouldn't do for Rudolph to see me all red and my undersleeves damp." She retrieved a clean handkerchief from her sleeve and patted her upper lip and forehead.

Belle tugged on her kid gloves, which she had saved from Mrs. Fairfield's waste bin and cleaned until the ink spot was almost invisible. *Lord, please help me,* she prayed, steeling herself for an awkward first meeting. Grasping the broken wooden handle of her carpetbag, Belle followed Angelique to the car door. She placed her shaking hand on the rail and viewed the platform as the steam lifted. She flinched at a loud clanging. At the furthest edge of the platform a man dressed in a black suit was hitting a gong with a wooden mallet as he shouted, "This way folks to the Harvey House! Get a hot meal that's the real deal!"

The girls stepped down onto the brick walkway that marked the station, the stench of horses and mud at once assailing her nostrils. Two men approached them with Stetsons in hand, the broad shouldered one with a coiled braided bullwhip on his gun belt and a shorter, round man with a rather limp bouquet.

The short man with the flowers stared at Angelique. "Miss Chauvin?" His forehead beaded with sweat as he waited for her to speak.

"Rudolph?" Angelique tentatively stepped forward, eyes brightening.

He grinned, revealing a gap in his front two teeth that Belle thought made him look kindly, but it seemed his picture must have been taken a few pounds ago.

He gave Angelique a small bow and thrust the wildflowers forward. "We heard about the hold up. It was a relief the telegram from the rangers stated that all were safe. I am mighty sorry it happened. But rest assured, Ranger Reid is the best Texas Ranger alive. He will catch those bandits eventually. Circumstances aside, it's a pleasure to finally get to meet you," Rudolph added, his tone disjointed as if the formality of his words hindered his tongue. Rudolph Smith extended his arm to Angelique, and the man Belle assumed to be Colt Lawson stepped forward.

Belle glanced through her long lashes to capture a glance of the towering man. His blond hair was combed neatly back, but a curl had escaped and caressed his forehead in a most becoming fashion, as if it wasn't used to being combed so and refused to behave. His dark brown eyes captured hers, sending her heart to fluttering as she waited for the most beautiful man she had ever seen to introduce himself. Her cheeks flushed at her thoughts as she took in his complexion, which was bronzed from years in the saddle.

He gave her a small bow, as if unsure of the proper greeting. "It's a pleasure to finally meet you, Miss Parish. You weren't hurt in the ordeal, were you?"

She shyly curtsied, the concern in his tone warming her. "It's nice to meet you too, Mr. Lawson," she managed to squeak out. *Get control of yourself. Certainly, he is handsome, but don't let him think you are a mouse. A potential rancher's wife needs to project strength.* "I am well. It will take more than a few bandits to scare me."

"Thank the good Lord for that. Please, call me Colt." The left side of his mouth quirked upward into a charming half smile. "You are even lovelier in person. Every day, I thought of how radiant your wide eyes were in your picture, but now that I know they are a deep blue . . ." Colt shook his head as if at a loss for words. "Breathtaking."

Her heart flipped as she dipped her head, unused to flattery. Not knowing what to say, she replied, "Thank you." *Very good work, Belle. Highly engaging.*

He offered her his arm as Rudy and Angelique made their way down the platform. Belle shyly slid her arm through his as he continued, "I hope you find Las Vegas meets your expectations. I knew from your letters and your picture that you were a lady." His brows lowered to a point. "I only hope you aren't disappointed in what you see, especially after what those bandits put you through. The Death Riders are a plague in the West."

Belle glanced across the platform and took in the grand building with two wings jutting forward to create a sort of courtyard with a massive live oak in the center. Above the tree rose a tower, declaring it to be the Castañeda Hotel. From what she could see beside it, the town continued down the way with small buildings, dusty sidewalks, and more scraggly looking trees. Besides the live oak, nothing looked like home. She thought of the bustling city she left behind . . . of her brother and his sharp-tongued wife and determined to make the best of it. There was nothing to return home to. In Charleston, the city was so vast it was difficult to make friends, but in this small town, perhaps she could have a better life—one filled with friendships, love, and joy. "I am certain I will come to love it here."

"I was mighty happy, as well as surprised, when Rudy and I received Miss Chauvin's telegram saying that you both accepted our hands and were already on your way. We thought our brides wouldn't be coming until Christmas."

Belle fought to ask what had been tormenting her the entirety of the journey. "Is it too soon? Should we have waited?" She looked back at the train. Even if she could return home, she didn't have the funds and no place to work.

"No, no. I like that. I like a woman who knows her mind." He took the carpetbag from her. "Is this all that you brought with you?"

"I packed light." *Because I had nothing left to pack, but you don't need to know that quite yet.*

"Well, if you ever find you have need of anything, Rudy, as you know, owns the mercantile now. The man who used to run it didn't keep much of anything for ladies, so all the women shopped at *Jones' General Store*, but now Rudy is giving the other store a little healthy competition. I think with Angelique's help, he will be able to give women exactly what they want on his shelves," Colt commented as he led her down the platform, following Angelique and Rudolph to a nearby wagon. "He's calling it *Rudy's Mercantile*." He chuckled. "Not very original, right? Anyway, I have credit there, and you can get anything you want. Just put it under my name, and I'll settle the bill at the end of every month."

He is certainly generous and talkative. She smiled up at him, hoping to put him at ease as she recalled him writing that he talked a lot when he was nervous. "Thank you. I appreciate your kindness."

"I know you are used to providing for yourself, but you're to be my wife, and I want to take care of you," Colt replied with a shy smile. He cleared his throat as he easily lifted her carpetbag into the bed of a waiting wagon. "We thought that you ladies might have some trunks, so that's why we brought the wagon." He turned to Rudolph. "Guess we didn't need the wagon after all, huh, Rudy?"

Rudolph laughed nervously as he settled Angelique's two

satchels in the wagon bed. "Colt and I thought that before we all get hitched, you ladies might want a bite to eat? As you can see, we got us a fine hotel owned by the Harvey House, and it makes for pretty good eating."

"What a lovely idea, Rudolph," Angelique's cheeks flushed with excitement. "We haven't had anything decent since we left Charleston."

"Really? There are Harvey Houses along the way." Colt's brows rose.

"We were saving our funds," Belle interjected. "We packed some food for the journey."

Colt nodded, but she could tell he was surprised that even the Harvey House's fair prices were too much for them. "Well, then. Let's consider this our wedding feast."

Relieved she needn't bind herself quite just yet to Colt, Belle agreed and gratefully followed them past the doorman into the Castañeda Hotel, a delightful, savory aroma greeting her. She glanced every which way for Miss Fairfield. Her last letter had told them of her engagement to Mr. Carver Ashton and of their impending marriage in October. Her heart ached for a glimpse of her dear lady.

"The lawmen are on high alert. I don't want you to think this sort of thing happens all the time in the West." Colt said as they paused at the dining room threshold.

Has he been talking about the robbery again this whole time? "Doesn't it?" She teased.

A girl dressed in a high collar black dress wrapped in an over large crisp white apron and topped with a white bow perched in her pinned-up hair greeted them. "Good evening, my name is Miss Harriet, and I will be your waitress today." The curvy blonde showed them to a small table for four in the corner of the room. "Do you know what you would like to order?" Miss Harriet asked as they took their seats.

Colt grinned at the waitress in a familiar fashion. "I know what I want, but I think the ladies may need a moment as this is their first time here. I'll wait until they are ready to place the food order, but I think it is safe to say coffee all around please."

"Of course. Welcome ladies and I hope you find your experience enjoyable." Miss Harriet smiled and left the menus with them before hurrying back to her other tables.

Belle felt Colt's gaze on her shaking hands as she gripped her menu, discreetly looking over the top, searching for the sight of her lovely former employer. It was difficult to imagine Sophia Fairfield bustling from table-to-table waitressing. Perhaps she had the day off?

"You okay there, little lady?" He placed a finger on the top of her menu. "Do you need some water?"

Belle's gaze darted to the dining room doors. *Stop it. You are not going to run. Smile! Act natural.* "I-I am fine. Why do you ask?"

"Because it's almost a hundred degrees in here and you are trembling like a leaf in a windstorm."

"I'm only a little nervous," she admitted as she focused on placing the giant dinner napkin over her pink skirt.

He chuckled. "Me too. I would wonder if you *weren't* nervous, Miss Parish."

Belle blushed. *I'm sure he meant that to ease me, but how improper of him to insinuate such a thing.* She attempted to select something from the menu before Colt could ask her another question, but with the arrival of Miss Harriet with the coffee pot, Belle couldn't help but notice the comfortable way Colt chatted with the waitress. *Is he flirting with her? Or are they old friends? Why would he ask for a mail-order bride when this house is run by single, attractive women? It just doesn't make any sense to me. Is there a reason none of them wanted to court him?* Perhaps she was overthinking and being sensitive because of her situation. She focused once more on the menu, but the humming of the restaurant and the constant flash of the black and white skirts of waitresses darting from table to table, filling orders, kept distracting her. Sighing, she set aside the menu. *I'll just have whatever Angelique is ordering.*

Harriet turned her wide smile to Angelique, which Belle thought looked plastered on to disguise her fraying nerves. *She looks like she is doing the work of three people.* Belle noticed that while most of the tables had two girls working them, there were three tables with only one girl serving.

"And you, Miss?" Harriet's eyes were pinned on her, pencil poised above the pad.

She snapped to attention. "Oh, I'll have the same as Angelique."

Harriet jotted it down. "Very good. I'll have your salads out in just a moment and your meal out in ten minutes."

Belle sipped her coffee, instantly comforted by the strong brew. *I can do this.* As Angelique and Rudy were whispering away to one another, oblivious to the rest of the world, she turned to Colt, giving him a smile. "I enjoyed reading your letters. They helped me get through some particularly rough days with Suzanne."

"And I read yours over and over again," Colt whispered as Harriet brought the plates of salad, "imagining what life would be like when you finally arrived. And now, here you are, and I don't have to imagine anymore."

Harriet bent and placed the salad before Belle, her back to Colt. Out of the corner of her eye, Belle caught Colt's gaze straying to Harriet's backside, widening, and bouncing away. *It seems I'm not imagining things after all.* But, as Harriet served Angelique and turned her back towards Belle, she noticed that the waitress appeared to have sat in something, which looked like whipped cream, stark against her black uniform. Belle bit back a giggle of relief.

While famished from the long days on the train, Belle's frazzled nerves kept her dry throat from enjoying the perfectly flaky buttermilk biscuits without more coffee. She craned her neck looking for Harriet and then decided it was probably for the best because even though their table wasn't served quite as quickly as everyone else's, at least the delay in service gave her a few more fleeting minutes before their nuptials.

Dinner passed without another cup of coffee, and her almost full plate was whisked away by Harriet and replaced with a sweet. Harriet gasped, noticing Belle's cup for the first time. "Oh, I'm so sorry. I never do this. We usually have more girls on staff so things like this don't happen. Please accept your dinner on the house for your inconvenience."

"Ahh, don't worry about it, Harriet. We won't complain to the management," Rudy whispered to Harriet loud enough for the whole table to hear as she refilled the cups.

"It's really quite all right," Belle added, not wishing for the exhausted waitress to be so hard on herself. She well knew the pressures that came with serving and the embarrassment of missing a step.

"Thank you, but I *am* the management and it's unacceptable for a customer's cup to ever dwindle down to the dregs. If one of my staff had allowed this to happen, I would've offered you the same reparation." Harriet turned on her heel, whisking away to see to the next task.

Belle looked down at the huge piece of apple pie, which was triple the portion of a normal slice. She stabbed her fork into it, admiring how the crust was a perfect golden brown, and took a bite—the sweet, soft tang bursting in her mouth. She closed her eyes and sighed.

"I see you enjoy sweets."

Belle snapped her eyes open and blushed under Colt's lopsided smile as Harriet returned with the coffee pot and topped off Belle's cup. She nodded her thanks. "I have a particular fondness for chocolate, but truly, who doesn't?"

"If you love chocolate, you have to try their cake. Miss Harriet, could you please bring a slice of your chocolate cake for Miss Parish? She can't leave here without trying it."

"I couldn't possibly eat another bite." Belle set down her fork as if to prove her point.

"Well, I shall have some then and if you wish to have a bite once you see it, I'll gladly give you a sample. I'll take one slice, Miss Harriet." Colt sent Belle a wink.

Uncomfortable with his ease toward Miss Harriet, she turned to Angelique, but she and Rudy's heads were bent together again, whispering. Dabbing her mouth with the oversized napkin, she noticed a Harvey Girl with lush red whisps escaping her bun kept glancing her way.

"This is Miss Parish?" The waitress commented as she approached their table with a brilliant smile directed at Colt. "*She's* your mail-order bride, Colt?" Her jaw dropped as she looked back at Belle. "And you thought she was going to be homely if she was desperate enough to answer your advertisement."

Belle choked on her coffee, the hot brew burning her nostrils and making her eyes sting.

Colt scowled, his cheeks reddening. "Why, Miss Dolly, I never said any such thing."

Angelique reached under the table and squeezed Belle's trembling hand.

Miss Dolly laughed. "Whatever he said, Miss Parish, I know he is mighty relieved that you are a true beauty. Mr. Lawson comes in here every Saturday morning on his way to the general store, the post, or station, and I've overheard him voice that particular concern to Rudy on multiple occasions as they sat reading and discussing their future brides' letters."

"Being in our situation, I'm certain we have *all* spoken our concerns about our intended's appearance and personality." Angelique laughed nervously, attempting to make light of Dolly's comment as Harriet brought out Colt's cake and refilled Belle's cup. "That cake looks divine. I'll take one too please, Miss Harriet. Afterall, it is our wedding day, and cake should be had."

Belle wrapped her hands around her coffee cup, praying she would make it through this trying dinner. Spots lined her vision. She needed fresh air, or risk fainting in the middle of the restaurant. Belle motioned for Harriet to come closer, intending to ask where the lavatory was located, but Harriet must not have seen her signal as she went back to the kitchen for Angelique's order.

Miss Dolly bent down beside her. "Yes, Miss Parish, may I help you?"

Belle whispered her need. Colt's reddening ears betrayed that he overheard, but he kept his full attention on his cake.

"Follow me." She held the back of Belle's wooden chair and led her out the door and around to the side of the Harvey House where the guest outhouses were located. Dolly touched her elbow, stopping her. "Miss Parish, I know you don't know me, and I'm not certain if I should even be telling you this, but I think it is only fair to warn you."

Belle turned to Dolly, her breath catching. "Warn me about what?"

"Colt. He's not the marrying kind of man. He showed up to town about three years ago to start up a ranch with his brother, Grant, who lasted about a week before returning to San Antonio. Whenever Grant is in town, he is always at the saloon and Colt is never far behind him."

"Oh?" Belle discreetly ran her palms over her sleeves, wiping away the sweat.

Dolly glanced over her shoulder, ensuring they were alone. "I see young girls all the time give up too early on their career as a Harvey Girl and marry the first guy to come along. I was almost one of them." She placed her hand on Belle's arm. "I only thought you should know Colt doesn't come from a shining past and maybe that's why he wrote for a mail-order bride in the first place. More importantly, I wanted you to know I overheard that he never intended on marrying you."

"What?" Her chest seized.

"This is just hearsay." Dolly lifted both her palms out to her. "You have to realize that. Just hearsay. I would *never* repeat gossip *except* if it was to perhaps warn an innocent woman who just met him. You may want to get to know him in person before *marrying* him. His brother, Grant, came in here on his way out of town last month and he was saying *he* placed the advertisement for Colt as a jest, wanting to see what could make a woman so desperate that she would marry a stranger, and dared Colt to reply to your letters."

Belle ran the back of her hand against her cheek, her vision swimming. *But his letters sounded so genuine, so raw. How could he fake that? What am I going to do, Lord?*

"On one of my night shifts, I saw Colt passing around a particularly personal letter from you. The men at the table were hooting with laughter." Dolly smoothed her apron. "If I were you, I'd hear it straight from the horse's mouth. Don't take the word of Grant, or me, but confront Colt and make certain it isn't true. You're a beautiful woman, and I'd hate to think that the only reason he's marrying you now is because of that fact."

"Thank you for warning me." She cupped her cheeks and moaned. "What am I going to do if it turns out to be true? What other option do I have if I don't marry him?"

Dolly shrugged. "I don't know what experience you have, but we are very short of staff at the moment, and I know they made an exception once before to have a girl trained here instead at the headquarters in Kansas, so you could try to apply for a job here. I'm sure Miss Harriet would be happy for the help as that same girl just up and left us a few days ago when she wasn't supposed to marry until October."

"Marry in October?" *Is that why I haven't seen Miss Fairfield?* Her stomach twisted. "It wouldn't happen to have been a lady named Sophia, would it?"

Dolly gasped. "You *know* her? Why, that would be recommendation in itself! Our Sophia was quite the diligent worker, even if it took her a little longer to catch on to our system."

"Thank you. I'll think on it." Belle hurried into the outhouse where she lost what little dinner she had managed to swallow. *Miss Fairfield is gone?* She leaned her head against the thin planked door, trying to still her racing heart. She should have written to her friend. She should have prepared better than to have snuck a peek at Sophia's first letter to the Fairfields and jumped on the next train, seeing it as a sign of God's blessing on her potential marriage. *Lord, how am I going to get out of this mess? Can I trust this woman I just met, or should I trust the man I have only known through his letters . . . if he even wrote them?* The stench pressed her to leave.

With a sigh, she dug out her worn handkerchief and

cleaned up as best she could before returning to the front porch of the Harvey House and sank into one of the rocking chairs, praying while she waited for the others to finish their desserts.

The front door swung open and the group spilled out, Colt looking eagerly about for her. Belle rose to join them, offering Angelique a smile.

Angelique took Rudy's arm. "I suppose it's time. Are you ready, Belle?"

Not at all. Belle's heart shrank back as Colt offered his arm to her once more, but she slipped her hand through his arm and the couples strolled down to the end of Main Street to the pretty little blue chapel beside a field of wildflowers that called to her. There may not be a bay in Las Vegas . . . but there was another sort of calming beauty with the foothills in the distance and the wildflowers covering the land. Her breath hitched as she climbed the steps. This was it. She had to make up her mind now or be bound to this man forever.

"You must be Miss Chauvin," the preacher greeted the ladies with a smile and stuck out his hand to Rudy. "Rudy has told me so much about you over *several* Sunday dinners. I'm Andrew Martin." His gaze swept over Colt and Belle. "Why, Colt, I didn't know you had sent for a bride as well."

Belle's eyes jerked to meet Angelique's. In his letters, he specifically stated he attended church with Rudy. If he did, wouldn't the preacher know about the mail-order bride? If he lied about attending church, what else had he lied about?

The preacher nodded to Belle. "Hopefully, now that you are taking a wife, I'll be seeing more of you on Sunday mornings like Rudy. It's important for a man to raise his family in church."

With those words, any hope for a future with Colt Lawson completely melted away as doubt coated every letter he had ever penned her. She had thought she might be able to dismiss what Dolly had said, but she couldn't dismiss this outright lie.

CHAPTER 2

*H*er fingers trembled in his as they stood before the preacher. Colt hadn't planned on marrying her. Grant was the one who started it all and even answered her letter that first time, beginning their courtship. When he dropped the small packet of letters atop Colt's dinner plate in the Harvey House, guffawing all the while, the men jeering, Colt was enraged at Grant's making fun of an innocent girl and made up his mind at once to end the farce. But after Colt read Belle's letters . . . he felt something in his heart shift that allowed the longing he kept buried deep within to break through the hardened soil. A surge of protection for Belle filled his being. His stern warning to the men silenced the mockers. There was some merit to being a Lawson brother.

And Lord help him, when Colt beheld the petite beauty stepping down from the train, he felt in danger of heat stroke. He stole a glance at her—such a pretty little thing. Why on earth would she need to go west for a husband?

"Shall we begin with you two?" The preacher looked expectantly at Rudy and Miss Angelique.

Rudolph held his hand out to Angelique, and, with a shy smile, she accepted his hand and Colt watched as his best friend bound himself in holy matrimony.

"I now pronounce you man and wife." He smiled at the newlyweds. "May God bless you and keep you."

Rudolph bent and gave Angelique's trembling hand a tender kiss. "He already has."

Angelique rewarded him with a radiant smile before turning and embracing Belle. "I did it! I'm Mrs. Rudolph Smith." She looked back at her husband and giggled. "Mrs. Rudy Smith."

"Congratulations, Mrs. Smith." The preacher gestured to Belle and Colt. "Will you both please come stand in front of me?"

Colt grasped her elbow as gently as he knew how and stepped forward, but Belle kept her feet firmly planted, pulling away. "Miss Belle?" He leaned down and whispered, "Is there a problem? Do you need a moment?"

"You lied about attending church here regularly." Belle yanked her arm out of his grasp with surprising strength for one so tiny and charged out the front doors, Colt on her heels. "I can't marry a man I don't trust."

He kept himself from jerking back from the hurt in her tone... even if her instincts were right not to trust him. He lifted his palms up and slowly approached as he would with one of his frightened horses. "It was one detail out of many, many truths in my letters, and I can explain it." He looked to the open church door. "The preacher can vouch for my character. I may not make it to church every single month... or quarter, but he knows I'm not a bad man." *Not anymore.*

Belle crossed her arms. "Going to church is not the point. The point is that you should've been honest with me."

"Maybe I exaggerated a bit, but everything else I said after

Grant's first letter was true." He gritted his teeth. He probably shouldn't have mentioned his no-good brother.

"So, Dolly was right. Your brother was the one behind the letters and not Rudy, correct?" Her eyes flickered with a pain that cut him. "That's another lie, Colt. You are up to two. Is there another you'd like to confess?"

"It started as a lie, but Rudy is one of my best friends in town and when he found out we both had mail order brides, we would meet up and talk about you both." He dipped his head but forced himself to meet her gaze. She deserved to know the truth. "Even if I did alter a few truths, there is one that needs no alteration. I came to-to love you."

"Love does not lie." A tear trickled down her lovely cheek as she picked up her skirts and bolted down the church steps.

She sank into the patchy grass and rested her back against the rough bark of the scraggly tree. Belle covered her face with her hands, trying to have an ounce of privacy while she regained her composure. What had she done in leaving her lovely Charleston? Her position? When she had first begun writing Colt, she hadn't even known where Miss Fairfield had gone, and when the Fairfields received her message only days ago saying she was in Las Vegas, Belle had thought it was God's direction, but to arrive to discover that Miss Fairfield had departed . . . "Lord, where are You in all of this? What am I to do?"

Angelique's slim hand rested on her shoulder as she sank down beside her. "Belle? What's wrong? This isn't simply a case of nerves."

Belle dropped her hands, drawing in a full breath that

turned into a hiccup. "Dolly, a girl at the Harvey House, warned me about Colt."

"But you're a perfect stranger to her. Why would she even care about warning you?"

"Exactly. What does she have to gain from giving me false information? How can I, in good conscience, disregard her warning and not take it into careful consideration? And you heard him, Angelique. He lied about being a regular attender. He lied about Rudy convincing him to place an ad when he could have easily said it was his brother. What else has he lied about? I can't marry him. I know I wasn't exactly excited about being a mail-order bride, but I didn't lie about my looks, or my beliefs, or standards. I was *completely* honest with him. I told him everything in my letters—my hurts and my dreams. I was open to becoming a bride. My heart was ready to love a man and be loved . . ." She blinked away her tears, swiping angrily away at them. *Suzanne was right. What good, honest man could ever love a girl like me?* "And Miss Fairfield is gone too."

Angelique rubbed Belle's back, knowing what Miss Fairfield meant to Belle. "What are you going to do?"

"I'm not going to marry *him* that's for certain."

"But what other choice do you have? He paid for your train ticket, and you don't have any way to get back, and we don't know anyone out here you could stay with until you found a way home to Charleston."

"I will pay him back once I land on my feet."

"But where will you go tonight?" Angelique gnawed on her bottom lip. "Perhaps I can ask Rudy if you can stay with us. With those outlaws roaming the foothills—"

Belle snorted. "On your wedding night? I think not."

Angelique blushed. "At least let me ask him for money for you to stay in the Castañeda where you will be safe."

"There is no need. Dolly said they could use me. You saw the waitresses. They were proficient but understaffed and overworked." Belle rolled back her shoulders and pushed herself to standing. "Hard work doesn't scare me. I will be fine. However, I wouldn't be fine if I married a stranger who doesn't even match his letters."

"Won't you at least give him a chance?" Angelique squeezed Belle's hand.

"I already have, and it took all the courage in my body to give him that one chance," Belle pulled Angelique into a fierce embrace. "I hope Rudy is everything you dreamed him to be. He seems to be a good man." Before her desperate courage could have a chance to turn into fear, Belle fled straight to the Harvey House, slowing only when she reached the courtyard, smiling to the doorman as she strode inside past the ornate lobby. She watched from the dining room threshold as the Harvey Girls dashed about cleaning the tables and preparing for the next train. She spotted the tall, curvy blonde who was giving orders to the rest of the girls, and she quickly made her way to Harriet.

Harriet turned a confused smiled to Belle. "Miss Parish? Did you leave something at your table?"

Belle kept her back straight and shoved confidence into her voice. "Whom might I see about applying to work here?"

The head waitress's brows furrowed. "That would be Miss Trent, but I thought you were marrying Mr. Lawson today."

Belle managed to keep her tears at bay and her tone strong. Suzanne's many scoldings had prepared her well. "I was, but I would've been foolish to miss all the signs telling me *not* to marry him."

Harriet motioned Belle to follow her into the immaculate parlor with beautifully stained hardwood floors in the center of the Harvey House. A few guests were lounging throughout, most seated before the row of windows facing the foothills. The furniture was in the highest of fashion. She hardly dared to take a seat on the red velvet mahogany settee lest she mar it.

"Have a seat, and I'll go fetch Miss Trent. She's the housemother to us Harvey Girls."

Belle sighed at the luxury. She had always seen the fine things of the Fairfield household, but being a servant, she of course was never allowed to touch the fine furniture except to clean it unless Miss Sophia Fairfield invited her to sit with her. The high ceilings of the Harvey House parlor added elegance while the giant stone fireplace gave it a homey feel even though it wasn't lit as it was stiflingly hot. On the side table was a beautiful red book of poems with gold lettering. Tilting her head to read the spine, she thought it said *Lord Tennyson* was the author. She saw out of the corner of her eye Miss Harriet speaking with a lady with red hair streaked in silver that must be Miss Trent who appeared to be reading a missive.

"It's a beautiful book," Miss Trent commented and took a seat and smoothed her gown that was the same austere black as the waitresses with a high collar, but hers had delicate white lace trim at the neck and cuffs, distinguishing her rank. At her side hung a chatelaine with about fifteen keys attached that clinked as she adjusted her seat.

Belle shot to her feet. "Yes, Ma'am."

"It was left by mistake by a girl, Sophia Bird Fairfield." She lifted a telegram. "Now, Sophia Ashton, who recently moved to New Orleans after joining the Harvey House staff rather unconventionally and leaving equally so."

"Miss Fairfield is married? To Mr. Carver Ashton?" Belle sank into the settee.

"You know her?"

Belle laughed, shaking her head that Sophia had actually done it. She had seized her future and married the man of her dreams. "I'd say so. I was her lady's maid."

Miss Trent exchanged glances with Miss Harriet who had drawn up a chair beside them.

"Well, that is the most recommendation I could hope of obtaining with such a short notice."

"I hope you don't mind, but I've informed Miss Trent of your situation," Harriet interjected.

"Of course." Belle clasped her hands to keep them from trembling. "I know little of your hiring process, but I hope you would consider taking me on staff. I'm a very hard worker."

"Well, it is out of the ordinary, but I understand your trying situation." Miss Trent leaned forward and rested her hand on Belle's knee. "Usually, our girls are sent to the Harvey House headquarters in Topeka, Kansas, and trained for six weeks before receiving their assigned stations."

"If you don't have a position as a waitress open, I have worked for five years as a scullery maid before becoming a lady's maid. I also served at dinner a few nights a month when the footman had time off, so I am already well trained in waitressing, but maybe I could work in your kitchen until a spot opens up?" Belle suggested, scrambling for a solution.

Miss Trent waved her off. "I'm afraid that won't do. We hire our head chefs from Europe, and we are fully staffed in the kitchen with men. However, we are woefully understaffed in the dining room at the moment because every time I turn around, three girls are getting married. At the moment, Topeka cannot supply enough waitresses for this new Harvey House quickly enough. But, if Harriet agrees, I think we might be able to find a place for you. She's our head waitress, so she would have the responsibility of training you."

"I know this will sound harsh, but I'll only take you on staff if you sign a year contract and if you break the contract, you will not suffer the normal one month pay penalty, but a two month pay penalty." Harriet pressed her lips into a thin line.

"While I agree with your reasons, don't you think that is unrealistic?" Miss Trent gestured to Belle. "She's breathtaking."

Belle's cheeks tinted at such praise. She had never been called anything near breathtaking before today.

Harriet gritted her teeth and turned to Belle. "I fear we must. I don't want Mr. Harvey to think we are constantly making exceptions to the training rule. If I am going to take a chance on you, I don't want to take the extra time to train you and then have you up and run off with the next cowboy who looks at you."

Belle laughed. "I assure you that will never happen."

"No offense my dear, but hiring a scared mail-order bride makes me a little hesitant and with you being so beautiful, you'll have your pick of men and will have ample opportunity to run off." Harriet offered her a smile to soften her judgement.

"I understand, but I'm not interested in getting married anytime soon. To be honest," Belle dipped her head, "my sister-in-law was threatening to see me fired, so I only accepted Colt's hand in order to put a roof over my head. I'd be happy to sign a yearlong contract if that's what it takes for you to take a chance on me."

Harriet's eyes softened. "I'm sorry to hear that was the catalyst in you coming west. Well, in that case, I think a month of forfeited wages will suffice. Miss Trent, if we are in agreement, could you get the contract together while I show Belle around her new home?"

Miss Trent grasped Belle's hand. "Welcome to the family!" She removed a few keys from her long chain and handed them to Harriet. "Here you are. Just bring them to me when you are done."

"Thank you, Miss Trent. Come along, Belle. I'll bring you to the supply closet and get you outfitted with two black dresses and four white aprons along with a few hair bows and some black stockings. You're responsible for supplying your own shoes." Harriet guided her through the hallway toward the supply room closet.

"When do I start?" Belle asked as Harriet flipped through the keys, trying to find the correct one.

"I know you are tired from your trip, so let's say tomorrow morning at five o'clock after you've rested up." Harriet pushed open the door to where uniforms and aprons hung. She selected a dress and holding it up to Belle, she sighed. "Even our shortest gown is a little too long for you, but if you hemmed it, it should work, and, as a lady's maid, it should be no problem." She retrieved the aprons, hair bows, and stockings, piling the items into Belle's arms. "Now, I'll show you where you'll be staying, and you can unpack your belongings."

"My things!" Belle's hand flew to her mouth, nearly causing her to drop her uniform. "I was in such a hurry to get away from Colt that I forgot to fetch my carpetbag out of his wagon."

"You better get it before Colt leaves town. He might be too distracted from your rejection to notice much, and he likely won't be back for a spell."

"I'm sure he left it with Angelique." Belle shook her head. *I hope.*

"Go fetch it, and I'll show you your room across the street in the Rawlins dormitory when you return." Harriet removed the stack from Belle's arms, pointing her in the direction of the nearest exit. "Go that way."

"Thank you." Belle hurried out a back door around to the dusty sidewalk. She spotted Angelique leaning against the wall of the general store, absentmindedly picking at her nail bed. Belle's old carpetbag sat at her feet.

When Angelique saw her, she jumped up and rushed to Belle, clasping her hands. "What did they say?"

"They hired me." Belle laughed with relief, embracing her friend. "Isn't it perfect? As the mercantile owner's wife, you will always be right around the corner, which is closer than if I was tucked away on Colt's ranch."

Angelique handed her the carpetbag and whispered, "Rudy is as sweet as his letters. He went and got your bag before Colt took off. Colt sure was mad. I don't think I've ever seen a man's face turn that red—not even when Mr. Fairfield stormed into the kitchens looking for Miss Fairfield."

"Oh dear." Belle grimaced. "Please tell Rudy thank you for me and do try to put me out of your mind. I am well looked after."

"I will tell him. Rudy seems so kind. I'm sure this will be and is the best thing for me, and I pray this will be the best for you as well." Angelique looked to the general store and back. "If you find yourself regretting the position—"

"It couldn't be any worse than working for Suzanne back home." She pressed her hand to her friend's cheek. "Now, enjoy your new life. You deserve every bit of happiness."

CHAPTER 3

Colt set his horse loose on his ranch, watching the mare toss its head as it ran free from constraints. He looped his thumbs in his gun belt, kicking at tumble weeds as the lowing of his cattle at the foot of the hill filled the air.

"Where's your woman, brother?" Grant drawled as he strolled down the ranchero's steps, releasing a stream of tobacco to splatter into the dust.

"She ain't my woman." Colt grunted, slapping his hat against his thigh, dust lifting from the brim. "She found me out in a lie or two and refused to marry me."

Grant snorted, crossing his arms. "Why did she go and do that for?"

"She's an honorable lady and sniffed out that I wasn't no honorable man." Colt gritted his teeth, hating the gnawing ache in his stomach that he had disappointed the sweet girl. If she had only waited until Christmas . . . everything he told her would have been true—besides Grant being the instigator.

"You going to let her get away with shaming the Lawson

name?" Grant scowled. "What would Pa have to say about that?"

"Seeing as he ain't here, I don't need to be worried about that, do I?" He gripped his mare's bridle and headed for the barn, thankful that Grant did not follow him to the tack room. He put away the bridle and reached for the bullwhip at his belt, scooping up the tin cans he used for practice and strode into the paddock. Tossing a can in the air, he gripped the swivel handle and released the twelve-foot braided leather, snapping the can in the air. He tossed the cans over and over as he prayed—brooded—over what he should do next to convince Miss Parish that he was the man in those letters.

Nine months ago, she would have been right to leave him at the altar . . . but that was before he met the Lord and before he struck a deal with the very Texas Ranger who would have seen Colt locked away for life.

BELLE HELD HER CRISP, new black uniform up to her chemise in the room she shared with Fannie Traverse and Dolly Matthews. With her ebony hair and dark dress, she thought she would look like a little sparrow in a giant white hair bow. As she wasn't allowed to wear any jewelry, she tucked her mother's wedding band on her lace necklace inside her dress. She ran her finger over the fine lace trim that was supposed to adorn her wedding dress—love's gentle promise that might never be used now. She buttoned the collar, comforted by its presence even as the heat already made her high collar stick to her throat, but she tried not to think about it for fear she might become claustrophobic and claw away the collar.

Her old kitchen shoes weren't fit to wear in such a fine

establishment as the Harvey House, so her tight Sunday shoes that she had saved from the Fairfield waste basket would have to do until she could make a desperate trip to the general store as soon as she could. Her Sunday shoes had an impractical heel that wouldn't do for long hours on her feet. She hated to spend any credit at Rudy's store while she waited for her first paycheck, but she knew it couldn't be helped. She sighed, the cost of Colt's train ticket pressing on her heart.

She slipped on her apron, crossed the dark street with the moon still shining, and hurried into the side door of the hotel, finding the dining hall empty save for the kitchen staff already preparing for the day. She was the first Harvey Girl down for the morning shift. She helped herself to some coffee and reached for a plate, taking a small portion of the delightful array and eating as quickly as she could. As no one else appeared, she reached for a second muffin, even as the ghost of Suzanne's ready reprimand bade her to leave it for the others. There was plenty. She stuffed the baked good in her mouth.

"Good morning! I hope you slept well?"

Belle shot to her feet and lifted her hand above her mouth, managing to say, "Very."

"Glad to see you are punctual as you will be working the lunch counter with me for the day. We call it the lunch counter, but of course, we serve meals there around the clock. Also, just so you know, I *never* work the lunch counter, but since you haven't had any formal Harvey House training, I will need to supervise you very closely for the next six weeks. You've been through one meal at the Harvey House as a guest. Did you notice how we run things?" Harriet held the door open to the dining room, waving Belle through.

Belle nodded as the girls began trickling into the dining

room on their way to the kitchens with some pausing to adjust a station. "I noticed a code for the cups. Cup up is coffee. Cup down is tea. Cup down and placed an inch away from the saucer is iced tea."

"And cup upside down and tilted against the saucer would be what?" Harriet quizzed.

Belle scrunched her brow in concentration. "Water?"

"Everyone has water. The cup tilted on the saucer would signify that milk has been ordered."

"Ah yes," Belle snapped her fingers as she remembered the little boy who had sat near her table the day before.

"You'll get it, but hopefully, it'll be sooner rather than later." Harriet laughed and glanced at her pocket watch. "The first train will be here in an hour, but guests from town will begin to arrive any minute."

A medium built man with bronzed skin and auburn hair strode into the dining room and took a seat at the counter, setting his Stetson on the seat beside him. "Good morning, Miss Hallie and you too, Miss."

Harriet smiled. "Miss Belle, please meet my childhood friend, Mr. Gilbert Elliot. He's recently returned home from attending university and seems to forget that I go by Harriet these days."

Belle attempted to give him a welcoming smile, though it was difficult with not even knowing the man. *This is the hospitality business. You must learn to smile at strangers.* "Mr. Elliot, a pleasure to meet you. What can I get for you this fine morning?"

Harriet raised her brows at Belle's initiative, but stepped back and allowed her to take the order.

"Call me Gil if you will. Mr. Elliot is my father." He grinned, sending a wink in Harriet's direction. "I'll have coffee, potatoes, a rare steak, eggs, and apple pie for dessert."

Steak for breakfast? And dessert? Belle jotted down his order on the pad without questioning his decision while Harriet filled his drink order.

Harriet turned to her, whispering. "Bring the ticket into the kitchen and call out the order to the head chef."

Belle stuck her head in the kitchen and called the order to the already busy chefs. Seeing a nod of confirmation from one of the chefs' assistants, Belle grabbed a coffeepot and filled it at the urn as she had seen others do the day before and filled Gil's cup.

"Honestly, Gil, you drink entirely too much coffee," Harriet muttered. "You downed that drink in one gulp."

He shrugged as he accepted another refill from Belle, grinning. "It's a gift."

Belle set the coffee pot beside the urn and stood behind Harriet with her hands folded, ready to do whatever was needed.

Harriet handed her a rag. "You'll need this in a minute. Whenever there is a lull at your station you can wipe the counters, and every ten minutes make certain the coffee urn is full, which will help the rest of the girls."

The dining room door swung open, and the jingling of spurs caught her ear. Her heart lodged itself in her throat and she caught hold of the counter, steadying herself at the striking cowboy in the doorway. Colt was here?

"Belle?" Harriet placed her hand on Belle's shoulder. "Are you quite well? Do you need to sit down for a moment?"

Belle released her grip on the counter and drew a deep breath. "I'll go check on Gil's order."

The chef's assistants had the food plated already and Belle hefted up the heavy dinner and dessert plates, backing through the swinging door.

Colt had taken a seat at the corner of the counter, his gaze burning into her as she set the plates before Gil.

Gil draped his napkin over his lap and inhaled the steam rolling off the food. "Love me some good cooking."

Gil was well looked after by Harriet and as this was her new livelihood, Belle forced herself to turn to Colt, smiling politely. "Good morning, Mr. Lawson. What can I get for you?"

He whipped off his dusty, dark Stetson. "Coffee please."

She retrieved a cup and saucer from under the counter, filled it and slid it in front of him. She set a pot of sugar and a spoon beside the cup. "Please let me know when you need a refill, Mr. Lawson."

"Please don't do this," he whispered, his eyes pleaded with her.

"Do what?" Her brows rose, attempting to appear oblivious as his meaning.

"Don't act like we don't even know each other, Belle. We have been writing each other for two months." He plunked a spoonful of sugar into his coffee, swirling his spoon around and around as if he didn't even have the heart to drink it. "I just don't understand what could've caused you so much doubt in the span from our concluding dinner and our standing before the preacher."

She gritted her teeth, forcing herself to keep a smile pasted on for the rest of the guests milling through the doors. "I think I was fairly clear."

"You left me at the altar and did not even give me a chance to explain myself. It sure seems like you were just looking for an excuse to run."

And maybe I was . . . Should she tell him that it was Angelique who signed her up to begin with? After all, *she* had never lied about it . . . she had simply not told him what led to the advertisement. Deciding not to cause him further pain, Belle topped off his coffee and nodded to the three new men approaching the counter. "Colt, I know you feel like you know me, but I don't feel the same because what you said in person and what you wrote in your letters doesn't align."

"I don't know what spooked you, but at least give me the courtesy of listening to my side. You don't know how disappointed I am that we didn't get married yesterday." The men at the counter shifted their gaze toward him. Colt sent them a blistering scowl, and they at once turned to their menus. He lowered his voice. "After all those long nights dreaming about holding my sweet wife in my arms that I have come to respect and cherish, I am left just holding the cost of a train ticket."

At that, she slipped the letter she had composed last night from her apron pocket and slid it across the counter.

Colt's head snapped up, his brow furrowing. "What's this?"

"A promise in writing to repay you."

Ignoring the envelope, he met her gaze. "I don't want your money. I'm sorry for bringing up the train ticket. It was just my anger getting the better of me. Will you at least allow me to call on you after work today and try to set things right?"

Belle glanced over her shoulder to find Harriet busy with Mr. Elliot. Someone had to see to the three cowboys. She nodded toward them, and, taking their orders as quickly as possible and alerting the kitchen, she returned to Colt, whispering, "I don't think that's wise. I don't want to encourage you."

"But you *did* with your letters. You have no idea how it feels to have this hope build and build inside of you only to have it crushed when it's within reach." At her silence, he sighed again, but this time, there was a hint of frustration. "I'm not used to expressing myself. I don't like this raw feeling. I am Colt Lawson. Around here, I am known as the brother of the burly Grant Lawson, and men know not to mess with me, but when I am with you," Colt's shoulders slumped. "Maybe it is just as well that you don't want me. I don't need to be a man with a weakness . . . having a weakness out here is like having a target painted on your back."

She extended the letter to him, giving it an impatient flap. "Please, take this. It isn't fair that you thought you were getting a wife and got left with the price of an expensive train ticket and no wife to go along with it."

"I don't need your money." Colt gulped down his coffee, clanking it down in the saucer.

"I want you to take it. It would make me feel not quite so cruel." She set the letter beside his cup and poured him another. "Please."

"Tell me. Did you ever intend on marrying me?" His eyes burned into hers.

Her cheeks flamed, but she owed it to him to answer honestly. "You weren't the only one who was disappointed that we didn't end up wed yesterday."

"Then allow me to call on you just once tonight. That's all the payment I want." His gaze dug into her, as if trying to make sense of the events that had transpired.

"I would rather you take your money," Belle mumbled and grabbed the rag and wiped away invisible dirt from the counter.

"Fine. I'll take the money if you will go for a walk with me or go to the other hotel for dinner. Please. Just give me a chance. My brother needs me in San Antonio, so I have to leave soon, and I'm not entirely certain when I'll be back."

Belle sighed, shaking her head. "You really are persistent,

but if it gets you to take your money, meet me after Sunday service when you return, and we can go for a *short* walk. I'm not promising anything—only a walk, and it's just for you to take your money back. I don't enjoy this feeling of being beholden to you."

"You may consider yourself guilt free after our walk." Colt grinned as he paid for the coffee and tugged on his Stetson. "You won't regret it."

I sure hope I don't. She whisked away his half-filled coffee cup. She strode into the kitchen to dispose of the cup as Dolly came charging through the doors, knocking the cup and sending its contents sloshing down the front of Belle's white apron.

CHAPTER 4

Colt dismounted in the hill country outside of San Antonio where the gang's shack was built at the base of the canyon. He led his horse to the creek and let the mare drink her fill after their ride from the Boerne train station where he had parted with Ranger Reid. The three-hour ride allowed him to set aside thoughts of his conversation with Belle this morning and focus on the matter at hand —the Death Riders.

He knelt beside the creek and splashed water into his face, washing away sweat and the dust of the trail. He pulled his bandana from his pocket and dried his face as he sank back on his heels. His parent's parcel of land was beautiful with its lush trees along the creek that was always cool. It would have been a perfect place to settle—too bad Grant had decided to use the shack of a cabin as the gang's headquarters, but what else could be expected when raised by a thief?

He slapped his Stetson on his thigh and rose, glaring at the cabin with its lazy curl of smoke from the stone chimney. It was time to get to work. "Grant!" He imagined his brother rolling from his cot, bottle gripped in hand as he shook away the haze from his eyes. "Grant!"

The door banged open, the thin planks wobbling on their hinges. Grant filled the doorway, pulling on his suspenders and squinting in the daylight. "What took you so long?"

"Took a later train. Wanted to speak with Miss Parish."

Grant finished off his bottle and flipped it into the bushes where it hit another bottle, shattering. "Russ is almost too drunk to talk plans."

Colt stared at his older brother—any apology would be seen as weakness. "Seems a little soon for you to be planning our next robbery."

"The train didn't yield enough gold, and jewelry is hard to get rid of quickly without it being traced back to the thief." Grant leaned against the door, pulling at his suspenders and letting them snap against his chest. "Boerne Bank is expecting a gold transfer from San Antonio tomorrow morning." He grinned. "But it ain't never going to get there."

"Sounds like a good pay day." Colt cracked his neck from side to side. "Got anything to eat, or do I need to go hunting?"

Grant spit toward the bushes. "Got some canned goods."

"I'll be back in an hour." Colt snorted and slid his rifle from his saddle, striding into the woods, sweeping his eyes for any signs of a deer and Reid. With any luck, this would be the raid that Reid could arrest Grant and set Colt free from the life his brother had pressed him into.

AFTER FIVE WEEKS OF TRAINING, Harriet was finally beginning to loosen her reins and not wishing to disappoint the kind headwaitress, Belle threw herself into her work. She was determined to avoid making even the slightest mistake as Dolly was always there, watching her and promoting her failures, so while the rest of the girls were having their late lunch break and waiting for the next train to come in, Belle bustled about the lunch counter and adjusted anything that was just a hint out of place.

"It seems as if I have created another me." Harriet called to her from across the room, grinning. "Everyone else is enjoying their lunch, yet here you are still working."

Belle shrugged. "I wasn't hungry, and I like working here. I enjoy the freedom that this job brings . . . I know what it is like being trapped, so I don't want to lose this independence for lack of trying."

"Exactly." Harriet wove between the tables, inspecting the settings with a ruler. "A lot of girls take this job as a way to find suitors until they are swept off their feet by magical bachelor number twenty, but I see the Harvey House as something far more than just a payroll and a holding place for a husband."

"Well, I don't think there is anything wrong with wishing to marry and start a family, but it would be hard to surrender my independence for any man." Belle bit her bottom lip. "Although, some would probably call me a hypocrite if they knew I came to Las Vegas as a mail-order bride. However, if they only knew the truth about my circumstances, they would know that I did not have any other choice."

"Most girls think I am here merely because I couldn't land myself a husband." Harriet laughed and picked up a glass in an impeccable place setting and held it up to the window. "Fetch a new glass for me? This one has a smudge." She continued her assessment. "The truth is, it would have to be some kind of man to make me take interest, because I've decided to be a housemother someday, and there are rarely ever exceptions to allow a married woman on staff." She accepted the clean glass from Belle with a nod of gratitude.

"But if marriage is forbidden and Fannie is engaged to Joshua . . . How is that allowed?" Belle caught sight of her hair in the mirror behind the counter and smoothed back the strands as she reached under the counter for a new glass.

"Engagement is allowed, but not marriage. If you get married while under contract, you forfeit a month's wages at least. As you have already proven yourself to be an amazing waitress, I am secretly glad that you chose to sign a yearlong contract. I'd hate to lose you after a short six-month contract."

"You won't have to worry about it. No man will propose to me in this town after they hear I jilted Colt Lawson."

"I'll believe that when I see it," Harriet laughed. "By the end of your contract, you will have had a hundred proposals, and you will be dying to marry the man of your dreams. Just wait and see." She sighed. "The best waitresses are always snatched up. But if a young man does take interest, and you wish to court him, you must get the approval of Miss Trent."

"Oh?" Belle's brows rose. "That's refreshing to hear that the Harvey House cares so much about our livelihoods."

"It's Mr. Harvey's way of extending his fatherly arm over us girls while we are away from our own parents. If you do fancy a young man, I would not be too worried about Miss Trent saying no. She has always approved the young men unless he is an outlaw or does something irrefutably evil."

I may be a great waitress, but a wife? My own family rejected me, and Colt lied to me, revealing his wanting character. Suzanne was right. I'll never find a good man. Belle swallowed back her thoughts and smiled. "Nope. I'm here until the day I die."

"Good! But you have hardly left the Harvey House grounds since you started working here, except for a short trip or two to the mercantile. You need to take some time outside to refresh yourself. Trust me. If you keep going at this pace, you will burn out before your day off comes around, and it only comes once every ten days *if* it isn't a full house. If it's a full house, all hands are required to work, and you'll lose your day off. So, I suggest that even though you aren't hungry, take your break outside today, or go visit your friend." Harriet surveyed the room, nodding her approval. "There's nothing pressing left to do in here, and the train won't be here for another hour and a half, so you should have a solid hour to relax. If anyone comes in, I'll take care of them."

"Well, I would like to go to *Rudy's Mercantile* to see Angelique . . . and my shoes are making my feet swell." She lifted her skirts to show Harriet her high heel.

Harriet inhaled sharply through her teeth. "You've been working this whole time in those? The sooner you purchase new shoes, the better. If you don't take care of your feet, your legs will never stop aching. You have had your wages since last week. I suggest you do some shopping."

"I'll be back in an hour." Belle slipped out of her apron, folded it, and placed it under the counter before running across the street to the dormitory and snatching her reticule. Belle cast a glance down either side of the street, looking out for the real reason she hadn't ventured about town—Colt. *Please Lord, don't let me run into him.* She gathered her skirts and hurried down the main street and into the mercantile.

"Belle!" Angelique called from behind the counter, duster in hand. She rushed around and engulfed Belle in her arms. "Every time I poke my head into the restaurant, you are taking some cowpoke's order and then, every church service, you have to dash away. I've been feeling quite neglected."

Belle leaned her hip against the countertop. "I'm sorry.

Work is difficult, but I'm pretending to be tireless so they won't ever have an excuse to kick me out like Suzanne. I never thought Suzanne was an easy taskmaster, but I've been averaging twelve hour shifts every day this week, and by the time I am done for the day, I'm almost too tired to climb the stairs to bed, much less walk to the general store."

Angelique squeezed her hand. "I wish I could come to see you in the evenings, but Rudolph prefers that I spend the evenings with him after working all day at the store, but I think he'll soon miss his friends, and I shall be free to visit you," she whispered. "Marriage is a delicate thing when you are a mail-order bride, and you still need to become acquainted with one another in ways a normal courtship would have revealed."

"Please don't strain your relationship on my account. Harriet has asked me to work the night shift for the week, starting tomorrow. Maybe I can come have coffee with you some morning if your work allows?" Belle picked up a pair of gloves from the lady's shelf and examined the petite stitches. "But besides trying to make a good impression, which I am sure you have, are you enjoying married life? Is it as wonderful as those romance novels you were always so keen on reading until the wee hours?"

Angelique's cheeks flushed. "Rudolph is very kind."

"Do you love him yet?" In all the romantical stories Angelique had told her about and read to her during stolen moments at the Fairfield house, Belle knew that love could happen at any time. Sometimes, all it took was a glance.

"I am certain I will grow to love him. He and I only need to get to know each other a little more." She cleared her throat and lowered her voice, "Honestly, the more Rudolph talks about Colt, the more I do not understand why he lied to you about attending church. He sounds like a good man, but

Rudy's accounts may be biased as I remember the preacher's comment, and I'm sure that the preacher wouldn't lie." She shook her head. "It is all so confusing. Have you spoken to Colt since my wedding?"

"He came by the Harvey House, and I about died from embarrassment." Belle quietly informed her of all, including his promise to leave her be after their walk as Angelique unpacked a shipment of ladieswear.

Angelique sighed. "Well, I'm glad you'll be done with him soon. I have to admit, it was awkward when he called on Rudy yesterday. I feel like I am a reminder of your absence to Colt."

"He's back in town?" Her knees weakened at the thought of facing him.

She nodded. "Anyway, I wanted to ask if you are settling in well with the girls? Are you happy? I am rather jealous you have so much female company, but this is what I chose." She laid out a delicate lace trimmed fan on the shelf, giving it a little pat.

"I love working at the Harvey House. For once in my life, I truly feel independent. I have a roof over my head, clothes on my back and a steady paycheck coming to me at the end of every month. Yes, I'm happy." Belle smiled. "I can even afford to get myself a new pair of shoes without feeling guilty for such a luxury. Speaking of which, I need a pair with the lowest heel possible if you have any my size in stock."

"That I can do." Angelique hurried to the far wall and pulled down a box from the third shelf from the top. "I believe this size will fit you if I remember correctly. I have a chair behind the counter if you want to try them on?"

Belle took a seat, unlaced her heeled shoes and slipped her feet into the plain, rather ugly shoe, but as she took a step, she sighed from the simple comfort a practical heel could bring. "So much better."

"And since you are my dearest friend in the world, I'll throw in a pair of black stockings," Angelique called, heading into the storage room as the brass bell over the door jingled.

"Oh, you don't have to tha—" Belle glanced up from her seat behind the counter and met the gaze of a ruggedly handsome man with the deepest, bluest eyes she had ever beheld. *Why, he's the ranger from the train.* She ducked back down, stuffed her stockinged foot into her shoe and fumbled to secure the laces as she covered her ankles with her skirt.

"Hello there." A deep voice rumbled.

She glanced up to find him leaning over the counter and thumped her head on the countertop overhang. She swallowed her pain and smiled up at him as she stood, taking in his ruddy complexion and dark brown hair. *He is almost too good looking for a man. Why didn't I notice it before?* She snapped her jaw shut and as if he could hear her thoughts, she blushed to the roots of her hair. "Uh, hello." Her eyes fell on his gun belt. She swallowed and took a tentative step backwards as the memory of the robbery surged to the surface, silence roaring in her ears as loudly as a train whistle. She gripped the shelf behind her, desperately pushing the memory of the bandit in the scarlet bandana away as she did with everything unpleasant in her past.

"I heard that Rudy found himself a bride, but the reports on your loveliness didn't do you justice." He tipped his Stetson. "He's one blessed man."

"Oh. I'm not Rudy's wife. That would be Angelique. I'm Miss Parish." Belle looked around for her friend as she came bustling from the storage room.

"Found them!" She sang out, giving the stockings a little wave in the air and then realized they were not alone. She tucked the unmentionables behind her. To her credit, she did not blush for her display of the intimates. "Good afternoon, sir."

He tipped his hat to her as well and smiled. "Good afternoon, Mrs. Smith, I presume?"

Belle mumbled that she had better run before her shift started. "I'll wear these out and stuff my old shoes in the box if that's okay with you?"

"Of course," Angelique discreetly passed her the pair of black stockings. "We can settle up later."

"I have the money with me," Belle withdrew the bills from her shabby purse. "Is this enough?" *Ankles showing and now money being spoken of in front of a perfect stranger!* The situation was beyond mortifying.

"I'll fetch two bits change, and you can be on your way." Angelique bent behind the counter and the sounds of a cash box rattling greeted them before she pressed the coins into Belle's palm. "See you at church?"

"Of course." Belle nodded to them both as the striking man smiled to her, and she bolted through the door. *Hopefully, he won't even remember me.* Thinking about his blue eyes, she amended her thought. *Hopefully, he will . . . just not my ankles.*

CHAPTER 5

*T*houghts of the ranger stayed with her for the rest of the week and to her annoyance, Belle found herself looking for him at her lunch counter. Day after day passed and no ranger, but with the church bell ringing, calling all to church, she felt foolish that her stomach twisted in hope of catching sight of him in service.

As the other girls dressed for church and Dolly placed the finishing touches on Fannie's hair, Belle was painfully aware that her Sunday best was not anywhere near as nice as her uniform. Seeing the other girls in their bright, pretty dresses bedecked with flounces, puffs, lace trim and fluttering ribbons, her blue dress that was passable the first handful of Sundays looked faded and shabby in comparison, especially after she accidentally left the iron on the back of the skirt too long and it left a deplorable scorch mark at the bustle.

Belle spread it on the bed and sighed. *What would be worse? Wearing my uniform black dress, or displaying how truly poor I am that I can't even replace my skirt that I burnt?* She shook her head. *What's wrong with me? Just because I met a handsome man at Rudy's Mercantile, I shouldn't go spending money on things I don't need to impress him on the chance that he attends service.* She bit her lip, remembering how Suzanne would make her wear the scorch marked dresses until she had grown out of them as punishment for daydreaming and being careless. *If I hadn't been daydreaming about that man, I wouldn't need a new gown.*

Dolly ran her fingers over the cloth. "It's not all that bad."

At Dolly's generous assessment, she returned the gown to the closet. *Uniform it is.* "I'll be down in a few minutes ladies."

She picked up her gown and held it against her chest, her hand skimming down over the waist and sighed. *I'll buy a store-bought dress tomorrow and then, I'll catch the eye of that handsome stranger.* Startled at her marked interest, she gritted her teeth, hung the dress in the closet, and reached for her austere uniform. *You had your chance for happiness, and you missed it. Once that stranger hears of your jilting Colt, he'll run for the hills.*

She buttoned her gown and decided to rearrange her hair into a delicate bun at the base of her neck. She released a tendril on either side of her face, allowing them to gracefully frame her face before pinning on her pale pink chapeau. The white plumed feather hung rather limply, but at least it added a splash of much needed color. She retrieved the envelope with most of her paycheck for Colt and carefully tucked it into her reticule, planning to give him the money during their walk.

She paused with her hand on the doorknob, glancing back at the hand mirror on Dolly's nightstand. Poking her head out into the hallway to make certain no one was near, she peeked into the small mirror. While her hairstyle greatly softened the somber look of her uniform, she could hear Suzanne's voice saying how she was still the little sparrow who would never be a bluebird like her daughter, Mary. *I'm not that weak little girl anymore. I don't need Suzanne's love, nor her approval. I don't need anyone.* She sighed, setting down the mirror with a *thump. Sure, you don't, Belle.*

COLT SHIFTED in the hardback pew. Sure, it had been a while since he attended church, but the seats seemed more uncomfortable than usual. Maybe it was that bullet Grant dug out of his backside and stitched up after the robbery, but he couldn't rightly sit on a pillow without drawing notice. Once again, Reid was unable to capture the gang and it was only because Colt "accidentally" got in the way of one of the gang's bullets that Reid was still alive today. He squirmed, beginning to rethink the ranger's creed of "one riot, one ranger." It hadn't worked so far in the nine months he had been working with Reid to clear his name. The Death Riders didn't become one of the most feared gangs in the West without having a clever *and* ruthless leader. The raid had resulted in the largest haul in years and would hopefully garner the interest of more rangers.

His share of the gold was buried under the floorboards of his ranchero, awaiting Reid's instruction. Before he had the ranger's direction, he would donate his portion to a few churches that he came across on the rides to and from the canyon shack. His fingers went to the two coins in his coat pocket as the church's offering plate was passed his way. He dropped them in—the joy in giving *his* hard-earned money from the ranchero filling his chest.

The back door opened, and Belle slipped inside in a black gown with a lace ribbon necklace. She was a vision. The whole of the sermon, he couldn't keep his gaze from finding the petite Belle sitting beside Angelique. He needed to plead his case. *Lord, I know how this all looks. I know I can't explain away some things, but help me not to lose her.*

"Our annual charity social will be held on a Friday evening in two weeks, so plan on being here." The preacher announced after the prayer. "This year, the funds will go into buying food as well as fabric to sew clothes for the needy. Now, our local seamstress would like to say a few words. Mrs. Curtis?"

Colt shifted in his seat again, itching to stand. He set his teeth against the fire from the healing bullet hole and attempted to keep a pleasant expression even as a sheen of sweat broke out on his forehead.

An elderly lady stood, leaning heavily on a cane. She cleared her throat and addressed the crowd. "Preacher Martin and Mrs. Martin have graciously offered to host the sewing circle at the parsonage. Anyone is welcome, and we will meet on Fridays at seven o'clock beginning the first Friday after the social, so if any of you young girls want to learn to sew by stitching clothes for the needy, come on by and I'll be happy to give some instruction."

He noticed Belle lean forward in interest.

"Thank you, Mrs. Curtis." Mrs. Martin rose from her place in the front pew. "Preacher Martin and I thought it might be fun to change things up this year. Usually, the ladies pack the picnic lunches and the men bid on them, but this year, the *men* will be supplying the basket dinners and the *women* will be buying them."

The young ladies in the congregation broke out into whispers, giggles, and excited peeks at the single men in the congregation as Colt caught the looks of panic in their eyes. Belle stole a glance around the room—was she looking for him?

The preacher laughed at the men's reaction. "And men, I know you're probably asking yourselves 'how in the world do they expect me to pack an edible basket fit for a lady?' Well, I already spoke with Miss Violet Trent at the Harvey House, and she has agreed to have their chefs prepare baskets with various meals for you to purchase at a low price, which is very generous of the Harvey House." He cleared his throat and looked pointedly at the nearest cluster of young men. "And I recommend that you gentlemen take her up on the offer and place your basket order directly after service today, so they can know how many baskets to prepare. Now, let's pray." He bowed his head, gave a quick blessing, and dismissed the congregation.

The pews creaked with relief as the congregation rose and made their way to the large arched doorway. Colt rose, hat in hand, his eyes on Belle as she glanced around the room again. He lifted his hand in greeting and the smile on her face faltered as she immediately averted her gaze and began fiddling with the strap on her reticule.

Dolly passed him, whispering to Fannie. "Do you think I should bid on Colt Lawson's basket? I've been aching for the chance to speak with him again."

"Do it." Fannie giggled as if he couldn't hear them.

His cheeks reddening, he bolted out the front door, seeking shelter under a copse of cedar trees as he watched Belle embrace Angelique and move as if she was about to dart down the street. He had waited weeks to see her. He swiped off his hat and stepped out from his place, clearing his throat. "Miss Parish? Do you have a moment for our walk?" He extended his arm to her.

After a moment's hesitation, she wrapped her hand around his arm. Colt tugged on his hat and guided her alongside the trees, down the road, and away from town. He cleared his throat once more, choosing at last to break the awkward silence. "Pleasant day, yes?"

"I love Sundays. It's so refreshing to spend the morning in song and listen to a much-needed sermon. How did you like it?"

"Like what?" He tugged a twig with a cluster of leaves from a live oak and twirled the stem in between his fingers.

"The sermon."

He released her arm and threw the leaf up into the air. In a single motion, he removed his whip and snapped the leaf in half with the tip of his bullwhip.

Belle jumped. "Why on earth would you do that?" She clutched the top of her hat to keep it from tumbling off.

He chuckled at her reaction as he rolled up his whip. "Sorry. Old habits die hard. When I used to walk home from school as a young boy, I'd practice my aim the whole way."

"No wonder you had to send for a mail-order bride. You probably made all the girls you courted faint from shock." She giggled. "I'm sure that skill became useful when you became a rancher though."

"It did. We always had a handful of longhorns in the canyon. Always thought them beautiful creatures and hated when we reached the last of the beef and another would have to go to feed us." He adjusted his Stetson to block the noon sun. "I liked the sermon just fine, and if attending regular-like is what it's going to take to get you to allow me to call on you, I'd gladly go to church every Sunday for the rest of my life."

"Colt, it's going to take more than you attending church to make me trust you again." She dug into her reticule and retrieved the blasted envelope. "Please take it."

"And I told you that I am not interested in your money. I have plenty." He kept walking, and, as he hoped, she followed suit. "You know, if you'd let me, I could keep you in style all of your days, and you wouldn't have to wear your uniform to church."

Belle blushed to the roots of her hair. "I think we've walked far enough."

Did I say something wrong? He pushed back his hat, his hands on his hips at her twitching lips. He had embarrassed her. He cussed under his breath—before cutting himself off, remembering that he was trying to kick that habit. "You'd look beautiful in anything, Belle."

She flapped the letter. "I wish you would take it, and release me from your so-called claim on me."

"I didn't mean to be rude, but you see, I don't want to release you." He picked another leaf and at once, Belle stiffened as if bracing herself against another whip outburst. "In the West, we don't take kind to thieves." He ripped the leaf into tiny pieces before crumpling the pieces in his hand and letting them scatter to the ground.

"I'm not a thief if I offered to pay you back!" Belle shouted. She ran her worn handkerchief over her perspiring forehead and swallowed, lowering her voice. "I'm not rejecting you because I only wanted a free ticket to the West. I am turning you down because you lied to me."

"You're a thief because you stole my heart, and now you're trying to give it back and it's too late for me. The damage has been done." He sighed, frustrated at his weakness. "I'll not give up trying to make you see me the way you did in your letters."

"I don't understand. There are plenty of other girls in town. Why didn't you just pick one of them instead of going through all the trouble of letter writing?"

"Well, part of the reason, as I told you, was my ranch, but the biggest part of the reason is because in these parts, people know my brother's name, and they fear me because of it. They know I'm good with a gun and even better with a whip, and I am capable of snapping out their eyes faster than they can blink if they take one wrong look." He kicked a rock and sent it tumbling down the path. "Not that I would, but Grant's ruined any chance I've ever had with a decent, good girl, and I desperately want a good, decent life away from my brother and his reputation."

"What has your brother done to make him so feared?"

He studied her as her lips pursed. She was a tiny woman, but there was a strength behind her quietness and something in her eyes that echoed the ache in his heart. And she hadn't run yet. "Nothing anyone can prove, but once, there was an outlaw who threatened him—a renowned outlaw. Let's just say my brother eliminated the threat, and word got around. He claimed his actions were self-defense, and he was acquitted." He shook his head. "No one wants their daughters marrying into a dangerous family, and that Miss Trent guards her girls like a mother bear."

"I'm sorry your brother has ruined your chances with the ladies of Las Vegas." Belle swallowed and turned on her heel toward town. "However, I will consider myself absolved from feeling any guilt because I offered you the money, and you refused. There's nothing else I can do, and I won't allow you to lord the cost of the train ticket over me any longer."

"I'm *not* trying to lord it over you," he retorted.

"Yes, you are."

The sound of a horse and buggy coming around the corner brought a flash to Belle's eyes . . . as if she *feared* him. He had been a fool to release his heart.

CHAPTER 6

The drop-front phaeton halted as the occupant scowled down at Colt. "Belle? Is everything well?"

Relief flooded her body at the sight of the head waitress. "Can I ride with you, Harriet?"

"Of course. I'm visiting my father's friends who live just outside of town, but you're most welcome to join me." She patted the leather tufted seat next to her as the horse stomped its hoof, not at all pleased at stopping so soon.

"Thank you." Belle ignored Colt's hand and gratefully clambered into the seat. Her gaze met Colt's fiery one. "Goodbye, Mr. Lawson."

He lifted his Stetson.

Harriet snapped the reins. "What were you doing walking with that Colt fellow?" Harriet guided the horse around the corner of the winding dirt road. "The Lawsons do not have a good reputation. You never know what might've happened with a Lawson brother."

Belle sighed and leaned on the seatback. "Thank you for rescuing me. I only agreed to go walking with him in order to pay him back for the train ticket, but in the end, he still wouldn't accept it." She shrugged. "I don't know what else I can do to rid myself of him."

"That makes things rather uncomfortable for you—having such a tie with a mighty Lawson?"

"It's frustrating." Belle took in the fine buggy and Harriet's beautiful hunter green serge blazer suit with large sleeves and wide collar. Her chapeau was trimmed with ivory and burgundy flowers and gold silk ribbons that fluttered in the wind. "Why, Harriet, are you from money?"

"What?" Harriet coughed. "Such a question. My father left me his modest savings and I have my monthly earnings, and, as I don't have a mother, or siblings to support like most of the other girls, my money is my own. There was a time that I took too much pride in that fact . . . not too long ago really. I was more than happy to parade in front of the girls and flirt with gentlemen, but then, something happened, and I could not care less about it now."

"What happened to change that?"

"Love hits us at strange times and in mysterious ways." Harriet sighed. "Anyway, I don't really wish to keep up that kind of lifestyle anymore. Even though I make my own money now and can support myself, my father's sister always wishes to dress me in the height of fashion. Her next *Harper's Bazar* will be here any day with this autumn's fashions, so I'm sure she'll want me in the next latest style." She glared at the road ahead.

"Is that such a burden?" Belle laughed. *You don't know how good you have it to possess money to spend and an aunt who cares for you.*

"It is when you're trying to be independent and are desperately not trying to place so much value in the latest fashions. My entire wardrobe will have to go through the minor tweaks with the latest updates. My aunt would like me to have all new things every year. However, it seems a little frivolous to me when I know how hard it is to earn a living. She thinks I'm like my old self, but now, I couldn't stand it if I had to throw out perfectly good clothes just for a tiny change in fashion, and it irks her to no end."

Belle tried to still her yearning for a dress such as Harriet's. "Maybe when the catalog comes in, I could borrow it for an hour or so? I've been needing to sew a new dress, and I'd like to model it after the latest fashions, if I could."

Harriet's gaze fell on her uniform. "Black looks very nice on you, but I think a deep blue would be the perfect color to set off your eyes, and I'm certain my Aunt Gertrude would be thrilled to have another female take interest in the magazine."

"Thank you." She smoothed her skirt. "I'm hardly in the state of calling, but who are your father's friends?"

"My mother, Louise, died in childbirth and I was only seven when my father, Clyde Lane, died. Mr. Elliot acted as a father to me for years. In fact, he wanted me to move in with his family, but my aunt objected and had me move in with her, my uncle, and their nephew, Gaston Reid."

"Gaston? Quite the fancy name for these parts." The buggy hit a rut in the road, sending her poor chapeau toppling to the side of her head. She removed the long hatpin, and repositioning the hat, she worked the pin through her hair to secure it against the bumpy road. Her flimsy chapeau's cheap feather drooped into her face, and she blew it away from her nose. She brushed her damp curls from her forehead and used her hand to block the September sun.

"He was named after our grandfather. Gaston Reid is her nephew. It's kind of complicated to explain, but her sister,

Penelope Reid, had to move back East for her health and she couldn't look after her son. So, Aunt Gertrude and Uncle Roger took Reid under their roof as well. Every other winter season and occasional summers, Reid would head East to be with his mother until he gradually grew too old to be forced to return East so often and joined the Texas Rangers."

"How sweet of her. She must love you both very much to take you both in." If Suzanne had loved her . . . she might have stayed in Charleston. "When my parents died, my brother had to force his wife to allow me to live with them. I don't have the best childhood memories, but at least I had a position as a scullery maid, a roof over my head, and food warming my belly every night."

"Oh, Belle." Harriet blinked rapidly. "I am so sorry for your loss."

"It was a long time ago." But a loss that was seared into her heart. Belle cleared her throat. "So, how often do you and your aunt come to visit the Elliots?"

"*We* don't as she doesn't care for the company of the Elliot family. I come alone because she doesn't approve of the Elliots, especially now that I am a woman of a marriageable age." She glanced at Belle, her eyes falling on her, no doubt, flushed face. "Are you feeling well?"

Belle waved her off as they passed beneath a giant archway made from two pillars of stone and a hewn log atop with a wood carving in the shape of a "E" hanging from the middle. Beautiful yellow flowers grew gracefully in and around the wheel tracks, which must have been worn away from years of wagons rolling in and out from the ranch. "I'll be fine, thank you. I'm just a little thirsty after my heated discussion with Colt. Why does your aunt disapprove?"

"Because she believes the Elliots are the reason my father is dead, and, as she owns half the town, Las Vegas practically turned their back on them." At Belle's gasp, Harriet continued, "My father visited the Elliots before they were aware they had been exposed to scarlet fever. My father died soon afterwards."

"I am so sorry."

"I am as well, but Mr. Elliot has been like a father to me all these years, and I would never end our friendship because of their tragic unawareness of the disease." She guided the horse down the dusty road and rolled to a stop in front of the large ranchero, which was composed of white stones in various shapes and sizes while the sides of the house were made of faded red planking.

Belle smiled her greeting as the Elliot family welcomed them and followed them inside. Her feet echoed on the stone floor as she stepped into the large room and took a seat at the table beside a massive stone fireplace with a small fire glowing in the hearth.

A petite, beautiful lady with kind eyes stepped into the room, a platter of food in each arm. The warmth in her smile enveloped Belle, and for the first time since her father died, she felt at home.

COLT TOOK a roundabout trail toward Ranger Reid's campsite. He halted his mare and check for the twentieth time that he was alone. Even if Grant stayed in their canyon for most of the time between heists, Colt couldn't be too safe. Spotting the tent through the clearing with a fire dying out, Colt dismounted and approached slowly, releasing the downward, slurring coo of a roadrunner.

The tent flapped open, and Reid stepped out. "Colt. You have news?"

Colt squatted by the fire, tossing in a few of the limbs Reid had stacked beside the circle of stones. "Grant is going to lie low for another few weeks after this gold robbery, and I don't have weeks to wait."

Reid frowned. "What do you mean? Is Grant on to you?"

Colt cracked a stick over his knee and stoked the fire with the longer of the two pieces. "I mean that I can no longer omit the truth from Miss Parish, or I risk losing her forever."

"I see." Reid pulled the tin coffee pot from the stone it was perched on beside the fire, pouring a tin and handing it to Colt. "I didn't know you two were anything to one another."

Colt narrowed his gaze. The ranger almost sounded... jealous? "She was supposed to be my bride, but she won't give me the time of day after she caught wind of my lies—lies I told to keep our secret. I need to bring her into our circle."

Reid shot to his feet. "There is no way that is going to happen. Your freedom depends on keeping everyone in the dark, lest Grant find out."

"We were supposed to have captured Grant by now," Colt reminded him. "You said that it would only take months. It's been nine, and I don't have any more time to give you."

"If my horse hadn't thrown a shoe, I would have caught Grant in the act of stealing that gold."

"And if I hadn't taken a bullet for you, you would be dead." Colt rose, ignoring the throb of pain leftover from Grant's inept doctoring. He should have been without pain for weeks now, but he couldn't even go to a doctor for his bullet wound without his secret being found out. "You need to call for a second ranger."

"I can handle it." Reid crossed his arms.

"So, I am supposed to lose Miss Parish because of your pride?"

"You are willing to lose your freedom for a woman?" He returned.

Colt's fingers itched to punch the man—to settle things the way he used to. But he was a new man who was shaking his old ways. "Just let me tell her. She will keep quiet."

"We cannot risk it. I am sorry, Colt, but that is my final word on the matter." Reid reached into his saddle bags and tossed Colt a piece of beef jerky. "Now, let's talk about what went wrong and how next time, we can insure all goes right."

CHAPTER 7

"I'm so sorry. I know you've already covered the nightshift for Millie after our visit to the Elliots yesterday and worked a full shift today, but as you are the only one of us not retching, you will need to run the counter by yourself tonight." Harriet patted a damp handkerchief at the nape of her neck, sweat glistening on her brow and matting her golden hair. "I never thought of a solution for a situation where all my girls were ill."

"It won't be a problem." Belle grasped Harriet by the elbow and steered her to a chair in the vacant dining room. "You all need to be in bed, not cleaning up after the dinner rush."

Dolly gripped the doorframe and her stomach as Fannie plunked her head in her arms on the lunch counter, moaning.

Belle poured them each a glass of water. "Did anyone ever figure out what was getting them sick?" She lifted up her glass, "After witnessing the aftereffects of what made you all sick, I'm almost afraid to drink water that hasn't been boiled until we know for certain."

"I heard it was the ham we had at lunch today. It apparently had sat in the sun a little too long." Fannie held her cool glass against her forehead before gulping it down. "But if that's the case, why aren't you sick, or did you eat something else for lunch? If you did eat the ham, this is your future in about an hour." She chuckled as she pressed her hands to her cheeks, her mirth fading. "I'm burning up."

"I skipped lunch," Belle admitted. "I met up with Angelique this afternoon on my lunch break."

"Fortunate for us because every girl is out." Fannie fanned a menu through the stifling air as she sank onto the stool behind the counter, leaning her head against the wall of windows that overlooked the foothills, the sunset casting the room in a pink glow.

"I might as well surrender the hope that I can work. I'm sorry Belle," Harriet mumbled into her hands. "I've got to lie down. I can't sit up for another second."

"I can handle it."

Harriet brushed back a lock of damp hair. "I appreciate it, and I'll let Miss Trent know you are more than pulling your weight around here. You'll get a full day off on Sunday as well as compensation."

"Stop worrying about me. Go to bed." Belle pulled Harriet to her feet and pointed her in the direction of the dormitory where the rest of the girls had vacated. "I can manage." *I hope.*

The first few hours blurred as she was the only Harvey Girl running the floor, but by ten o'clock, the dining hall emptied of customers. Belle wiped down the counters, checked the coffee urn, and made sure her station was spotless before settling down in a chair as she waited for any guests to wander in. *Under the circumstances, I don't think Harriet will mind that I neglect the busy work.* The pull of the chair against her aching, overworked body was more than she could bear. *I'll close my eyes for a second. No sleeping, just resting.*

Sensing someone was standing over her, Belle jerked her hand up to block her face from a strike as she sank from the chair to the floor with a cry.

"Whoa! I am so sorry I startled you, Miss," the man swiped off his Stetson to reveal himself to be the handsome ranger from *Rudy's Mercantile*, still wearing the loaded gun belt.

Belle let her hand drop, discreetly wiping the corner of her mouth as if that had been the reason she had lifted her hand instead of instinct and rose. "I'm so sorry. I fell asleep, and you startled me awake. Everyone is ill, and I had to work a double shift." She brushed off her perfectly clean apron and grabbed her notepad. "What can I get for you, Sir?"

"Did you think I was going to strike you?" He slowly set his hat on the counter, concern etched in his brows.

She lifted her chin, unwilling to admit or recall anything she had endured under Suzanne's heavy hand. "I was startled. Can I help you?"

"To start, coffee please." He sank onto the lunch stool, but his knowing gaze revealed she had not fooled him.

"The coffee urn is likely not as hot as you would prefer." Belle escaped to the kitchen and smoothed back her hair, splashing a little water on her cheeks to wash away the memories, begging the Lord to help her forget them. She grabbed the piping hot coffee pot, which she had been keeping on the stove, and returned to the man, fetching a cup and saucer from under the counter. She filled it to the brim, watching the steam curl as its welcoming aroma filled the air. "What else may I get for you?"

"Five eggs, eight pieces of bacon, two pieces of toast, and a slab of ham." He snapped his fingers. "And I almost forgot. Some hot apple pie, please. My friend tells me it's the best he's ever tasted."

She gritted her teeth against the mention of ham, but she couldn't dare tell him the real reason they were out of ham, lest word circulate about town. "Uh, the ham is currently out of stock, but I'll make sure you get some extra bacon free of charge for your inconvenience."

He dismissed her apology with a wave. "No inconvenience whatsoever, but I am surprised you are out. Seems like it would be a staple."

"Oh, it is, but there was a problem with the last shipment and uh—" She searched for a way around telling him that every privy at the Harvey House was occupied because of the wretched ham. "We had to throw it out. We only serve the highest quality at the Harvey House." *Perfect. Miss Trent would be proud.* "Please excuse me while I get this order to Chef Harold." She darted through the kitchen door and cleared her throat, hoping it would be enough to wake the large man napping in his chair. "Chef?" Her voice squeaked, "Chef Harold?" He snorted and shifted in his sleep. "We have an order, sir." She repeated a little too loudly.

"Huh?" He jerked awake and narrowed his gaze at her as he snatched the order from her hand and stood, stretching before he shuffled to work, mumbling about the joys of the nightshift.

"Thank you." She quickly made a fresh pot of coffee, and, unable to think of an excuse that would keep her from returning to the counter, she pushed open the door, disconcerted to find the man watching for her. She silently poured him another cup of coffee, knowing she wasn't supposed to engage in conversation during the day, but she supposed it would be unfriendly not to talk when there's no one else to talk with the guest.

"I don't believe I've properly introduced myself. I'm Texas Ranger Reid."

"A Texas Ranger in New Mexico? My niece, who is only a few years younger than myself, has read about the Texas Rangers, and she is quite fascinated with you. She's positively in awe how one lone Ranger can dispel a crowd of outlaws."

"Well, I hope I live up to what your niece has read," he chuckled. "Most of those magazines and stories greatly exaggerate the day-to-day life of a Ranger." He shrugged off his coat and Belle caught sight of his silver star pinned on his vest. "It's a lot of dust and a whole lot of tracking, which brings me to New Mexico, but it sure feels good to finally arrest outlaws and criminals when I do catch them."

The smell of coffee called to her as the long day began to take effect on her weary eyes. *Desperate times call for desperate rule bending. Sorry, Mr. Harvey.* She poured herself a cup. "Do I call you Ranger Reid, or Mr. Reid?"

"My first name, Gaston, is such a stuffy name, so my friends all call me plain Reid and I'd say we're friends, wouldn't you?" He gulped down his coffee, reached into his vest pocket, and retrieved a ring, absentmindedly flipping it into the air and catching it.

"Wait . . . Gaston?" Recognition flooded her. How could she not have known? "You're Harriet's cousin and a friend of the Elliot family. Miss Harriet brought me out to the ranch last Sunday for dinner, and they told me so much about you."

"Order up!" The chef called from the kitchen.

Belle retrieved the dinner plate and pie, setting them in

front of him and made herself busy by wiping down the already clean counter and stealing a gulp here and there.

"Thank you, Miss Parish, isn't it? I didn't get your name." He shook out his napkin and draped it over his thigh.

"Belle." She smiled shyly at him. "Belle Parish."

"Parish. That's not a name you hear in these parts. Where are you from?" He dug into his food.

"Charleston," Belle poured him a glass of water in case he wanted something besides coffee.

"That's right. I've heard things about your southern cooking from Harriet when I saw her on her break the other day. Is it true?" He stabbed a forkful of eggs.

Belle laughed. "Well, I don't know what you've heard."

"She told me that yesterday you served them some seafood dish that was the best she ever tasted." He took a swig of coffee. "You'll have to share your recipe with Harriet, so she can make it for me one of these days."

Belle blushed with pleasure at Harriet's praise. "Since she loved the dish so much, I might be able to share the secret family recipe as long as she doesn't tell anyone else. My sister-in-law would have my hide if she knew I let the recipe out. You are either born or married into the recipe, she says." Belle laughed, stopping short as she realized how that sounded. *I hope he doesn't think I was insinuating something . . .*

"Then your fellow is one lucky guy." He started on his pie. "Could I get a glass of milk too?"

"Of course." She bustled into the kitchen and fetched the milk from the icebox. Belle placed the full glass in front of him and whisked away his finished plate, setting it in the dish bin under the counter. "And I don't have a fellow," she corrected him and then blushed, realizing again it sounded like she was hinting that she was available, so she quickly added, "I only just arrived to Las Vegas, and I'm sure I'll sign on for another year at least when my contract is up, so I won't be seeing anyone anytime soon." *There, that didn't sound too eager.*

His brows shot up at her confession. "Well, you aren't like most Harvey Girls, then. Most of them joined up only for the minimum allotment because they're here to find themselves a husband."

Well, I did come here to get married, but you don't need to know that. Feeling the conversation was getting a little too personal, Belle nodded to his glass. "More milk?"

He pushed back his empty dessert plate. "No, thank you. I'd better be off. I need to make my rounds. The sheriff is a friend of mine, and well, I'm sure you've heard about the cattle thieving that has been going on around these parts?"

Belle placed his dessert plate in the dish bin. "Harriet and Gil told me all about it. Apparently, the Elliots are missing more cattle. Just a few here and there, but Gil said it wasn't a wild dog that was taking them down. It's strategic. He's afraid that if he doesn't get this figured out soon, they might get the whole herd."

Reid nodded. "It's gotten so bad that the rangers took notice. I've been searching the Elliots' property for days and all I found was this minimus ring." He held it out to her.

She looked at the inscription. "'To G.L. with love A.W.' I'm guessing you do not know what G.L. stands for?"

"I have an idea, but I can't say anything until I have the means of proving it, and I *will* find proof. It's only a matter of time, but let me know if you hear anything please. Anything at all." He tugged on his hat just as a man stumbled through the door, the scent of whiskey clinging to him.

"Hey pretty lady, how about some coffee?"

Not knowing how to respond, Belle quickly retrieved a

cup and poured the drunken cowboy a cup before stepping as far away from the ranch hand as possible.

Reid strode over to where she stood at the corner of the counter, leaned forward, and whispered through his gritted smile, "Is anyone else working with you tonight?"

"Everyone is ill. The chef is in the kitchen, but as you heard, almost nothing will wake him."

He reclaimed his seat as he slid his coffee cup toward her. "I'll have another if you please."

Rain gathered on the brim of Colt's hat, dripping down the front as he guided his mare over the foothills. It was a miserable afternoon to be out, but it had been three long days since he had spoken to Belle, and with every passing hour, he seemed to get more and more agitated, so he saddled up to check on his herd, or risk losing his mind.

The cow lowed, dangerously close to the cliff edge that dropped a hundred feet to the creek below. Colt guided his mare toward her and snapped the bullwhip at the air to her right to scare her away and keep her from tumbling, but she danced to the side and at once returned to the edge, lowing once more when a high pitch bleat caught his ear. Her calf. He hopped off his mare and slowly inched toward the edge, keeping an eye on the cow. About eight feet below, her calf was lying on a ledge, blinking its wide eyes up to her mother and releasing another bellow.

"Poor girl. You must have been knocked out, or I would have heard you calling for help." Colt lassoed the mother and tied the end to his saddle horn, guiding his horse away from the edge and pulling the mother with her. "Stay, Pepper." He rubbed the mare's nose and grabbed his backup lasso from his saddle bag. He wrapped the rope around a small boulder and dropped it down to the calf. Hand over hand with his feet against the cliff, Colt slowly approached the frightened animal. "Easy girl. Easy." Both feet on the ledge, Colt wrapped the rope around the waist of the calf and climbed back up. Hand over hand, he pulled the rope, gently lifting the calf from the ledge, ignoring its pitiful bellows. He grunted. The calf seemed to be a little over two months old, judging by its being over two hundred pounds. He drew it over the cliff and panted as he set it free, watching it kick its hind legs as she ran to her mother.

He sank back on his heels.

"There you are."

Colt's spine stiffened, and he slowly turned, the rain spilling from the brim of his hat. "Grant. I thought I just left you at the canyon."

Grant shrugged, leaning on his saddle horn. "Got bored. I figured it was time we rustle up some cattle for our meals back home and put a little fear into the hearts of the good townsfolk of Las Vegas."

"Wouldn't it be easier to spend that gold on a meal?"

Grant grinned. "I'm saving it for something special. What's the point of having a brother who is an expert cattleman when I can use him to steal me a few head."

Colt knew that if he offered his own steer, Grant would smell out his true feelings on thieving, and Colt knew what happened to family members who were not inclined to follow in the family business.

Colt sighed. "Which ranch did you have in mind?"

"Elliot's." He jerked his horse's reins toward said ranch.

"What, now? In the middle of a storm?"

"Don't want to wait until dark and besides, they won't be expecting us to make a strike during the day. The rain will cover us." Grant narrowed his gaze at Colt, daring him to question him again.

There was no way Colt could alert Reid in time, but perhaps he could minimize the damage done by Grant. Colt sighed, mounting up. "Wasn't really expecting to go on a raid, but you are the boss."

CHAPTER 8

"What else do you have for my readymade options?" Belle asked Angelique even as the deep blue gown in the mercantile window with puffed sleeves and a white accordion pleated mousseline de soie called to her. She traced the delicate laced cuff with her fingertips. It was too luxurious for her. She needed something that would last—something more sensible.

"That one is inspired from a Parisian gown in Harper's Bazar." Angelique reached up to the top shelves, fetching silk and cotton shirtwaists and some skirts.

"It's stunning." She gasped at the price tag. *So much, but I'm certain I'd catch Reid's eye in such a gown.* She shook her head at the thought, but something inside of her wanted this dress more than anything, more than her good sense and money.

"I know the social is next weekend." Angelique removed the dress from the window despite Belle's weak protests and held it against Belle. "This would look lovely with your raven locks. The men would be falling over themselves asking you to dance."

Belle examined the flawless stitches, her head spinning with possibilities as her hands grew clammy at the thought of spending so much. "I've never had a dress like this before."

"You could set up an account with us and pay in installments if you need more credit to buy the rest of the things you need," Angelique suggested as if reading Belle's thoughts and removed a ledger from under the counter and flipped it open. "We only open accounts for a few patrons, but I'm *sure* Rudy wouldn't mind because he knows we are practically sisters."

Belle nodded sharply, dismissing her qualms. "I'll take it."

"Wonderful." She grinned and marked Belle's name in a blank column. "I'll wrap it up for you while you select anything else you need and put it on your tab."

With those magical words, Belle selected a chemise with Valenciennes lace, a new corset with jersey webbing, a pale pink nightgown with a shirred front, a cream and an emerald tailor-made shirtwaist, two sturdy, but pretty skirts, a scarlet jacket, and a pair of gloves. Belle piled high her items, her pulse racing as she withdrew her funds and set them on the counter to pay against the tab.

Angelique folded the skirts with a giggle. "I am so happy you finally bought something for yourself, and the scarlet skirt and matching jacket are so daring." She wrapped them in brown paper and snipped the string, tying them securely.

"Who knew shopping could be so much fun?" Belle looked down in the small glass case, eyeing a gold chain. *It would be nice to put my mother's ring on something other than a ribbon.* She stepped back, laughing at her frivolous mood. "But I better stop before I owe you *three* months wages."

Angelique leaned over the counter. "What's the point in

being best friends with the mercantile owner's wife if you can't get a little discount?"

Though sorely tempted, Belle shook her head. "You've already done me the favor of extending store credit. Besides, I have a job now. I don't have any expenses, and I can pay in installments." She sighed in delight at the pile of clothes that were *hers* alone. "Can you believe it? For the first time in my life, I can afford *new* clothes and not just those dreadful hand-me-downs from Suzanne."

"It really is." Angelique smiled and raised a single brow. "Now, I know you are going to protest, but since you are in my debt, as you say, for extending you credit, you *must* at least allow me to give you this." Angelique rustled to the back room and brought out a chapeau draped with a delicate sapphire applique and ivory ribbons cascading gracefully from a cluster of matching silk roses on the right side. "Isn't it lovely? I just noticed that you forgot to select a proper chapeau, so you can't disagree that you need it." She cooed as she settled the hat onto Belle's hair and slipped a hatpin through her raven tresses. "You wear this to church, and you will catch the eye of that handsome ranger I know you are so keen on impressing." She grasped Belle by the shoulders and turned her to the small looking glass in ladieswear.

Belle's eyes widened at the sight of the fetching hat. "It's too fine for me."

"Nonsense. It looks like it was made for you. It will go perfectly with your ensemble. It would be a shame not to have a chapeau to do that pretty scarlet suit justice." Angelique boxed the hat and set it beside Belle's packages. "It's a gift, and you are not to deny me the pleasure of blessing you after all you've done for me in coming west with me."

Belle threw her arms around her friend. "Thank you."

"If it hadn't been for you, I would've never had the courage to come out here, and if I didn't come out here, then I wouldn't have met my Rudy, and I would still be stuck in that awful, hot kitchen in Charleston." Angelique stacked Belle's items neatly into a wooden crate. "Do you need help carrying this home? I think this is more than you have in your closet at this very moment."

"So very true, but after years of carrying Miss Fairfield's trays up those flights of stairs, I'll manage." With another round of thanks and her trappings piled high, Belle reached for the door just as the brass bell jingled, sending her jumping aside to avoid being hit by the door. A broad form filled the door, sending her heart to skittering despite herself.

"I'm so sorry, Miss—Belle? Is that you behind there? Let me carry that for you." Colt reached for her crate.

"Mr. Lawson, I hope you are well." She kept a firm grip on her crate and swiveled it away from his grasp.

"Very well now that I've seen you." His gaze never left her face. "Would you like me to carry that for you? It looks cumbersome."

"I'll manage. Thank you, sir." The crate was beginning to make her arms ache. Not wanting him to know it was so heavy, she nodded towards the door. "If you'll excuse me, I really must return to the Harvey House."

"You don't have to be so unsociable," he called from behind her. "I know how to be a gentleman . . . even if no one else thinks me capable of it."

She turned in the doorway, keeping the door ajar with her back. "I don't mean to seem aloof, but I'm afraid any association between us must only be that of the lunch counter. I've signed on with the Harvey House for a year, and

I can't possibly entertain any gentlemen callers." She shifted her crate again. "I'm sorry."

His lips pressed into a thin line as he sighed and tipped his Stetson. "As you wish."

"Have a good day." She charged down the sidewalk for fear Colt would follow her. Rounding the block for the entrance to the dormitory, she ran straight into Ranger Reid, knocking the crate from her grip. The corner of the crate fell directly onto her foot as the parcels came tumbling out. Tears sprang to her eyes as she stumbled back, and the Ranger caught her by the arm.

"I am so sorry, Miss Parish. Are you hurt?" Reid's blue eyes pierced hers as he set her to rights.

She swallowed back her pain, blinking back her tears. Her foot throbbed. "Nothing that won't heal." *I hope it doesn't swell.* She bit her lip as she wondered how to cram a swollen foot into her new, tight shoes.

He collected the scattered packages and stacked them neatly in the crate.

Belle inwardly groaned at the thought of the delicate new underthings. *How could he possibly know what's inside them?* She snatched a long, narrow parcel from his hand, which could only be her new corset and tucked it into the crate, trying to hide her utter mortification. "I would say no, but I don't think I could manage to make it another yard with this heavy thing."

Reid lifted the crate, his eyes widening at the weight as he straightened. "You made it all the way from the mercantile with this? I'm impressed."

Belle shrugged. "I'm used to doing heavy lifting. In Charleston, I was the one who toted the heavy baskets from market each week filled with groceries." She glanced at him from the corner of her eye. His olive cotton shirtsleeves were rolled up to his forearms, the load making his muscles flex. He caught her observing him, and she quickly averted her gaze, blushing as she tried to hide her limp. *Compose yourself!*

"So, I see you'll let *him* carry your crate," Colt said from behind them.

Belle grimaced.

Reid turned, his eyebrows rising in surprise. "Lawson?"

"Reid." He nodded his greeting. "Glad to see you back in town."

"Figured it was time to land those outlaws in jail," Reid drawled. "There were six more steers taken from the Elliot farm."

"That's a right shame." Colt shook his head. "Maybe you should send for back up?"

Reid's gaze narrowed. "Any news for me, Colt?"

"Nothing too pressing. I'd like to meet with you later though." He tipped his hat to Belle in passing.

Why on earth would he meet with a Texas Ranger? "How do you two know each other?" She endeavored to keep her tone congenial and conceal her shock of their unlikely acquaintance.

"We met a while back," Reid replied, not offering any more information and closing the matter as he set her crate at the threshold of the Rawlins building.

If they are friends, does Reid know that Colt sent for a bride? Does he know it was me? Pausing in front of the dormitory, she reached for the crate. "Thank you for your help."

"Anything for you, Miss Parish," he smiled, creating a fissure in the wall she had carefully constructed around her heart.

She darted inside, groaning under the weight of the crate as she trudged to the top of the stairs and down the hall to her room. The door was wide open. Belle peeked around the door to find Fannie and Millie piled onto Dolly's bed pointing and chattering over a magazine.

Belle set down the crate on her side of the room and peered over their shoulders. "What are y'all going on about?"

"Dolly's *Harper's Bazar* just came in!" Fannie squealed. She pointed to a collar and sighed. "I will need to adjust my trousseau for Joshua. He can't have a dowdy bride. What would people say?"

"You just finished making those dresses last week, so I'd hardly call them dated," Belle surmised. Glancing over their shoulders, she added, "Besides, it looks as if the styles have barely changed since last year. I'm certain you'll be fine with what you have."

Dolly's face pinched as if she were struggling to keep from rolling her eyes. "To the untrained eye, yes, they may appear the *exact* same as last year, but there are hints all over the gown promoting the latest fashions. Don't display your ignorance of women's fashion, Belle. It doesn't flatter you."

Belle swallowed back her retort that as a former lady's maid, she made many such alterations over the years when Miss Fairfield had a favorite dress that she couldn't bear to part with.

"Dolly," Fannie reprimanded her softly. "I can see how she could think the styles are so similar." Fannie cleared her throat and looked to Dolly. "So, will you help me alter my dresses a tad? You are the best at alterations."

"Of course." Dolly agreed. "As long as you let me wait on that Texas Ranger the next time he comes to the Harvey House."

"I thought you had set your cap for Colt?" Fannie lowered the magazine to her lap.

Belle stiffened as Dolly's smile skittered. *Did Dolly exaggerate about Colt?* She slowly turned her back to the group and unwrapped her packages, piling them onto her bed in the corner. She lifted out her precious corset, tucking it away in her dresser drawer and waited for Dolly's answer.

"I-I might have, but that doesn't mean I can't think Gaston Reid isn't attractive."

"Might have? Before I was courting my Joshua, you said it was a shame Grant had such a dubious character, or we could marry a set of brothers." Fannie sighed as she pointed to a wedding dress sketch. "So lovely. We'll have to adjust my collar to match this one."

"Easy." Dolly grabbed a white Harvey uniform ribbon from her nightstand and draped it across the page, marking it.

Belle crossed her arms, staring at Dolly. "If Colt is such a catch, why did you persuade me to leave him?"

Dolly pursed her lips. "I simply thought you did not know him well enough to go marrying him."

Fannie cleared her throat, interjecting, "So, will you be able to make it to the bonfire tomorrow, Belle?"

"What bonfire?" Belle blinked, trying to gather her frayed nerves and keep herself from saying something that she might regret.

"You were so busy snapping at me that you neglected to check the invitation on your pillow." Dolly snorted and resumed perusing her magazine, turning each page with an indignant snap.

Belle opened the card and read as Fannie interjected, "It's an invitation to my Joshua's birthday party. I would've told you sooner, but he only just told me that he has *never* had any kind of birthday celebration. He was orphaned as a child, and now that he has me, I intend on throwing him a birthday party every year for the rest of his life to make up for all those he missed."

"I have to admit it seems silly to throw such a lavish birthday party for a grown man," Dolly commented, "but any excuse for a bit of fun in this stuffy place is fine by me."

"I think it is sweet and a bonfire sounds lovely," Belle continued, ignoring Dolly's negativity as she returned the card to the envelope. "Who will be chaperoning?"

"Chaperoning? My, aren't we playing the fine lady?" Dolly chortled, keeping her nose in her magazine.

Belle wrenched the magazine from Dolly's hand and tossed it to the side of the bed. "Why do you feel the need to be so ugly to me? You and I both know Miss Trent would never allow us to attend a party if it wasn't chaperoned, and I am just *curious* as to whom it will be."

Dolly leapt up and snatched up the *Harper's Bazar*, her eyes glinting with anger. "You are just too straight-laced for your own good, but if you must know, my mother will be coming to help Miss Trent. She wanted to meet my roommate and discover if you were as awkward as I told her." She smirked.

Belle's feelings were bruised, but she swallowed and wouldn't allow herself to reveal how much Dolly's mean spiritedness affected her. "It would be an honor to celebrate with you, Fannie. I'll be there."

CHAPTER 9

Where is Harriet? She's a half hour late! Belle wove about the guests in the Harvey House parlor, searching for her. With its already elegant décor, Fannie only enhanced the parlor's charm by decorating the buffet table with vases bursting with wildflowers and lighting a crackling fire in the massive stone fireplace. In one corner of the room, there were two galvanized tubs filled with apples with the names of guests carved into them, one for the ladies with the men's names, and one for the men with the women's names. Fannie had explained that whatever apple a guest managed to capture with their teeth, the name on the apple would reveal the persons future husband or wife. The housemother stood by the tubs enjoying herself as the young ladies and men bobbed for apples, laughing at the results.

Belle poured herself some punch into a crystal glass and reached for a cream puff. She enjoyed her treat and wove through the guests, trying to avoid unwanted advances from a rough looking fellow named Russ who had tagged along with Joshua's brother Jesse. She sighed with relief as Russ was drawn into a conversation with Dolly.

"Happy birthday!" Harriet called to Fannie's fiancé as she arrived on the arm of Gilbert Elliot, meeting Dolly's gaze as if daring her to say something. While every guest, besides Fannie and Miss Trent and Belle, seemed to judge the daring couple as no one else came up to greet them.

Dolly hissed to her friend, "I cannot believe she would bring *him*. The whole town knows what his father did."

Belle strode across the room. "Harriet and Gil." Seeing Gil's beautiful, auburn-haired sister behind them, she gave Lorna a smile. "So glad to see you as well, Lorna."

Gil extended his hand, giving her a warm smile. "Nice to have another friend here."

"So, what games did Fannie plan for tonight?" Harriet's eyes danced with anticipation.

"Bobbing for apples and tossing three chestnuts, each representing a potential spouse, into the fire to see which bursts into flames first. The flaming chestnut is your soul mate." Belle waved her hand dismissively. "Such utter nonsense, but it is fun to see how seriously Dolly is taking the games."

Harriet giggled. "Quite."

"Sounds fun to me. Where do I get some chestnuts?" Lorna craned her neck, searching the crowd.

"Are you going to name them all Ranger Reid and see if he is your match?" Gil laughed and Harriet playfully swatted his arm.

"Time for the bonfire everyone!" Fannie sang out and waved them to the side door. "It will be in the field far beyond the Harvey House, so as to not cause an accidental fire, or panic."

Lorna glared at Gil. "See how late you made us? You just had to stop and find the perfect flowers. Now, I won't be able to find out to whom my heart belongs."

To avoid the squabble to come, Belle excused herself and followed the large group. The brisk weather stung her cheeks, and she hugged her arms to her chest, wishing she had grabbed a shawl. The grass scraped at her stockings, and she desperately tried not to think about the snakes lurking beneath. The party trailed past the privies and out into the open meadow before the foothills to where Joshua had built an enormous bonfire. Surrounding the fire were logs draped in burlap sacks for seating. Fannie had set a linen covered table with refreshments of pie, muffins, and a pile of apples along with a few pots of what seemed to be hot chocolate.

Belle caught a glimpse of Harriet and Gil sidling up near the fire, their heads bent together, eyes shining with hope as Lorna caught a glimpse of a new guest arriving, striding across the field. The ranger was not wearing his hat and his dark brown hair glistened in the firelight as if he had just washed and raked it into place.

"Reid!" Lorna shot to her feet, hurried around the fire, and grasped his hand. "I didn't think you were going to come after all."

"I'm sorry. I was finishing up some work and lost track of time." He must have felt Belle's intent gaze as his eyes snapped up and met hers, his grin flashing. He waved her over to join them.

"Hello, Reid." Belle strolled up to them.

Lorna's scowl deepened before she schooled her expression into a smile and returned her attention to the ranger.

"What did I miss, Belle?"

"We were late as well, but there are apples for roasting,

and I know how much you love roasted apples," Lorna interjected and tugged on his arm. "Come on, they are this way."

If he was surprised by the young woman's boldness, his demeanor did not betray him. "Please excuse me." He tipped his hat to Belle, laughing at Lorna's antics as she towed him away.

Still a little hungry and anxious for a cup of hot chocolate to warm her bones, but not wanting to appear over eager, Belle edged near the table where Fannie and Joshua stood and poured herself a cup, wrapping her hands around the warm mug. "Everything looks amazing. You really outdid yourself, Fannie."

Fannie beamed. "Miss Trent was kind enough to let me borrow the supplies from the house. She really is the kindest housemother in Harvey House history. She even allowed me to purchase some of the food from the house at cost." She turned to the dessert table and began dishing up the pecan pies, handing one to Belle. "You have to try it. I made it myself."

"You don't need to ask twice." Belle giggled.

"Colt! You finally made it." Joshua slapped Colt on the back.

The sweet pie turned gritty in her mouth. Had she been foolish to trust Dolly even though Colt had told a lie in his letters?

"I'm sorry. I had a few things I needed to finish up for the cattle drive tomorrow," Colt explained as he snatched a plate of pecan pie. "Delicious. Miss Fannie, you have outdone yourself." He caught sight of Belle and as his mouth was stuffed, he smiled through closed lips.

Belle dipped her head and gave him a small smile in return and took another bite of the sweet pie, trying to appear nonchalant. *When am I ever not going to be nervous around him?* While Colt's blond hair was meticulously combed back, a stubborn curl escaped and caressed his forehead. *Probably never. I wish he weren't so wretchedly handsome and kind. Maybe it would help me forget how much I wish we could've worked out.*

Fannie grasped her by the arm and drew her into the small circle of friends. "Wait? The drive starts tomorrow, Colt? I thought y'all were leaving in two days."

"Sorry, sweetheart. It was moved up to tomorrow, which means I am in charge of the ranch by myself." Joshua rubbed his head. "Ugh. I should've stayed to help you prepare for the drive, Boss, but I didn't know about the change in train schedule."

Colt swallowed and dismissed his remorse with a wave of his fork. "Nonsense. You'll make it up to me by seeing to the ranch while the rest of us are on the drive."

Did he just call Colt his boss? "The drive?" Belle asked before she could stop herself. "So, you two work together?"

"Sure do. Colt here is the best boss I have ever had," Joshua helped himself to a piece of pie.

Her eyes widened as she quickly took another bite of pie to disguise her surprise. *How did I not know this? I should've never believed Dolly. If Joshua works for Colt and is an honorable man then maybe . . .* She couldn't keep changing her mind. *I'm here to work now. Why, I'm almost as bad as Dolly—the professional husband hunter.*

"My brother Jesse also works for Colt," Joshua continued as he polished off his plate and Fannie reached to take it for him. "Aw now, you don't have to wait on me, Fannie. It's your night off."

Fannie laughed and pulled her grey wool shawl tight against the chill of the night air. "Don't be silly. This party is for you, my darling." She set aside his plate and poured him a cup of hot chocolate, handing it to him and pouring another for Colt.

"I won't keep you standing, Boss. Come have a seat by the fire," Joshua motioned Colt toward the logs that had been arranged for seating surrounding the fire.

"You coming, Belle?" Fannie asked.

"Be right behind you." Belle topped off her hot chocolate and turning around, she found herself facing Russ' barrel chest. She stepped aside, trying to avoid him, but he sidestepped with her.

"Whoa there, little missy. I've been aiming to speak with you all night, but every time I get you alone, you scurry off." He grinned down at her, revealing a gap between his front teeth. "You ain't on duty now, so I know you can talk to me."

Her eyes alighted on the dribble of pecan filling in his wiry brown beard and she rubbed her arm, hinting that she needed to stand by the fire, and gripped the handle of her cup. "If you'll please excuse me, I need to warm up by the fire."

His mouth twisted into a lustful grin as his eyes roved over her torso and whispered, "I can think of another way to warm you right up. That's what you Harvey Girls really want, right? Your high and mighty ways are just a trick to make us want you more. You ain't no better than them girls down at the Whistlin' Coyote."

"How dare you." Belle tossed the hot chocolate into his face.

He wiped his face with one hand and with a growl, took an angry stride toward her, his fists clenched.

COLT'S NECK BRISTLED. He twisted on his log seat and spied Belle at the refreshment table with Russ, her cheeks scarlet. He rose slowly so as not to garner attention from Dolly Matthews, who was determined to trail him all night. Outside the circle of log seats, he strode through the tall grass as Belle tossed her drink in the man's face.

Colt shot between them, his fingers itching above his whip. "Leave now before it's too late, Russ."

The man glared at Colt. He didn't dare disobey the brother of the leader . . . not after the gold robbery when Colt had reminded Russ who was the stronger man. Even with a bullet in his backside, Colt's whip had found its mark around Russ's shooting arm, keeping the man from killing one of the guards.

Russ cracked his neck and spit at Colt's boot, but Colt did not flinch, waiting for him to reach for his gun belt. Russ grunted and moseyed away.

Belle exhaled, gripping her cup tightly, as if attempting to settle the tremors in her hands. She glanced at the fire, but everyone was so enraptured with a story Joshua was reenacting that their laughter had concealed her encounter from all but him.

"Are you okay?" Colt whispered, his brows rising with concern. "Russ is a coyote."

"Yes." She gave a quick nod, pressing her hand to her chest. "Thank you. I don't know what came over me, throwing hot chocolate into his face. I've heard worse in my days as a maid, but this . . . this time it felt different."

She's endured worse than Russ's lude words? The thought of others treating her less than a lady set his teeth on edge. "He deserved it." He glanced behind her and lowered his voice. "I need to speak with you."

She nodded, though her eyes darted over to Harriet—her

hesitation evident, but he could tell that she no longer feared him.

"When we went for that walk, I couldn't tell you why it seemed like I lied, but if you are willing to listen, I can explain everything." At her nod, he took her hand in his and set aside her cup on the table, gently guiding her a little further from the group and toward the grove of cedar trees. "I couldn't tell you why because my boss wouldn't allow me for fear of jeopardizing the plan."

She held up her hand. "Your boss? I thought you owned your ranch?"

"I do, but that's not all I do." He raked his fingers through his hair. "I asked my boss for his permission again to tell you what I do besides ranching, but he still said it wasn't safe, but I know that if I don't tell you and dispel that lie, I will lose you forever, and I couldn't bear it." Seeing her shiver, he slipped off his coat and rested it around her shoulders, the piece engulfing her.

"Thank you." She hugged the coat close and if he wasn't mistaken, she sniffed the collar, a little smile playing at her lips.

Emboldened, he leaned forward. "I know it may have seemed like I lied. You see I am an informant for—"

"Miss Parish! There you are. Harriet was asking for you." A voice boomed from behind them, making Belle jump.

Colt tensed, longing to throw a punch at the interfering ranger who seemed bent on wooing Miss Parish away from him.

"She was?" Her gaze lingered on Colt as the Ranger extended his arm to her.

"You look positively freezing, Miss Parish." He lifted the coat from her shoulders and tossed it back to Colt. "Let's get you back to the fire."

She glanced over her shoulder to stare at Colt, the firelight shimmering against her dark locks. Colt could tell she wanted to hear him out, and for now, that was enough.

Knowing Reid would dominate Belle's attention, Colt mounted up and rode for home, his horse following the trail without so much as a nudge from Colt. He crested the hill to his ranch's entrance and pulled back on the reins as lowing caught his ears.

Why were his cattle so close to the fence line? They preferred to be as close to the mountains as they could manage. He kicked his mare into a trot, following the fence line until he crested the foothill, his jaw dropping at the sight of at least twenty head of cattle on his land . . . cattle that he did not recognize. He wheeled his horse about, looking for his brother. Russ had been at the party, which meant Grant was not far behind. He swiped off his hat and beat it against his leg. Grant was determined to ensnare him in his thievery.

"Grant!" He shouted, kicking his horse and surging around the edge of the herd. "Grant!"

"Hello brother," Grant rode out from behind the cedar trees. "Got you a little present."

"A present that could see me hung." Colt shot back. "Where did you get all—?"

"Save your questions for later. You are going to help me brand these cattle with your symbol and add them to your cattle drive, which will be leaving as soon as we are done."

Colt gritted his teeth. These cattle were someone's livelihood. Grant had pulled this while Colt was busy because he knew Colt would never agree to steal so many. "I won't do it, Grant. I am going to have them returned at first light.'

"And risk getting hung? You think anyone in this town is going to believe a Lawson? Especially when I stole these out from the mayor's son?" Grant grinned, leaning on his saddle horn. "You know I'm right."

Colt gripped his fist. He could not fetch Reid without Grant knowing, and to refuse Grant would risk Colt's cover—something he could not risk . . . even for someone's livelihood. "Start a fire. I'll get the iron."

CHAPTER 10

〜✥〜

*B*elle waited until Dolly and Fannie left for church before donning her pretty cream silk blouse, canary yellow skirt and matching blazer with billowing sleeves. She tilted her head in Dolly's hand mirror, and for the first time in a very long while, she felt beautiful. Pulling on her delicate lace gloves, and grabbing her lovely new straw hat, Belle gave a little twirl before hurrying downstairs to meet Harriet in her room.

"Belle." Harriet's jaw dropped. "When you said you'd bought some things, I thought you meant a new skirt, but this," she motioned at Belle's fashionable ensemble, "is a whole new look. I wish I could see Dolly's face when she sees you walk through the church doors."

"Aren't you coming to service?" Belle asked, confused as Harriet was already dressed in a rich emerald gown with ivory lace trim at the neck and cuffs.

Harriet sighed as she unpinned her chapeau, her golden hair catching in the morning light cascading through the large windows. "Apparently, Miss Trent isn't feeling well, so I won't be able to make it to church. I can't leave her here all on her own while she has one of her migraines. Normally, I wouldn't mind taking over for her, but . . ."

"But the Elliots' Sunday meal is today, and we were supposed to go together?" Belle finished for her. "Poor Miss Trent. But surely, one of the other girls can see to her needs?"

Harriet rubbed her forehead. "I can't possibly leave now. Someone has to supervise."

"Can't I take over while you go?"

Harriet unfastened her pearl necklace and settled it into a small, velvet lined box. "It's kind of you to offer, but you are not ready yet for that kind of responsibility. You're close to that level, but not yet and until then, I'm not comfortable leaving the Harvey House when Miss Trent is unavailable to supervise and provide the girls with protection from Dolly's iron fist."

"I could stay with Dolly and make sure she doesn't get too carried away with bossing the girls around." Belle helped unbutton Harriet's dress, the action reminding her of dear Miss Fairfield, her heart aching from so much change and the loss of having her friend near. Not for the first time did she regret declining Miss Fairfield's offering of her address so that they might converse. At the time, Belle had been too afraid of being caught by Suzanne and tossed out by the Fairfields . . . and what did her caution win her? She had been fairly tossed out in any event.

"There's no need for you to miss out on seeing Gaston Reid and showing off your pretty dress, and besides, you know Dolly would *never* listen to you." Harriet sighed, pressing her lips in a tight line. "I was really looking forward to seeing Gil."

"At least let me try to take your place here because you know it'll mean more to the Elliots if *you* attend than just me." Belle pleaded. "I can hardly go without you. I've only had the one dinner with them."

"They will understand. I've had to miss one or two dinner parties before. It's one of the sacrifices of being head waitress. I have to do this." Harriet hung up her dress and donned her uniform. "You, however, don't have to work today, and I really want you to go for them as much as yourself. You know how the townsfolk have slighted the Elliots after my father's death. No one wants to be associated with the people who killed the beloved town mayor who was set to become governor, so it would mean a lot if you go."

"I know what being made to feel like an outsider is like." Her childhood flashed to mind, and how Suzanne treated her as the hired help rather than family. Belle swallowed back her discomfort at attending alone. "Very well. I'll go, but how will I get there?"

"You can take my phaeton, or ride on horseback," Harriet offered and started for the dormitory door.

"Uh, I barely know how to drive, much less ride on horseback," Belle retorted, squinting in the morning light.

"Good morning, ladies!" The tall ranger called to them as he swiped off his Stetson. His grin broadened at Belle's small wave. "Gil asked me to escort y'all out to his place. With all of the criminal activity happening lately, he didn't want you to travel alone today and risk running into the bandits, which I thought prudent," Reid explained, resting his hands on his gun belt. His deep blue shirt pulled tight against his chest and his Sunday jacket did little to hide his broad, dangerous shoulders.

"Well, I'm afraid I won't be able to make it after all." Harriet gestured down at her uniform. "Duty calls, but Belle can still go. Why don't you escort her to church, and y'all can leave directly after service in my phaeton."

Belle gave Harriet a sideways look as she scrambled for an excuse. Her mouth went dry. *That little matchmaker. First, she tells me she doesn't want me marrying, but the minute she finds out I think her cousin is handsome, she is all giggles and starts scheming to throw us together. I'll have to come up with an hour's worth of conversation. I've never been alone with a man for an entire hour in my life—much less a ranger.*

A smile played at the corners of his mouth. "I would be honored to escort you if you'd be willing, Miss Belle."

Of course, she would be willing. Who wouldn't be willing? "Thank you, Reid."

He tugged on his Stetson. "I'll have her back before dark."

"Perfect and I'll tell the stable boy to have the phaeton ready for you both after service," Harriet called after them, already heading across the street to the Harvey House.

Following Reid, she secured the hatpin through her darling straw hat with its blue ribbons. She was happy to know that the new hat was most becoming and made her eyes even more blue.

Reid offered her his arm, and seeing as there was no polite way to refuse, she threaded her trembling hand through his arm, praying that he wouldn't pick up on her nervousness. "Lovely day," Belle ventured as they made their way down Main Street. In her ensemble, she felt brighter than she ever had before in her life. *There's no sinking into the shadows in yellow. I hope I didn't make a mistake in choosing such a bright color.*

He looked up at the sky as if noticing his surroundings for the first time that day as they climbed the steps into the pretty pale blue church. "I'm glad we'll be taking Harriet's buggy. It would be a mite windy on the back of a horse. At least with the phaeton, you can block the wind on the back and sides."

Swiping off his hat, Reid held the door for her at church and they quietly took a seat on the back pew behind her roommates. She glanced about before recalling that, of course, Colt was not in service. What had he been so eager to tell her?

Seeing Reid, Dolly's eyes sparkled as she gave him her sweetest smile, which faded the instant she realized he had escorted Belle. She clenched her jaw and pursed her lips as she turned around without so much as a nod of acknowledgement to Belle.

Belle did her best to follow along with the sermon but having Reid beside her and Colt in her thoughts, she was a bundle of nerves and couldn't absorb a single word the preacher was saying. She had to compose herself. It wouldn't do to be so preoccupied on the journey to the Elliots'. *You can't just be quiet the whole ride to the Elliots'. You're smart. Think of questions to ask him.*

When the preacher called for the final hymn, Belle stood, but forgot that she still had the hymnal in her lap, and it tumbled to the ground. Thankfully, the rest of the congregation was in the process of standing, so the sound was muffled. Reid bent, retrieved it, and handed it to her with an encouraging smile as the hymn began. *Wonderful. Not only do I look like I'm clumsy, he is about to find out that I sing like a crow.* Singing as low as she possibly could, Belle managed to get through the three hymns without another blunder. The preacher called for the closing prayer and dismissed the congregation with a blessing for the week to come.

Before Dolly could pounce, Reid touched her elbow and guided her out to the stables. As promised, the phaeton was ready and waiting for them. Reid held her hand and averted his eyes as she lifted her hem to step up into the buggy.

She smoothed her skirts as he tied his horse to the back

of the buggy and settled in beside her. *Time to try small talk, Belle.* "Thank you for escorting me."

"Of course. I was heading that way anyway, so it's no trouble at all." He snapped the reins.

The buggy rolled down the road, and while he seemed content with just exchanging pleasantries, she felt it her duty to at least try to make conversation. Having thought about which would be her first question the entirety of church service, Belle cleared her throat. "So, any news on the bandits?"

"I've been following them for months, but the trails just mysteriously end near Las Vegas and San Antonio, and I am left wondering where I went wrong." He grunted as he slapped the reins again. "I've caught dozens of bandits and murderers, but this group . . ." He shook his head. "The Death Riders are smart. They don't leave many tracks, but they are bound to mess up sometime. And when they do, I'll be there to arrest them."

"Have any of the other ranches besides the Elliots' been robbed?" Belle fiddled with her lace trimmed sleeves, still unused to such delicate finery belonging to her.

He tilted his hat further back on his head. "I hate to say it, but at first, the townsfolk didn't care when the Elliot family was robbed. However, the moment the mayor's son's ranch was broken into, they began holding meetings and set a rotation of men in the community taking watches each night in town to ensure their safety."

"The mayor's son? Where is his ranch?"

"Wesley's ranch is just beyond the Elliot ranch. The bandits stole their entire herd during Fannie's party two nights ago, and if that wasn't enough, they managed to get their hands on the Wesleys' life savings buried behind one of the stones in the fireplace. Apparently, the leader threatened to shoot the wife."

She shivered. "How horrible."

He cleared his throat. "But enough about robbers. Tell me about yourself."

"Well, my life isn't nearly as exciting as capturing outlaws. My family comes from a long line of servants, mainly cooks." She lifted her hand to block the sun from her eyes.

"That explains your family's secret recipes that you told me about."

He remembered. Belle's cheeks heated. "Indeed."

Reid guided the horse under the hanging "E" sign. "So, now that I know you come from a family of southern cooks, what brought you all the way out here?"

Not wanting to reveal she was a mail-order bride just yet, she wracked her brain for a truthful answer. "What brings everyone else out here? I came for a chance at a new life—an adventure!" *That's close enough. Adventure led from desperation . . . and the hope of finding love.* "When did you join the Texas Rangers? You seem young, but whenever I hear the men talking about you at the lunch counter, it sounds as if you have been at this for quite some time. And, from what I've heard, you are very good at what you do."

He smiled as he leaned back on the tufted leather seat. "I met my boss, who was friends with Mr. Elliot, when I was twelve and I hung on his every word, enamored with the life of a Texas Ranger. He told me that if I ever wanted a job, come see him, so I ran away when I was fifteen and have been with the Rangers for a little over ten years now, but I've only officially been a Ranger for seven years as I was just the errand boy until I was old enough to join."

"Fifteen? So young." Belle whispered.

"I didn't like being sent East every other winter or

summer. My mother and her family back East were too controlling, so the moment I had an opportunity to get away from their scrutiny, I took it." He shrugged.

"Harriet told me how you lived with your mother every other winter season back East, so why didn't you refuse to go with her since you could have just stayed with your aunt?" She held onto her hat as the buggy hit a rut.

He laughed. "You obviously have never met my aunt. She would go East in a second if her husband would sell the ranch. She thought I was foolish not to live East all the time, so I ran. I didn't feel young at the time, but looking back, it does sound kind of young." He shrugged. "I didn't like it in the East as much as I did here. Every summer, I'd spend my days with my father's best friend, 'wild' Bill Elliot. Harriet and I, of course, are not related to the Elliots, but they treat us as if we were their flesh and blood family."

Except for Gil, Belle thought as the phaeton bounced down the dirt road and rounded the corner to the Elliot home. *He thinks of Harriet as something much more than a sister. And Lorna certainly does not think of Reid as her brother.*

CHAPTER 11

Lorna batted her dark lashes at Reid, smiling at him throughout the meal. Belle's gaze leapt back and forth between the two of them. She hadn't noticed him sending Lorna any special looks. He treated her like a little sister. *Maybe she's sweet on him and he just doesn't reciprocate.* She gave her head a little shake and stabbed her fork into her steak and cut off a small, ladylike bite. *Why do you care? You won't be marrying any time soon. Your contract has you bound for almost a year, and by then, Reid will have long left New Mexico, and you, behind for his first love, the Texas Rangers.*

"Pa, don't you think it's time for me to feed the stock?" Lorna asked, her tone dripping with feigned innocence as everyone finished their meal.

Mr. Elliot slapped his portly stomach, laughing. "You really are incorrigible. You *never* feed the stock. You seem to think that I have a surprise for you hidden in the barn. I don't know where you've gotten the idea because it's not even close to your birthday, or Christmas."

Lorna grinned. "I still think we should go check on the stock."

Mr. Elliot threw down his napkin and sighed. "I can't seem to keep her at bay any longer. Mother, looks like the secret is out." He winked to his petite wife across the table.

"Secret?" Belle whispered to Gil, who was seated next to her.

Gil grinned. "She's been pestering Pa for months for a new horse and he finally met with the horse trader yesterday, and Lorna assumes that means he bought something for her."

Lorna giggled, scraped back her chair, and hurried to the door with everyone scrambling to follow her. Before she was halfway across the yard to the stables, Mr. Elliot caught his daughter's hand. "Wait here, my dear." He chuckled and headed into the stables. Lorna's cheeks flushed a pretty pink, her eyes glistening with pride as her father led out a beautiful silky black stallion. "I searched for ages for a horse that matched your description," he said, watching his daughter as she stroked the horse's mane. "Is he to your liking?"

"He's lovely." Lorna threw her arms around her father. "Thank you, Pa."

Reid shook his head, disapproval in his eyes as he whispered to Gil, "Won't that horse be a bit much for a wisp of a girl like Lorna?"

Overhearing him, Lorna's eyes flashed toward Reid. "You forget I can ride better than any man in this town. Including *you*. How about we all go for a ride before we take dessert?"

Gil shrugged, nodding his consent. "It wouldn't hurt to check a fence line or two and set my mind at ease that the rustlers are gone for now."

Reid turned to Belle. "How about you, Miss Parish?"

"My ensemble won't allow for riding." *Thank the good Lord*

for such a perfect excuse. She sighed as if saddened to miss out on the ride.

"I'm sure Lorna can lend you a split skirt." Gil looked to Lorna, his eyebrows raised in question. "Will you lend Miss Parish what she needs?"

Belle protested, but Reid sent her a wink that said she had already lost as he turned to join the men in saddling the mounts. Lorna motioned for her to follow her into the house.

"Thank you, but you really don't have to. I can wait for you all here," Belle said as they entered Lorna's bedroom, which didn't match the rest of the house. It was decorated only in the highest of fashions with silk papered walls, Louis XIV furniture, and a petite crystal chandelier. It looked quite out of place in the ranchero, but it brought Belle back to the Fairfield's mansion.

"If you volunteer to stay, then Reid will insist on staying as well and then it wouldn't be a party, and I've been waiting for my stallion far too long to have my fun spoiled now. You would be doing me a great service to join us." Lorna threw open her armoire and riffled through her clothing, tossing a skirt and cotton shirtwaist into Belle's arms before proceeding to change into her riding clothes.

Belle slipped into the brown serge riding skirt and buttoned the shirt. Stepping in front of Lorna's mirror, she blushed at how the skirt hugged her slender body and showed off her figure more than she preferred. *I actually look like I have a figure. I suppose eating three solid meals a day is finally showing.* She tucked the shirt into the skirt waist as Lorna handed her a small Stetson. "It stays on better than a straw hat and you don't want to burn that ivory nose of yours."

In order to make the hat sit right, Belle released her raven locks from her high coiffure, allowing them to spill uninhibited over her shoulders. Securing the chin strap, she took a deep breath and followed Lorna outside.

Leading a paint from the barn, Reid's eyes widened at Belle's new attire and a smile crept into the corner of his mouth. "You look like you were born to ride, Miss Parish. You will be riding Lorna's old gelding, Jumper."

Belle placed her hand on Jumper's nose and gently stroked him as Reid tightened the girth once more. She whispered in the horse's ear, "You take care of me, you hear?"

"You are safe with me." Reid nudged the horse closer to her, his gaze piercing her.

Her heart raced as she clenched the saddle horn, staring up at the saddle seat. How on earth was she to manage it on her own?

"Don't be nervous," he whispered into her ear.

She cleared her throat, hoping that confidence would once again reside in her tone. "Is there a mounting block?"

"You could use the fence rail, or I could help you like this," Reid wrapped his hands around her tiny waist and easily lifted her onto the saddle. Lorna's eyes blazed and then lowered into a simmer as she leaned against the rail, watching them.

Belle shifted her weight in the saddle, trying to get comfortable as the horse let out a disgruntled whinny and bucked. Belle lost her grip on the horn and tumbled head over heels from the saddle, slamming onto the manure trodden ground.

"Belle!" Reid wrapped his arm around her waist and gently raised her into a sitting position. His gaze darted up to the horse, "What in blue blazes set him off? He's normally such a calm animal." He took her by the shoulders, examining her. "Belle, answer me. Are you hurt?"

"No." *My rear just feels like it might never be able to sit again. Apparently, I'm the only woman in New Mexico who has never been on a horse.* She pressed her palms to the ground, struggling to stand. "Again, please."

"Are you sure? That was a pretty hard fall you took there." Reid pulled her up, scrutinizing her petite hand. "And you scratched yourself on the landing."

Ignoring the sting from the cut, she drew her hand from his. "I'm fine. It doesn't hurt." *However, my tailbone begs to differ.* She shifted her stance, trying to alleviate any pressure from her lower back.

He leaned close to her ear, "Have you ever ridden before, Miss Parish?"

She pressed her tongue to her cheek and sighed before admitting, "My brother is a coachmen for a family in Charleston, but my sister-in-law would never allow me near them for fear I would injure a horse after I accidentally gave one too many oats and made it sick. And if I hurt a horse, I'd force the whole family to leave the household because of my clumsiness."

"You were just a little girl though. Surely, you don't feel such apprehension even now? Because if you do, the horse can feel it."

"If you are well enough to ride, Miss Parish, we really should be on our way. We still have dessert to finish," Lorna called from her saddle, her tone exuding eagerness to ride and agitation with Reid's attention to Belle.

"I'm not comfortable with you riding Jumper by yourself." Reid retrieved his mount. "Miss Parish, why don't you ride with me?"

"With you?" Belle waited for him to declare that he was in jest, yet he looked at her as if it was the most normal suggestion in the world and why would she object?

"It would be better than you falling off Jumper, breaking your neck and me having to explain to Harriet that she will need to hire a new girl." Gil patted his mount's neck. "Reid's horse is gentle as a bunny and faster than a pack of wolves."

I suppose things which would be deemed improper back home would not be deemed so here as necessity compels people out here to do strange things. She slowly nodded, and Reid guided his horse to where she could easily grip the saddle horn. He lifted her into the saddle and waited for her to adjust her split skirt before grabbing the saddle horn in front of her, carefully sitting behind her. "Normally, if I had someone in the saddle with me, I'd put them behind me, but I think this would be a perfect time to teach you to ride properly."

He lifted the reins and grasped her hand in his rough, tan one and threaded the reins through her fingers and demonstrated how to grip it with her hand. "You pull this way to go right and this way to guide him left." The horse moved its head back and forth, obeying Reid's commands. His arms brushed against her own as he gripped the reins ahead of where she was holding. "I'm going to instruct the horse to start walking now."

Conscious of his nearness, all Belle could manage to do was nod.

"Hold onto the saddle horn until you're comfortable enough to take the reins." He gave his horse a gentle kick.

The horse took off as if eager to catch up with Lorna's stallion, sending Belle's curls whipping about her face as the horse's gait almost tossed her out of the saddle. Reid's arm encircled her waist and held her steady as the horse lengthened his strides into a gallop. Every time she felt herself slipping, she could feel the muscles in Reid's arm tighten, reassuring her that she was safe.

Lorna halted her mount on the top of the hill, breathless

from her ride but immaculate in her appearance. "Reid!" She called as their horse slowed to a walk, "Isn't it beautiful? Don't you wish you could settle down on a ranch like this with a nice girl?"

Gil coughed at the undeniable flirtation and raised his brows at his sister, but if she saw, she didn't care to heed him.

"It would be nice, but my job doesn't necessarily allow for the luxury of owning my own ranch, much less marrying." Reid adjusted his Stetson.

Lorna laughed. "Well, of course, you're enthralled with your work *now*, but I'm sure one day, you'll wake up and be tired of being a ranger with its lonely, nomadic lifestyle and will want to become a rancher like Gil. Maybe you'll even buy the piece of land next to us?"

"I don't think I'll ever tire of being a ranger, but you never know what God has in store." He shrugged, dodging her hints.

At his noncommittal reply, Belle felt the little bloom of hope in her heart die. *You knew he was against being married. Serves you right for even thinking about his handsome eyes, strong arms, and his dark brown hair. You don't really even know him.*

Gil hopped off his horse and checked the fence line, grunting in frustration. "They did it again. I just checked this stretch of fence yesterday."

Reid joined him, studying the cuts in the barbwire fence. "They are getting bolder, busting a fence so close to your ranchero."

"They know our family isn't in good standing with the rest of the town." Gil slapped his hat against his thigh, dust lifting from the brim.

"I'll find them." Reid rested his hand on Gil's shoulder. "But I'm not comfortable keeping the ladies out when the rustlers have been here so recently." Reid mounted behind her once more and wheeled his horse around. "We better head back. Miss Parish will need to be home before dark."

Reid pressed his mount, returning them much faster than the journey out to the fence line. With a brief farewell to the Elliots, Reid ushered her into the buggy as the sun began its descent. Despite Reid's urgency, Belle reveled in the beautiful golden sky, ignoring the fear skittering in her heart about the bandits. "It's so beautiful out here."

"I can't argue with you. To me, there's no place prettier than the West. So, you never did answer my question. What adventure brought you out to New Mexico? Was it only the job of being a Harvey Girl or do you have any acquaintances around?"

Belle swallowed. *I suppose he will have to find out sooner or later.* "Um, well, I came here with Angelique Chauvin . . . now, Mrs. Smith."

"The mail-order bride of Rudy's?" His eyebrows shot up.

"Yes, um, well, I . . ." she stumbled. *Just say it.* "I actually moved to become a mail-order bride myself. When I met him, he didn't match his character description. Taking account of all of the stories of his actions from one of the Harvey Girls and his conversation with Preacher Martin, I decided that I couldn't marry a man when our relationship was based on lies."

"So, it is true. You moved your life to marry a stranger." Reid's jaw tightened. "And his name?"

Belle glanced down to her hands and began picking at the skin around her nails. "I'd rather not say. I don't wish to cause him any more distress than I already have. I offered to pay back the price for the train ticket, so he wouldn't think I was using him for his money, but he wouldn't take it."

He pushed his hat back and scratched his forehead. "Why

didn't you just return to Charleston? I'm glad you didn't, but why didn't you?"

Her heart bounced at his admission. "Well, uh," she cleared her throat, "I couldn't. My sister-in-law found my letters to Col—I mean, my former fiancé—and she threw me out of the Fairfield's home for my deceiving her again after my helping Miss Fairfield escape her impending marriage to Mr. Payne. Las Vegas was my only option, unless someone fired a lady's maid in Charleston, which does not happen often."

"Oh." He snapped the reins and kept his eyes on the road. "Well, I'm glad you didn't marry him. There's nothing worse than being bound to a cruel man. My father was cruel. That's why my Aunt Gertrude hated him so much. He hurt my mother, which made her have to return East and leave Aunt Gertrude alone in Texas with her husband."

So his father didn't die. "Where is he now?"

"My father is in jail." His jaw clenched. "I never wanted to be like him, so I chose an occupation that is his exact opposite. As a Texas Ranger, I put men like him behind bars and hopefully, I can protect helpless women. When I was a child, I couldn't protect my mother." He halted as his voice grew hoarse and cleared his throat. "By the time I was big enough to stand up to him, she was too hurt to continue living out here, and she had to return East."

"I'm so sorry, Reid," she whispered. She blinked away her tears, knowing the sting of a heavy hand from one who was supposed to love you.

"It's been a long time since I've seen her, but I think of her every day and every day, my strength for this job is renewed, kindling my passion for justice."

"I know you said you disliked it back East, but that was

when you were a child. Why don't you move to be with her now?"

"Because my calling is here where I can help women who are trapped in situations similar to my mother. Out West, it's easier for cruel men to get away with treating their wives poorly."

Belle shivered as a breeze swept through the valley, sending the ribbons on her chapeau spiraling in the air.

Seeing her tremble, Reid looked under the seat for a blanket. "I guess Harriet doesn't pack for cold weather in the fall. If I had a jacket, I'd lend it to you, but if it's not too forward of me . . ." He slowly eased his arm on the back seat, letting his arm drape over her shoulders.

Her stomach flipped at his touch. Too cold to protest, Belle leaned back on the seat, relishing his closeness. She gazed up into the stars, inhaled his musky scent and savored the last few moments of Reid's company, wishing the ride home would never end.

COLT SWIPED the sweat from his eyes as he steered the remaining twenty-five head of cattle into the canyon. After three days of leading the cattle drive with Jesse, Russ, and Grant, Colt guessed Grant's motives for stealing only a thousand dollars in cattle was power. He wanted those townspeople to fear the Death Riders and doubt the rangers, and he wanted Colt to bend to his will.

Colt flicked back the brim of his hat to study his brand on the rump of a nearby steer. It covered the former owner's brand quite nicely, but all Colt could think of was the months of sweat and love that went into cattle raising. His stomach twisted at the pain his brother caused this family. If he hadn't been so busy at Fannie's party, maybe he could have convinced the drunken Grant to let things be. *If Reid had been patrolling instead of wooing Belle, perhaps I wouldn't be driving stolen cattle into my family's canyon and instead, be telling Belle the truth.*

Grant shot three times into the air, skittering the cattle toward the paddock. The cabin door burst open as Colt kicked Pepper and corralled a few that were trying to escape the danger and lassoed a pregnant cow, gently guiding her into the pen. He locked it and turned a glare at his brother.

Grant holstered his weapon, grinning at Colt. He lifted his hands in greeting to the last member of the Death Riders who trotted down the steps, rifle slung over her shoulders.

"Welcome back, sweetheart."

"You are a sight for sore eyes, Jill." Grant hopped down from the saddle and pulled his wife into a deep kiss, the men whooping behind them.

Jill gave Colt a saucy grin. "Good to see you too, honey. I overheard some news at the Boerne General Store, and I have an idea for our next robbery—and it's a good one."

CHAPTER 12

She wiped her hands on a rag and threw it down on the counter, tapping her foot as she waited for the cowpoke to place his order. After almost a week of not seeing Reid, Belle was growing nervous. *Where is he? He always takes at least one meal a day here. I wonder if he left town? But why would he leave without telling me unless he's avoiding me because of the I-was-a-mail-order-bride conversation?*

"Just go ahead and *order*, Frank." She jammed her hands onto her hips and glowered at the man. "You always do this. You lollygag for thirty minutes, order seven cups of coffee and then finally, place the exact same order you have every single day. Save me some time and get your biscuits with an absurd amount of honey, one medium rare steak, a side of potatoes and green beans and one piece of apple pie and be done with it. I've got things to do."

His jaw dropped, making his long, scraggly beard dip into his coffee cup. "But what if I decide that I want a change?"

Dolly swooped in, grabbed Belle by the elbow and yanked her aside. "Miss Belle," she said through a gritted smile, "that's no way to speak to our guests." She turned and gave a brilliant smile to the offender. "Mr. Jenkins, you take as much time as you wish. And allow me to get you another cup on the house," she cooed and poured him a fresh cup, the action seeming to mollify him.

Harriet rustled over and studying Belle's flushed cheeks, she asked, "What's wrong with you? Tonight is the social. You should be excited and not agitated."

"I don't know what's come over me." *Liar.* "I'm so sorry." She sighed. "It won't happen again."

"It'd better not or you're fired." Dolly shot back as she passed by with a hot coffee pot. "Fill the coffee urn. I don't have time to keep running back and forth, fixing your problems."

"Excuse us, Dolly," Harriet steered Belle to the corner of the lunch counter. "Why don't you take a break for the rest of the afternoon because unfortunately, I'm going to need you to work an extra shift tonight after the social." Harriet grimaced as if she were afraid of Belle's cantankerousness.

Chastened, she smiled, eager to appear helpful again after such an outburst that even made Harriet afraid of her. "Of course. It won't be a problem."

"Thank you. May I ask what has you in such a dither?"

"There are a number of reasons." Belle reached for an empty coffee cup and whisked it into the dirty dish bin.

"Like Reid?" Harriet's eyes sparkled.

Belle felt her cheeks blaze, but she grabbed a damp rag and wiped away flecks of dried coffee from the last cowboy.

Harriet chuckled and crossed her arms. "I don't know why you even bother denying it. It's obvious you like him."

"But he's a Ranger and his duty comes first . . . he won't ever have time for a wife—" Belle scrubbed the counter with a vengeance as if to scrub away the sentence she almost finished.

Harriet took her by the hand, stopping her. "Take the rest of the day off. No one is in here now besides Mr. Jenkins."

Knowing she needed to get her mood under control, Belle thanked Harriet and crossed the street and lumbered up the stairs to her bedroom, unbuttoning the top few buttons of her dress to let in some air and collapsed onto the bed. Opening her nightstand, she retrieved her father's watch and cradled it in her palm, allowing the gentle, steady ticking to lull her to sleep.

"Does it say who it's from?"

Belle blinked awake to find Dolly and Fannie with their backs to her, studying something on the dresser top.

"No, it just says. 'Save a dance for me.' How is she supposed to know who to save the dance for if the note doesn't say who is asking for it?" Dolly turned the note over and scoured it for hints of the sender. "The penmanship is flawless."

Swinging her legs off the bed and stretching her arms, Belle was mindful not to step in the bowls of water where the feet of the bed rested, which had, so far, remained scorpion and insect free. She gently tucked the watch back into the cigar box before peering over to see what they were examining. A bouquet of hot house roses. "Who are they for?"

The girls started and Dolly's hand flew to her mouth to keep from squealing. With a sheepish shrug, Fannie handed her a small box of chocolates with a note tied together by a deep blue silk ribbon. "This was left at the dormitory door with a note addressed to you."

"So, you decided to read a note, which was intended for me?" Her cheeks flamed as she unfolded the note. *I wonder who sent it?* She examined the penmanship but didn't recognize it.

"Do you know who it's from?" Dolly sidled up next to her and stared at the note as if it would suddenly make sense to her now.

"Not in the least." Belle drew in the scent of the beautiful blooms. She had seen Miss Fairfield receive her share of costly hot house blooms, but never had she been offered such an array.

"Aren't you going to open the box of chocolates?" Fannie clasped her hands to her throat. "My Joshua hasn't brought me chocolates since we were first courting."

Belle pulled the ribbon of the paper box that was embossed with an intricate design of leaves and flowing vines, which surrounded the script label of the candy company, *Loft*. Opening the box, she pushed back the lace cut paper as the scent of the sweets wafted into the room and beheld a dozen delicate chocolates. Belle selected one in the shape of a heart and closed her eyes, relishing the moment. Before she took a bite, she lifted the box, offering one to Dolly and Fannie, "Would you like to try one?"

Fannie carefully selected hers, while Dolly just snatched one up at random and popped it into her mouth.

"These are heavenly. He must have had these special ordered. None of the stores around here carry *Loft* candies." Fannie's eyes danced. "You simply must tell me who it's from."

"I'm not entirely certain," Belle admitted and folded the lace paper over the chocolates and replaced the lid. *Well, the note is flawless, and I know Reid must have attended only the best of schools.*

Dolly rolled her eyes. "You're probably just ashamed of who it is. It's that old ranch hand who works for Harriet's uncle, isn't it?" She giggled. "Old Frank Jenkins who is always proposing to one of us."

"I believe they're from Ranger Reid." Seeing the color fade from Dolly's face filled Belle with guilt as she hurried to her side of the closet and fetched out her new Parisian styled blue gown that she had finished altering at last.

"Reid sent these?" Dolly's gaze darted back to Fannie. "You already turned Colt loose and practically announced that you have no intention to marry. Why are you toying with Reid's heart?" She withdrew her gold locket from her jewelry box and fastened it about her neck.

"I'm not." Belle stepped into her gown, enjoying the delicate softness of the fabric against her skin. *I'll never tire of this dress.* Belle smiled to herself as she smoothed down the white accordion pleated mousseline de soie.

"I've been waiting for him to court me for a year, and you better not lure him away from me just out of spite." Dolly crossed her arms over her mint gown, glaring.

"I would never lead a man on, and Reid does not belong to you." Belle retorted as she pulled her hatbox from the shelf. "And what of Colt? I thought you had your cap set for him."

"Colt is too busy for courting. And as for Reid, you're just jealous that you don't belong to anyone anymore," Dolly mumbled.

Belle's heart slammed against her ribs. "What did you just say?"

"I said, Colt doesn't belong to you anymore and now you've signed Mr. Harvey's contract, Reid can't either. He's fair game just like Colt." Dolly pinned on her hat and whirled about. "Come on, Fannie. Let's go."

Belle pressed a hand to her corseted waist and gripped the foot of her bed. *Oh Lord, did I misjudge Colt? I know the preacher confirmed he lied, but maybe Colt isn't as bad as Dolly made him out to be. Was she only trying to distract me from him to give herself a chance with him?* She crossed the room and flung open the window for a desperate breath of fresh air, her gaze landing on a tall Texas Ranger riding away. She leaned her head against the window frame and sighed. *What am I to do?*

CHAPTER 13

Belle clutched Harriet's arm, giggling with her over the excitement of the auction as the preacher's wife led the crowd in polite applause as another bachelor's basket was claimed. The ladies of the town had decorated the white church rails with wildflowers and had the pulpit moved to the small front porch to serve as the auctioneer's table. The churchyard was lit with rows of torches and sprinkled with lanterns hanging from the cedar branches, creating a festive air. In the spirit of the fundraiser, the Harvey House brought out almost all of the tables, chairs, fine china and linens from the restaurant. In the center of the churchyard, strategically placed hay bales designated a large circle for the dancing to come.

The auctioneer waved the next young man forward. Gil stood on the second step with his basket and gave Harriet a broad grin before directing his attention to the auctioneer, who raised his hammer and opened the bidding.

Without waiting to see if anyone else would bid, Lorna made a bid for two bits. The auctioneer called for a second bid and without waiting for a response, began to bring his hammer down.

"Harriet." Belle squeezed her arm.

"One dollar!" Harriet shouted, waving the bill in the air with a carefree giggle at her boldness.

Lorna grinned and if Belle wasn't mistaken, sighed with relief as the townsfolk turned to see what lady would want to bid on a lunch from an Elliot, much less pay so much. Harriet strode through the crowd, proudly paid the auctioneer's assistant and claimed Gil's arm. Smiling, they slipped away to the outskirts of the group to enjoy their tasty basket along with each other's company, despite the murmuring of the townsfolk.

Belle caught Aunt Gertrude giving Harriet a scowl that could melt the hide off an alligator. She sucked in her breath. *No wonder Harriet was so afraid to court Gil— the woman is absolutely terrifying.* Murmuring among the ladies announced the arrival of a particularly eligible, handsome man's basket.

Belle's heart raced as Reid climbed the platform with his Harvey House basket in hand. The four dollars in her pocket burned. *I hope it's enough. Surely, no one will bid over two dollars, much less four dollars.* But with one glance at the crowd of girls, Belle knew her chances of a lunch with Reid were slim.

"One dollar!" Belle called, setting the bid high. Reid's twinkling eyes met hers as he smiled, giving her a nod of what she thought to be encouragement. *Why, he wants me to win.* She smiled back, confidence filling her heart.

"Two dollars." Lorna strode forward as if to announce her claim on him and daring anyone else to bid.

Belle closed her eyes and tried to find courage. *It's for charity.* "Two dollars and a quarter!" Belle hollered.

"Two dollars and fifty cents." Dolly refused to look at

Belle, her cheeks flushing with suppressed anger at Belle's daring.

I'm going to pay for this later. Belle bid away all the money in her pocket.

"Five dollars." Dolly called out, grinning at Belle as if she knew she had won.

Lorna whispered into her father's ear and at his nod, her lovely eyes lit up. "*Ten* dollars!"

The crowd gasped at the unheard-of amount and the auctioneer looked to Dolly and Belle, but Belle shrugged and gave a small laugh, waving her hand dismissively.

"Sold!" The auctioneer shouted and slammed his hammer down. He waved the next man up on the stage as Reid met Lorna at the bottom of the church steps.

Colt. Her heart lodged itself in her throat. The handsome rancher stood beside the platform, uncrossing his arms and setting his hands on his hips. He had a wrapping about his wrist. *Is he hurt?*

"And now, we have this beautiful basket prepared by the Harvey House for Mr. Colt Lawson," the rotund auctioneer called from the church steps down to the gathered crowd as he held up a large picnic basket decorated with a white ribbon and a sprig of fresh violets tucked into the knot. The auctioneer held the basket up to his nose and took a dramatic sniff. "Well, ladies, this is going to be one tasty basket. It smells like fried chicken. I can't tell what the sides are, but from the weight of it, there are quite a few. Let's start the bidding off at two bits."

A young lady next to Belle lifted her hand to bid, but her mother slapped it down before the auctioneer spotted her. "Don't you dare bid on his basket. Only bid on possible suitors," her mother hissed. "Do you want to ruin your chances for a decent husband by getting involved with a *Lawson*?"

Colt met Belle's gaze and his smile faltered as Dolly bid against another lady. Having the winning bid of fifty cents, Dolly waltzed through the crowd and daringly threaded her arm through Colt's, throwing a victorious glance over her shoulder at Belle.

A young gentleman named Jesse, who Belle recognized as one of the Harvey House regulars and from Fannie's party, stepped up. A few girls placed small bids here and there but determined not to be embarrassed by not winning a basket at all, Belle bid seventy-five cents and won. Belle paid the auctioneer's assistant, the preacher's wife, Mrs. Martin.

"Thank you," Mrs. Martin's eyes sparkled as she accepted Belle's payment. "Such fun bidding on luncheon hampers, isn't it? All these years, we've been letting the young men have all the excitement."

Jesse clomped down the stairs, grinning as he offered Belle his arm.

"Looks like I lucked out. You are the 'Belle' of them all." He chuckled and led her over to a cedar tree. Before she knew what was happening, she realized all too late that he was leading her directly to the table where Colt was luncheoning with Dolly. "Howdy, Colt. Mind if we sit with y'all?"

"We don't want to disturb them," Belle choked out. "They probably want a private meal and there are, um, those tables over there." She picked up her skirts, turning to bolt for the empty tables. "I'll go claim one."

"Aw shucks, you don't have to do all that." Jesse grabbed her elbow, stopping her. "The boss man don't mind and he's easier to talk to than most of the townsfolk."

Boss man? Exactly how many men does Colt employ?

"Join us." Colt waved them over. He picked up his basket

from the chair on his left and placed it on the ground. "You don't mind, do you Miss Dolly?"

From the glare she sent Belle, she *did* mind.

His heart raced at the sight of Belle. After wishing all week to speak with her, his hired hand was escorting her to his very table. He rose as Dolly unnecessarily scooted her chair nearer to his, giving Jesse a wide berth. Belle sat to his left, keeping her gaze focused on the plate before her as Jesse rummaged through the basket.

Colt resumed his seat, casually glancing at her. She was nervous. He knew from her letters of her shy nature, but it hurt to see her and not be with her. How could someone know one another on such a deep level and suddenly forget all the sweet words written between them? He certainly had not.

"Mind if we join?" Reid smiled to Belle as Lorna clutched his arm.

Well, this will be a relaxing dining experience. Colt unpacked the last items in the basket lunch and was relieved to find fried chicken with mashed potatoes and green beans. He hadn't even bothered to look when he picked up a basket. All he had been thinking of was seeing Belle again.

"Do you even need to ask?" Dolly patted the seat next to her.

Lorna spread the feast before Reid, saying how she was so glad he didn't buy the fried chicken basket.

Belle turned to Jesse. "How was the cattle drive?"

"Short, which was nice," he replied, smacking his lips as he chewed his chicken. "But Colt here, got his hand smashed by a horse on the last day while he was shoeing it."

Belle whipped her attention to Colt, alarm in her eyes. "Did it break your hand?"

"Nah, just left it mighty sore." He lifted up his right hand. "I didn't need to add the bandage, but I figured it would look a sight better than for everyone to see how bruised and swollen my hand is."

"Thank goodness you are well," Belle whispered, her expression pained as Dolly parroted the sentiment.

"There is no need to worry you Harvey House ladies," he laughed and sipped his lemonade, shifting in his seat at the women's eyes on him.

"Shoeing a horse on a cattle drive isn't ideal, but when you work in the Wild West, you have to be prepared for that kind of thing," Jesse added, smacking his lips. "When Colt hired me and Joshua about a year and a half ago, I took a kick to the backside when I was digging out a rock from a hoof. I didn't sit for days!" He slurped down his glass of sweet lemonade.

Belle blinked as if she were trying to concentrate on his words and not the crumbs flying out of his mouth. Colt ran his hand over his mouth to suppress his laughter.

Dolly's eyes brightened. "Your ranch must be doing very well for you to be paying for two ranch hands." She turned her gaze back at Belle. "Bet you wished you hadn't been so hasty in your decision that first day after all?"

Belle choked on her mash potatoes, and she reached for her glass, her eyes wide. Her gaze flitted to Jesse and back to Colt and then to Reid.

Colt frowned. "No need to bring that up. It's water under the bridge." His eyes met Belle's, and she nodded her thanks to him.

"Water under the bridge? When I told you that Reid had sent her a box of chocolates and asked her to 'save a dance' for him, you turned redder than tomato basil soup." She snorted. "I'd hardly call that water under the bridge."

That's because I bought them from Rudy. If my hand wasn't hurt from the horse and Rudy hadn't written the note for me, Belle would have known they were from me.

CHAPTER 14

The fiddlers began to play, and the young men and ladies of the town fairly leapt to take part in the dancing, ending the most uncomfortable meal Belle had ever experienced.

"So did you decide if you were going to save me a dance?" Reid touched her elbow, turning her to him.

She smiled up at the ranger, the light from the lanterns hanging in the cedar trees casting a glow about him. "You should have signed your name. I might've never known it was you."

He shrugged. "Not saying it was, but if I did admit to sending it to you, where would the mystery be? So, did you?"

"Yes, in fact, I saved my very *first* dance for you." She allowed him to take her hand and lead her towards the dance floor, but before they reached the circle, Lorna planted herself in front of them.

"There you are, Reid. It's time to dance." Her eyes fell on their clasped hands. "You said you'd dance with me before anyone else."

"I did?" His eyebrows shot up. "That's right. I did. Didn't I?" He turned to Belle. "I am so sorry."

Belle slipped her hand from his. "No, no please don't mind me at all. Go ahead and dance with Lorna."

"Maybe the next dance?" He cast Belle an apologetic smile.

"I would love to," Belle fidgeted with her lace cuffs, eager to escape the awkwardness of the evening as people's gazes began to fall on them, "but I need to return to the Harvey House. I am on duty tonight. I probably shouldn't have accepted even for the first dance, but your note was so sweet, how could I refuse?"

"Note?" Lorna frowned.

"It was nothing." Reid coughed. "I'll see you home then. With the outlaws still on the loose, I don't think you should be walking anywhere by yourself."

"You really don't need to go to all that trouble. I'm used to seeing to myself." She reassured him, already backing away. "Enjoy your dance."

"Only if you promise to wait?" He pressed his lips into a firm line. "I would not allow Harriet to walk home unescorted with that gang on the loose."

"Very well."

Satisfied, Reid led Lorna out onto the dance floor as the dance began.

"I'm rather surprised you aren't out there spinning around on Reid's arm instead of Lorna," Harriet whispered.

Belle jumped, her hand flying to her mouth. "Oh! You frightened me."

"I heard about the mysterious note from Dolly, so I had thought you two would be the first on the dance floor." Harriet sipped her lemonade, wincing against the tartness.

"Lorna had already claimed him, and he forgot, which led

to a rather uncomfortable exchange. Besides, I have to start my shift in a few minutes, but he insisted on escorting me back." She blushed. "However, Lorna seems quite determined to attach herself to him tonight."

"Well, I'll make certain that you two walk back alone." She winked at her. "I truly am sorry about you having to work tonight. I'll be joining you shortly."

"Absolutely not. You have the night off and you aren't going to sacrifice your time with Gil again if I can help it. It will be a slow night with the social going on down here. I'll basically only be there to supervise the coffee pot," Belle said as she studied Lorna's upturned face, smiling at Reid. Belle turned her back to the dancing and leaned close to Harriet. "How's your time with Gil?"

Harriet squeezed Belle's hand. "He's even more wonderful than the first time I fell in love with him."

Belle's jaw almost fell, but she caught it in time. "You're in *love* with him?"

Harriet tucked a strand of golden hair behind her ear. "It may just be the moonlight, but I'm not sure I ever really *stopped* loving him—believe me I tried, but no one else compared."

Before she could ask more, Reid approached with Lorna clinging to his arm. "Are you ready, Miss Parish?"

Lorna shifted her body to maintain Reid's full attention. "Will you return for another dance before the evening is over?" She asked, her eyes flitting to Belle.

"I would never let a lady like yourself be a wallflower." He tipped his hat to Lorna. "I'll be back as soon as possible after I safely deliver Miss Parish to the Harvey House, and we will have one more dance."

"Thank you for keeping my Harvey Girl safe, Reid."

Harriet grasped Lorna's arm, distracting her with a question to keep her from asking to accompany the couple.

To Belle's surprise, Reid offered her his arm. Lorna's eyes kindled, but it was his closeness that made Belle's heart race. She swallowed as they strolled beyond the flickering light of the torches and lanterns. "It's been a while since you've come into the restaurant."

"I know. I've missed the coffee, so that's part of the reason I am walking you back." He chuckled. "I've been out scouting. I'm only back to gather supplies and rest up as I'm going to have to leave town next week for a little bit."

"Oh? How long is a little bit?" Belle stepped up onto the boardwalk, her blue skirts trailing behind. *I hope that wasn't too obvious.*

"Just a month." He halted at the front steps of the Castañeda Hotel.

Trying to hide her disappointment, she lifted her gaze to the moon and stars filtering through the leaves of the giant live oak in the courtyard. "Well, I hope you catch the outlaws sooner rather than later. They've been causing far too much trouble around these parts lately. I hear a lot of stories at the lunch counter about missing cattle and stagecoach robberies. I'm just waiting to hear about another train robbery." She shivered.

"I agree. With each new robbery under their belt, they seem to be getting braver and bolder, but to my annoyance, not *careless.*"

He helped her up the steps, which she didn't need, but was happy to use any excuse to keep clutching his muscular arm and he didn't seem too eager for her to be away either.

COLT KEPT HIDDEN behind the massive live oak in the center of the Castañeda Hotel's courtyard, keeping an eye on the couple, but when Reid presumed to step so close to the woman he loved, he couldn't remain quiet a moment longer. "Miss Parish?" He swiped his hat from his head and stepped away from the shadows, mindful of the oak's roots. "May I speak with you for a moment?"

"Colt! I mean, Mr. Lawson, um, I was just about to start my shift." Her gaze traveled to Reid and back to Colt. "Would you like to discuss it inside?"

"It's private. It won't take long," he assured her. There was no way on God's green earth he was going to pour his heart out in front of *that* Texas Ranger.

Reid's brows lowered to a point. "Lawson—"

"Reid, why don't you go inside and pour yourself a cup of coffee? Miss Parish will be just a moment." He glared at the man and at Belle's directive, Reid relented at last.

Belle strolled with Colt to the other end of the porch, waiting for him to speak. Her fingers went to the ring on the ribbon about her neck—a habit he was beginning to notice she did whenever she became nervous.

"After our parting . . . after the reason for our parting, I feel like I should be honest with you even in the littlest of things." He flicked back the brim of his hat and leaned against the handrail. "The chocolates weren't from Reid. I don't need to take the credit, but I just thought Reid misled you into thinking they were from him."

"Oh."

Was that disappointment in her voice, or confusion . . . or pleasant surprise? He rubbed his forehead. "I'm sorry. I should've corrected Miss Dolly, but I was nervous. Her comments made me uncomfortable, and I didn't want to embarrass her by correcting her."

Her cheeks flamed. "Why were you uncomfortable? *I* was the uncomfortable one. She was taking aim at me, not you." Belle twisted her hands. "The whole meal was . . ."

"Uncomfortable?" He supplied, chuckling before sighing. "But why was I feeling that way? You know why—you left me at the altar, Belle. I had tried to keep our letters to myself, but when my brother discovered that I actually wished to continue our courtship and that I poured my heart out to you in my letters, soon the whole town knew, and when you jilted me . . ." He cleared his throat and crossed his arms, shifting. "I can't go anywhere without people judging me. I'm the man who a Harvey Girl left because she didn't trust him. No mothers trusted me with their daughters before and now, they feel like they can boast about how right they were."

"Well, they could also assume that you left me too. I could have a wretched personality and that's why we didn't get married."

"Who would ever assume that? You're perfect."

"I'm not, but thank you," she whispered.

A breeze pulled a loose curl from her low coiffure and set it to dancing about her face. He ached to run his fingers down the lock and tuck it behind her ear. "I don't think you fully realize how much Suzanne poisoned the way you think about yourself. I could see it in your letters. You need to let go of her lies. You're so afraid I'm lying to you even now because way deep down in the core of your heart, you know she has lied to you your whole life. Her lies have a hold on you, and you can't seem to escape them because every man you met in Charleston treated you as she did—as less." He reached out to brush her hair back, but paused midway, thinking better about it and let his hand drop to his side. "You must remember the truth. You are anything but less. You are everything to me."

Belle leaned against the wall across from him, blinking away.

"I wish we could just start over. I wish I had never exaggerated to you in my letters. I wish that Miss Dolly would've kept her comments to herself, and you would at least allow me to be your friend."

Belle swallowed. "But I don't want you to take a friendship as an excuse that I am interested in something more."

"*You* know I am and always will be interested in something more when it comes to you." He reached for her hand. It felt so good in his, so right, so perfect.

"Colt, you know I can't," Belle whispered, gently tugging her hand from his. "Trust . . . it's not easy for me."

"And yet you trust that Texas Ranger? He doesn't want to settle down. He's about to leave town for a month and that's short for a Ranger."

"Where did you hear that he was leaving town?"

"He's always about to leave town." He shrugged, shoving his hands into his pockets and leaning against the rail. "Belle, I know I don't deserve your trust, but I'm begging you to give me a chance to earn it."

Belle's shoulders fell. "I want to, Colt. I really do, but how am I to do that when I gave up everything to marry that man from the letters when you and he don't match up?"

His heart pounded in his chest. "I can explain it. I can, but if they found out I told you, they would not hesitate on harming you."

"Who are they? You've alluded to this before. If you want me to trust you, then *tell* me."

Hearing footfalls on the boardwalk, Colt stiffened. Everyone was at the social, or the saloon. Colt scowled into the night, his eyes roving, searching for someone hidden in the shadows. "Wait a few more weeks for me and I can explain everything, please," he whispered and gently grasped her by the shoulders. "If you had waited until Christmas to come to Las Vegas, this would've never been an issue. Everything would be done, and there would be no need for secrets to protect you from the truth."

"The truth about what, Colt?"

"I'm afraid you might get hurt if I tell you." He groaned. This conversation was not going the way he had hoped.

"Miss Parish?" Reid poked his head outside. "There isn't any coffee in the urn, and I didn't want to trespass into the kitchen."

"Would you mind your own business?" Colt snapped. "We are trying to have a private conversation here."

"I will if the lady wishes me to." Reid glared at Colt.

Colt rose to his full height, straightening his shoulders. "You think I would ever hurt her?"

Reid strode out onto the porch, closing the distance, stopping directly beside Belle. "Watch your tone, cowboy."

Colt clenched his fists. "Back out of this, ranger. This is *not* your affair."

Belle pressed a hand on each of their chests, pushing them away from one another. "Stop this." She glared at both of them. "There's no need for you both to behave this way. Now, if you'll excuse me, I have work to do, and Reid, get your coffee at the social. Lorna is waiting for you." Dropping her hands, she made her way inside as the men glared at one another.

"You know the danger," Reid warned. "Keep the truth to yourself if you care anything at all for Belle Parish."

CHAPTER 15

*B*elle bent over the laundry basket as she twisted her undergarments free from droplets. While the Harvey House laundered her uniforms and aprons for free, she still had to clean her personal wardrobe. Shaking her chemise out, she reached up to pin it on the line behind the dormitories. Reaching into her empty basket, she sighed with relief as her fingertips scraped the wicker. She placed her hands on her lower back and stretched. *Laundry is the worst.* Raising her face to the sun, she basked in its warmth, recalling the early days in Charleston when she never left the kitchen. *No, I take that back. Dishes are the worst. At least with laundry, I can be outside.*

Someone caught Belle's hand from behind her and twirled her around. "Gil and I are to be married on Sunday afternoon at the ranchero and I want you to stand with me."

"What? Harriet! Congratulations!" Belle embraced her friend, eyes dancing with excitement as they sank onto the bottom step of the small back porch. "I want to hear everything."

"Gil was at the lunch counter for breakfast, which I thought was odd given how late the social was last night and that his mother is an excellent cook. He drew me outside to the courtyard and said he couldn't go another day without knowing if I still loved him . . . like I did before he went to the university. I rejected his proposal then out of deference to my aunt. I replied telling him that moment was my single greatest regret."

"And?" Belle breathed.

Harriet beamed as she squealed into her apron, her feet stamping in quick succession. "And I told him I loved him and wanted to spend the rest of my life with him and that I didn't care about what people said or thought about our marriage. I know he is the right man for me, and I have known it for the longest time."

"Oh Harriet." Belle blinked away her tears. "How lovely and—wait, did you say Sunday afternoon?"

Harriet leaned back on the third step with her elbow, using her hand to shield the sun. "Reid is leaving Monday, and Gil wants him to be his best man, so Sunday afternoon is the only time we could do it. I've already spoken with Miss Trent, and she agreed that the best person for being second head waitress is you, if you accept?"

"You want *me* to be the second waitress?" Belle gasped, pressing her hand to her chest.

"Miss Trent agrees with me. You go above and beyond to make the Harvey House sparkle. You work far more extra shifts than any other girl. You are devoted, and Miss Trent recognizes your efforts. She wants me to bring you up to the parlor to discuss your transition. We don't have much time to get you prepared to take over." Harriet rose, holding out her hand to Belle. "Come on. Miss Trent is waiting."

The days leading up to the wedding passed in a flurry of

preparation, and to her surprise, Dolly was far more cordial now that she was named the head waitress and even congratulated Belle on her new position.

On the morning of Harriet's wedding, before anyone else was awake, Belle slipped into her old Sunday best blue dress, which she had long since demoted to her off-duty work dress. Not bothering to pull up her curls, she simply ran her brush through her hair to catch the largest tangles before snatching up a green wool shawl and creeping down the stairs to the hall closet and gathering four flower baskets. With two baskets on each arm, she rounded the corner of the Harvey House and ran smack into Colt Lawson.

"Whoa there!" He chuckled as he caught a tumbling wicker basket. "We've got to stop meeting like this." He pointed to the rest of her baskets. "Where are you off to with all of these?"

"To the meadow beyond the churchyard. It's overflowing with wildflowers, and I need to pick as much as I can fit into these baskets and adorn the Elliots' arbor. Harriet mentioned wishing to be married surrounded by yellow flowers and I intend to give her that after she asked me to stand with her." Belle explained all in a rush as she adjusted her baskets.

Colt reached over and took the rest of the baskets from her. "It'll take you a spell to fill these. Would you like some help?"

Belle stiffened but remembering their recent conversation of trying to be friends, she allowed him to take the baskets. "I won't say no to help." Belle offered him a shy smile.

The birds called to one another in the cedar trees as Belle drank in the beauty of the sun rising over the foothills, her heart fluttering at the thought of with whom she was sharing it. When they reached the meadow, she knelt and collected the wildflowers. She placed them all carefully in one direction so as to not crush the blooms.

Colt knelt beside her and handed her a flower with an inch stem. Belle giggled. "You have to pick it close enough to the base, so I can weave it into the arbor. This is too short to be of any use."

He pulled up a flower with clumps of dirt spilling from its roots, sending Belle's laughter bubbling out into the meadow. "Like this," she said as she leaned over and plucked a flower, demonstrating the perfect length.

Colt glanced at the short-stemmed yellow flower in his hand and tucked it behind her ear. "There. Now, it won't go to waste. It matches your heart perfectly."

Belle blushed but was so pleased he gave her a flower that her hands trembled for a moment before she took a breath to get control of herself. *What has come over you? It's only a flower.* But in his actions, she caught a glimpse of the man she had allowed herself to hope to marry—a kind and tender man. *Lord, what would You have me do? I know he wasn't honest . . . but part of me wishes to give him a second chance—a true second chance.*

REID'S WARNING filtered through his mind as he carried the baskets of flowers for Belle. To tell her the truth before Grant was behind bars *was* foolish. He couldn't allow his affection for her to make him careless now. But part of him had to wonder if Reid had other motives in his pressing Colt into silence.

"Why do you want to marry me, Colt?"

Colt halted in his tracks. "Why?"

"Yes. You hardly know me."

"We've written each other for months. I'd dare say I know you a sight better than anyone else." He looked sideways at her as she continued up the hill in pursuit of the perfect wildflower.

"Colt!"

He stiffened at the man's intrusion. *Not now, Grant. Not now.* He turned as his brother rode up, grinning down at them.

"Well now, you must be the woman who was going to be my sister-in-law." He swept his leg over the saddle and hopped down, extending his hand to Belle.

Colt longed to throw himself between them to keep his brother from even touching the innocent woman, but he watched Belle, waiting for her que.

She nodded to Grant, ignoring his hand. "And I heard you are the one who placed the advertisement in the first place."

Grant's gaze roved over her. "I'm a little upset I didn't place the notice for myself, but I suppose my wife would be even more upset." He chuckled at his own jest, slapping Colt on the shoulder.

"I best be on my way. I've a busy day ahead of me." Belle dipped her head and reached for the baskets.

"Let me walk you home," Colt insisted.

She shook her head. "I don't wish to keep you from your business." Belle fairly ran away from him with her partially full baskets.

Colt glared at his brother. "What are you doing back already?"

He shrugged, petting his horse's mane. "The wife was annoying me, and I wanted to stretch my legs while we wait for the next robbery and think out some things."

"Like what?"

"Like there is a stinking rat in the Death Riders and I am aiming to find out who."

CHAPTER 16

Belle wove around the grove of trees just beyond the Elliots' ranchero. Reaching the lush green aisle, she sprinkled yellow petals as she passed the rows of guests. She took her place to the left of the arbor as Fannie followed close behind and stood beside her. Reid, who was sitting in the front, caught her gaze and she could see something spark within him. Her cheeks flushed and she broke the spell as she glanced at the small crowd of some of the Harvey Girls, Gil's friends, the Elliot family, Miss Trent, and four elderly couples. Her aunt and uncle were not present. *I hope Harriet isn't disappointed.*

Harriet strode down the flower-strewn aisle in a fashionable ivory wedding gown as everyone stood in her honor. Harriet didn't notice for she only had eyes for Gil. Her bouquet of yellow flowers accented the blue ribbons that Belle had woven into the wildflower crown resting on Harriet's golden locks. Her veil floated behind her, love shining in her eyes.

The ceremony was simple and sweet as Harriet and Gil

spoke their tender vows to one another beneath the arbor of wildflowers, and, in a matter of moments, Preacher Martin lifted his hands and said, "I now pronounce you husband and wife."

Standing, the guests clapped as Harriet and Gil turned with pride to face the small crowd. Gilbert lifted his bride's hand to his lips, whispering something to her. The rest of the Elliots rushed forward to hug Harriet, welcoming her into the family while the Harvey Girls clapped, giggling amongst themselves.

Lorna called out, "If everyone wants to make their way back to the house, we have some delicious food prepared by my mother, a cake from the Harvey House's chefs, and dancing in honor of this fine couple."

The wedding celebration dancing wasn't like anything she had seen at the Fairfield's house in her stolen glimpses as she helped serve food for one of their daughters' weddings. The dancing in the Charleston house had been stiff and formal, but this was an uninhibited lark. Fiddlers played and stomped their feet as the Harvey Girls were twirled around the dance area by Gil's friends. Laughter and cheer skipped in the air as the young couples two-stepped while the older couples perched on bales of hay, watching and enjoying the fun in the cool of the evening.

Belle filled her plate with barbeque beef, mashed potatoes, green beans, and a flaky buttermilk biscuit. Taking dainty bites to make her plate last longer, and, therefore, keep her from having to interact with others just yet, she spied Reid with his head bent low, speaking with Lorna. Belle found a seat on a hay bale at the edge of the dance area where she might eat and still enjoy watching the dancers. Out of the corner of her eye, she snuck a peek at Lorna's rather animated, yet hushed conversation with

Reid. *What in the world is she telling him to make him look so serious?*

Harriet sank down beside her, breathless from dancing with Gil. "Oh Belle, I wish every woman could be as happy as I am today."

Belle rested her head on Harriet's shoulder. "You deserve to be this happy."

"Everyone does." Harriet sighed, her gaze on her new husband who was motioning her over to the cake table. "Looks like it is time to cut the cake. See you soon, dear Belle."

Belle glanced around for Reid once more, and his eyes met hers, sending Belle to blushing for being caught staring at him. The guitarist called for a slow dance and began to pluck a gentle tune that the fiddlers joined as Reid wove around the small crowd to Belle, his hand extended to her.

"May I finally have that dance you've been saving me?"

"You mean the one I was supposed to save for Colt, but you decided to take for yourself?" Belle stated before she could stop herself.

His smile faltered.

"I'm sorry. I know you never actually *said* the note was from you." She placed her small hand into his rough, bronzed hand and allowed him to guide her in a waltz in the sunset.

"But I did not correct you, which is basically saying it was from me." He whirled her in his arms, his eyes holding hers. "You look lovely tonight."

"Thank you," she whispered as the dance caused him to pull her close again.

"You know, for the first time since I left Las Vegas, I have to say that I'll be missing this town when I leave," he said as they swayed back and forth to the rhythm of the fiddlers.

Belle's eyes widened and her breath caught. "I'll be missing you as well."

"You'll be missing me?" Reid's gaze burned into hers.

Belle's belly churned at his question. *Wasn't that what he just insinuated he wanted me to say?*

He groaned. "I promised myself not to allow this to happen again and like a fool, I let my guard down."

Confused, she tilted her head. "You can't allow *what* to happen?"

"I can't allow you to fall in love with me." His gaze lifted skyward as he released a heavy sigh.

Her face couldn't have stung any harder than if he had slapped her. "Excuse me?" She halted, dropping his hands. The façade of his genteel yet flirtatious ways ripping away and exposing his true feelings about her. She was merely another lady to fall for the ranger who could not be caught. *Colt may have lied in the beginning, but he would have never been so arrogant as to assume such a thing.* "Who says I am falling in *love* with you?"

"Well, aren't you?" His brows rose as he reclaimed her hands and spun her around. "I heard how your breath caught when I said I would miss this town. You thought I was saying I would be missing you."

"Of all the nerve." Hardly believing what she was hearing, she loosed herself from his grasp, left him on the dance floor, and stomped away to the barn. She could barely see through her tears as she led Harriet's horse to the phaeton and harnessed him up. Harriet would understand why Belle had to leave without saying farewell.

Having seen her brother do it often enough, she was confident she could hitch a horse without any man's help. *How dare he imply that I am falling in love with him?* She fumed as she tightened the harness before scrambling into the phaeton, nearly ripping the hem of her skirt as it caught on the hub of the wheel. She hopped back down, freed it from the hub and threw her skirt behind her, blinking back her anger as she marched over and gently grasped the horse by the harness. "Let's get home."

"Belle, where are you going?" Reid leaned against the barn door, arms crossed.

"Home." She clenched her teeth together to avoid saying something she'd regret and guided the horse through the door.

"It's dark and the outlaws are out there. They are overdue to make a raid and they could strike at any time now. It's not safe. You can't go back by yourself."

"Watch me." She glared at him and snatched up the reins, holding them in one fist as she scrambled inside.

He caught the bridle, causing the horse to jerk its head at his rough touch. "I can't allow you to do this." The horse stomped, taking a step backward.

"You have no claim on me, Reid. Release my horse."

With a grunt he released the bridle and raised his hands. "At least give me a moment to saddle my horse and allow me to follow you and make certain you arrive to the Harvey House safe and sound."

She narrowed her eyes, her chest burning. "I can take care of myself. I always have." Not waiting for him to move, she flicked the reins. Reid leapt to the side, and she darted into the night. She wanted to cry, but as always, she suppressed her tears. *How could he humiliate me that way?* She snapped the reins, charging down the moonlit road. *The nerve of him to accuse me of falling for him and then, essentially calling me a helpless female.*

A coyote pack began to howl nearby, but nothing could frighten her enough to make her turn around and accept that arrogant ranger's offer to escort her home. Passing under the hanging "E" sign, she urged the horse to increase his pace. The coyotes' howls grew nearer. Her horse skittered to the side and reared.

"Whoa. Whoa!" Belle cried, pulling back on the reins. The horse reared further. Fearing he would tumble backwards into the buggy, Belle scrambled out and rubbed his neck like she had seen her brother do countless times. "Easy, boy," Belle whispered in what she hoped was a soothing tone. She reached for the bridle, but he threw back his head, away from her reach.

"Whoa, boy." She took a tentative step toward him, wary of his hooves. He snorted before bolting down the road, pulling the phaeton along without her. "No!" She cried out as she sprinted after the animal, but her fancy heeled shoes wouldn't allow her to run longer than a few yards. "No." Belle laced her fingers behind her head and tried to keep from yelling in frustration.

She kicked at the dirt. "Surely, someone will be coming this way from the wedding." She counted off the guests and soon realized that all of the townsfolk had already headed home before her, besides the Harvey Girls who would stay until the very end of the party, and the only guests left were the ones that lived beyond the Elliot ranch. "Great," she mumbled and began the long walk back into town. *Like you said, five miles isn't that bad.*

The march home allowed for too many thoughts to surface—memories of her encounters with Reid that she now viewed in a different light. He had flirted with her, of that she was certain, but he did mention on many occasions of his attachment to the rangers. *I'm no better than Lorna in hearing only what suited me, but he should have known better than to flirt so and give a girl such a false impression.*

The coyotes called to one another and with every howl, Belle's pace quickened until the point she was almost trotting. *Blasted heels.* She considered pausing long enough to pull off her shoes, but didn't dare stop, not with the howls. The sound of hoofbeats coming towards her made her halt, her heart pounding. *Please let whoever it is be a better option than the coyotes, Lord. Not the bandits.* "Hello?" Belle called out, waving her arms.

"Belle?" The rider exclaimed when he was almost upon her.

"Colt!" Belle cried with a mixture of relief from being rescued, but also embarrassment that it had to be Colt doing the rescuing. "You didn't happen to see a buggy flying past you on the way here, did you?" She released a nervous laugh. "I seemed to have lost my horse."

He hopped down from the saddle, holding fast to the reins. "I didn't see any horse and buggy. How did he get away from you?"

"Not relevant." Belle waved away his question, grimacing. "I have to find him. I'd die if had to tell Harriet I lost her horse."

"We'll find him." Colt chuckled. "So much for an early evening. Looks like I'll be going back into town."

"Oh." Belle fidgeted with her gloves. "You really don't need to—"

He raised his hands to stop her protest. "Yes, I do. I'm not going to leave you out here to find your way back to town on your own. Now, I'm sure you would be just fine without me, but it would give me peace of mind knowing you'd made it safely to the Harvey House."

At a coyote's howl, she relented with a nod, and he fell into step beside her, leading his horse. "Thank you. I didn't fancy a walk home in the dark alone."

"Would you like to ride in front of me, or walk?"

She shivered. "Walk. I've had quite enough of horses tonight."

Colt led his horse beside him, keeping himself between Belle and the beast. "Did you enjoy the wedding? I'm not well enough acquainted with the Elliot family to be invited."

Belle crossed her arms for warmth. "Harriet was lovely, and Gilbert beamed with pride to call her his bride. The food was tasty, and the cake was made by the Harvey House chefs, so it was, of course, delightful."

His horse paused to tear up a bite of grass. "Did you dance?"

"A couple times. The dancing here is unlike anything I've experienced before." She patted down a wild curl that had managed to escape her low coiffure, realizing she had forgotten her chapeau at the ranchero.

"I'm surprised Reid let you leave without him." He pulled his horse onward. "If he couldn't escort you, he should've at least sent someone else."

"I didn't want him escorting me," Belle held her chin high.

"I'm sorry to hear that," he murmured, not sounding sorry at all.

She stumbled forward. Colt caught her by the waist, holding her against him for a split second before releasing her. "You okay there? You didn't twist an ankle, did you?"

She shook her head, her cheeks flaming and gently pushed herself away. Hearing rustling up the road to her left, she fairly jumped back into Colt's arms. "What's that?" She clutched his taut forearm.

Colt slipped his bullwhip from his belt and uncoiled it as he handed his horse's reins to Belle. Striding toward the sound, he disappeared into the darkness.

Belle whispered, "Colt? Colt, where are you?"

"Found someone." Thin branches and brush snapped underfoot as he returned, leading her escaped horse and phaeton. "Miraculously, the buggy is in one piece and he's unharmed. He was just having a midnight snack on the side of the road." He chuckled and halted the buggy to examine the horse's legs in the moonlight.

Sighing with relief, Belle rubbed the naughty horse's nose. "Thank goodness you found him. Do you think I'd be okay to drive the rest of the way back?" In the distance, lanterns illuminated the edge of town.

"Well, considering we are only a mile from town, I think you'll be perfectly safe, but I'll ride with you the rest of the way if you would prefer?" Colt gave Harriet's horse a pat and adjusted the harness.

Belle chewed the side of her cheek, not wanting to admit she was afraid of being alone in the dark, wild West. "Are you certain you wouldn't mind?"

"You know what, buy me a cup of coffee for the road and we'll call it even." He tied his mare to the back of the buggy.

"Deal." Knowing how his touch sent her pulse to racing, she hiked up her skirts and settled into the seat and picked up the reins before he could offer.

"Oh, you're driving, are you?" He laughed as he sat next to her. "I better hold on to my hat."

She laughed and gave the reins a little snap. "What were you doing in town this late?"

"My brother is in town. He enjoys the saloon, but I don't particularly care for it anymore, so we ate at the Harvey House and now, he's at the Whistlin' Coyote and I'm here with you. I have the much better arrangement." He adjusted his Stetson to the back of his head as they rolled into town.

"I appreciate your willingness to help me."

He sighed. "I'll always help you, Belle. Just because you

didn't marry me, doesn't mean those feelings I had for you went away overnight."

Not knowing what to say, she shifted in her seat and directed the horse into the stables where the young stable boy, Jimmy, grabbed the harness as Colt hopped out and trotted around the phaeton, lifting his hands to her.

They were no longer in the dark where a flash of petticoats from an ungraceful descent would be hidden. She rested her hands on his shoulders and he lifted her out, slowly setting her down, his steady gaze never leaving hers. His broad hands nearly encompassed her corseted waist and here, between his arms, she had never felt safer.

"Excuse me, Miss Parish?" Jimmy swiped his dirty cap into his hand.

"Yes, Jimmy?" She felt her cheeks heat as she broke away from Colt and retrieved her reticule from under the seat, relieved it was still there. She could not afford to lose the two dollars tucked inside.

"Miss Lane left this for you. She wanted me to give it to you when you dropped off her horse this evening." Jimmy handed her a thin envelope.

"Thank you! Have a good evening." She tucked the envelope in her reticule and strolled away with Colt under the stars back to the Harvey House. "So, what kind of work is your brother in? He seems to be in town quite often for not even living here."

Colt's expression tightened and he cleared his throat. "Well, he was supposed to go into the ranching business with me."

"But?" Belle lifted her skirts, stepping up to the Castañeda's porch.

"But he prefers getting his money by a different means, which is what I wanted to talk to you about." He paused with her, pulling her under one of the arches of the porch. He glanced about as if nervous to be heard by anyone. "I know I told you that I could explain everything away, and I am tired of waiting for permission to tell you, especially with the next cattle drive around the corner. I can't leave without you knowing everything."

"Wait for permission? Why would you—"

"Colt!" Dolly sang his name as she tapped on the windowpane, waving at them from the dining room window before throwing it open. She pressed her hands to the windowsill as she leaned out. "Whatever are you doing here? And Miss Parish, aren't you supposed to be at the wedding?"

"I met Miss Parish on her way home and decided to escort her and as payment, I thought I'd have a cup of coffee."

"I'll fetch it for you right away." Looking at Belle's disheveled hair, Dolly pressed her lips into a thin, disapproving line. "Miss Parish, I think you should retire. You have a big day tomorrow."

"Ah yes, now that Miss Harriet is married, who is the new head waitress?" Colt looked to Belle for the answer.

Dolly laughed. "Me, silly." She looked pointedly at Belle. "To bed, Miss Parish. I'll see to Colt."

"Of course." Belle gave Colt a small curtsy. "I won't forget your help, Colt, and I look forward to our talk in a couple of weeks when you return from the drive. I don't plan on going anywhere."

At the sound of his given name coming from her lips, he grinned, tipping his hat to her. "Anytime you need rescuing, you just let me know, and I'm your man."

Belle giggled as Dolly rolled her eyes behind him. "*Goodnight*, Miss Parish."

Belle darted across the street. The dormitory was unnaturally dark with so many at Harriet's wedding. She knocked on the door and waited for someone to unlock it. At the grating of a lock being inserted on the other side of the door, Belle looked over her shoulder to ensure no one else was near. She heard once about a drunk cowboy trying to force his way inside by overpowering a Harvey Girl.

Jenny pulled the door open, her golden braid draping over her shoulder. "Back already?"

Belle nodded to the Harvey Girl she hadn't gotten to know too well yet as their shifts did not align. "I'll catch you all up on the wedding in the morning. Thank you for opening the door."

She covered her yawn. "Someone had to and as the housemother wanted to attend the wedding, the task fell to me. Goodnight, Belle."

After hanging her dress in the closet, Belle remembered the letter from Harriet that she had stuffed into her reticule. She slipped on her simple cotton nightgown, retrieved it, and lit a taper.

> Belle,
>
> As my dear friend, I need to make sure you can come see me. Please accept my horse and phaeton as a small token of my appreciation for the encouragement and support you have given me in accepting Gilbert's hand. The censure from the townspeople will be too much to bear at the moment and frankly, I might hurt someone if they say one more judgmental comment against my sweet husband, so I won't be doing much visiting to town.

Please, don't argue. Rogue is yours. I've spoken with the stableman and Jimmy, and he'll send all his room and board bills to me. All you have to do is take him for a few long rides each week . . . to see me. Don't worry about your new position as second girl. You were born to be a Harvey Girl, and you are certainly good enough to be head waitress and will be one very soon, I'm sure.

Your friend,
Harriet Elliot

P.S. I giggled like a schoolgirl when I wrote my last name as Elliot. How many times did I imagine my name linked with Gilbert's growing up? And now, thanks to you, it is.

Belle blinked the tears from her eyes. What had started as a frightening venture had turned into the greatest time of blessing she had ever known—a new friend, a position she loved, a horse and phaeton of her own . . . and the hope of a fresh start with Colt on the horizon.

CHAPTER 17

Colt strode passed the saloon the next morning, hoping to catch Belle on her shift, when the high pitch laughter of one of the saloon girls caught his ear. She sounded like Grant's favorite. It had taken a heap of talking Grant down last night that there was no rat in the Death Riders—convincing that ended with Grant heading to the saloon to take the edge off.

Colt glanced over his shoulder and spied two men stumbling through the swinging wooden slat doors, squinting in the sunlight. He strolled behind the saloon, knowing they would follow. He leaned against the back wall of the saloon and crossed his arms, studying the windows above him and ensuring they were closed before he asked, "Couldn't ask you at the Harvey House, but what are you doing away from the ranch? You were supposed to be discreet."

"Don't you have some chores to do?" Grant lifted his sloshing glass bottle, taking a long draft as Russ chortled. "Figured we'd kill some time before the next robbery. A week is a long time to stay cooped up."

Colt knocked a clump of mud from his boots against the wall. "Not my problem. You know Las Vegas isn't a safe place for you until that ranger decides to move along."

"I don't know why you didn't just shoot him the first time you saw him." Russ bit off a chaw of tobacco, handing it to Grant who followed suit.

"Um, I don't know. Maybe because he is a *Texas Ranger* and if he goes down, ten more rangers will be on their way and will put an end to us before you can blink." Colt spat back, whipping off his Stetson and whacking it against his leg, pausing at the gasp from around the corner of the building. He stiffened as Grant's eyes sparked and he strode around.

"Don't you know it's rude to listen in on other people's conversations, girly?" Grant spat a wad of brown tobacco juice at her feet. "I know you think you probably need to tell somebody about the big bad man and his plans, but I would strongly suggest you refrain."

Belle. Colt's heart stopped as her eyes reflected his fear. What was she doing away from the Harvey House? He strode forward, placing himself between her and his brother.

"I, uh, um. I'm so sorry. My shoelace came untied and—" Belle stumbled.

"Don't scream, Belle." Colt whispered, his hands raised at his brother. "Grant, we don't need to hurt her."

"Shut up," he fired back. His hand flashed and seized her by the wrist. "You've let this little snip of a girl run all over you. It's time you show her who is boss in this town."

Belle gasped from the pain.

"I said there's no need to hurt her." Colt growled, ripping Grant's hold away from Belle and tucking her behind him with the other arm. "I think she is frightened enough to not talk. There's no need to harm her further."

Belle trembled against him. "You are the leader of the Death Riders?"

The man ignored Colt as he sneered at Belle. "You seem surprised. Yeah, I'm the leader. Colt might be the better looking of us, but I am the strongest, and out here, a man's strength is what counts. Now, lucky for you, you're the prettiest little flower this side of the Mississippi, so I'm feeling generous. Keep what you heard to yourself, and I'll let you live. Don't let that pretty face disappoint me by letting your brains talk you into doing something you'll later regret."

Colt swallowed back his relief and kept his gaze on his brother. "She won't."

"Good. Because I'm afraid I might have to put an end to her precious Texas Ranger if she does."

Belle paled. "I don't know who you are talking about."

"Mmhm, are you sure?" He shrugged. "Suppose you were misled, Colt. Oh well, I suppose the girl won't mind if I go kill a ranger tonight then."

"No!" She cried, clutching Colt's arm. "Colt, you can't let him."

Grant grinned. "We know where he goes to sleep at night. You say one word and we'll put a bullet in between his ears before your sentence is through. I've wanted to put an end to that man for some time, so please, give me the excuse I need. If you don't believe me, remember what I did to your train. If Colt hadn't stopped me, I would have taken your valuables too. Maybe I should have and put a healthy amount of fear in your heart toward the Death Riders."

"It was you?" Belle looked up at Colt, the hurt in his eyes incapacitating him. "I-I won't breathe a word."

"If you do, Ranger Reid is as good as dead." Grant tipped his hat. "Have a nice day, Miss." He turned and headed back toward the saloon, Russ stumbling behind him.

Colt caught her hand, pulling her close. "Whatever possessed you to come behind the saloon?"

"I-I saw you and thought you might be in trouble when those two men followed you," she whispered, tears filling her eyes. "How could I have known you were in league with them?"

Colt gently grasped her by the shoulders. "Please, for your own safety, do *not* tell anyone. Grant doesn't think twice about killing. No matter how pretty you are, he'll shoot you without a moment's hesitation."

"Was *this* what you were trying to tell me? That you were part of the gang that robbed my train?" She tore away from his grasp, her chest heaving. "How could you do this? This isn't you. I know you. You are kind, true, a-and honorable." Her breath came in gasps. "You can't be a murderer. You can't."

He groaned, rubbing his face. "I'm not. I can't explain everything right now, but—"

"You told me you could explain if I waited, but I can't wait anymore. You said your 'boss' wouldn't let you tell me. Is that because your boss is Grant?" She grunted through gritted teeth, trembling as she blinked away her tears. "I'm such a fool. I believed your letters. I thought you had showed me your true heart and it was kind . . .you were kind." She pressed her hands against her stomach. "I don't understand. Why would you get mixed up in this? Have I misjudged you so grossly?"

"Why would anyone begin to do this?" He countered. "When I was eighteen, my family needed money and I couldn't refuse Grant. I never wanted to rob that first family, but Grant was just getting started."

"Well, get out of it," Belle whispered sharply. "Your

brother is a killer, Colt. How could you stand by and let him do that?"

"I wasn't with him that time," he replied, his face ashen. "If I was, I would've stopped him."

"But you are part of your brother's outlaw gang, the Death Riders, no? That doesn't sound like you are trying to stop him." She brushed away her tears with an angry cry. "Why didn't you at least try and leave? Surely, he would've understood. You're his own brother for goodness' sake."

"You want to know why?" He paced the exterior length of the saloon, his heart at war within him. To tell her everything could put her in danger, but if she did not understand the gravity of the situation, she would unwittingly put herself in danger. "Because at one time, there were three Lawson brothers."

Belle paled. "You don't mean that he—"

"My kid brother, Abel. He only helped with the first couple of raids, all small-time robberies, to help keep us brothers together, but when Grant started to get out of control, Abel and I talked about how to get out. Abel stood up to him." He gave a short laugh. "Abel. Just like the Bible stories my Ma told me about." His throat swelled. "And 'Cain rose up against Abel, his brother, and slew him.' Grant shot him down right before my eyes. I didn't even have a chance to step up and tell Grant I agreed with Abel. He just heard Abel say that he was done and was going to turn himself in. Grant shot him. Grant says the only way out of the Death Riders is death." He laughed without mirth. "Fitting."

"Oh, Colt," Belle covered her mouth with a shaking hand.

"Grant saw him as a threat. Grant doesn't care much for threats. He eliminates them." He took her hands in his. "Can't you see? If I tried to leave the Death Riders on my own, I'm a dead man, which is why I've sought help from the rangers."

"What? You did?"

"Please, don't say anything to anyone. I promise that I will explain everything later, but it's too dangerous to tell you my plan now when Grant might be listening. Please promise me that you will stay silent. I couldn't bear it if you . . ." he swallowed, "if you were hurt. It would kill me."

"Why?"

"You know why. I love you."

She jerked her hand out of his. "How can you possibly love me when you rob and kill innocen—"

"I told you. I didn't have any part in that." He placed his finger on her lips. "If you won't stay quiet for the sake of yourself, think about your ranger. Grant would kill him and do unspeakable things to you before finishing you off as well. Don't tell anyone. I can't stay any longer with you, or Grant will get suspicious." He tugged his Stetson over his eyes. "I can't protect you from him if you tell anyone what you heard here today."

FOR DAYS, Belle was afraid to go to and from the Castañeda hotel alone for fear of running into Grant and soon, that fear turned into guilt as the weight of the knowledge pressed heavily onto her heart. She shoved aside her guilt as she anxiously waited for news on Reid's return. The moment he returned, she planned to rush to him and warn him of the threat against his life and reveal the identity of the leader of the Death Riders, but while he was still out there alone, she wouldn't breathe a word for fear Grant would make good on his ill promise.

"Did you hear the latest news?" One of her regulars,

Frank, asked at the lunch counter as he stuffed his face with a honey-covered biscuit.

Belle stifled a jaw-breaking yawn. "What news?"

"There was another stagecoach robbery last night—some family on their way in from the East. Them outlaws shot the two drivers, took the cash box, the family's lifesavings, and stripped them of all their valuables. They took the horses and left the family and drivers for dead." Frank slurped at his coffee. "And it's a sure thing that they would've died if Ranger Reid hadn't found him when he did. He got 'em into the nearest town and telegraphed us."

Belle plunked the coffee pot onto the counter, sickened. "How horrible. The family is unharmed?"

"They were lucky. These Easterners come out West thinking it is some kind of dime romance novel, but it ain't. It's a hard life, and you need to learn to protect your family." He slathered his biscuit in even more honey as if his story did little to affect him.

"I-is it the same group of outlaws that have been robbing around here?" The knot in her belly grew, her thoughts drifting to the Elliot family and Harriet. *She's out on the far corner of the ranch in that tiny cabin and when Gil is out, she's all alone with no one near enough to hear her.*

"Yup. That ranger fella confirmed it was the Death Riders."

Belle gripped the countertop. She could have stopped them. She could have saved that family from being robbed by simply being brave enough to speak . . . if not for the threat against Reid. "How far away was the stagecoach?"

He smacked his lips as he coated his next bite in butter. "That's the scary part. They was only thirty-five miles from here. That's the *second* time in a single month that the stagecoach has been hit so close to Las Vegas. You'd think they would be scared to rob near the same spot twice, but I guess they figured we'd figure that they wouldn't have the gall, which kind of makes sense actually. We'd thought that with their last robbery, they were done, but I guess they are coming back for more. Maybe that Elliot boy was right. Maybe they were just testing the waters of Las Vegas and we're about to get hit big time. There are rumors around town that the bank is next."

I need to get word to Harriet and Gil. Until the dust settles, he needs to move them into the ranchero. Belle looked around to see if Dolly had arrived for her shift in hopes that she could depart early for the Elliot ranch. She motioned Fannie over to the counter. "Watch the counter for me?"

Fannie whisked away a dirty plate. "I'll send someone for you if need be."

That was the nice thing about being second in command—no one questioned her. Belle removed her apron and wove through the kitchen staff to the side door. She draped the apron over the side porch rail and picked up her skirts to rush to the stable.

"Belle!" Harriet called from the dormitory door across the street. "There you are."

"What's wrong?" She ran down the steps and caught her friend as she fell into a heap of pink skirts, sobbing. "Is someone hurt?"

Harriet hiccupped and curled her arms over her head, rocking back and forth. "It's Gil. They took him."

"Who took him?" Belle stiffened, her heart already knowing the answer.

"The Death Riders." Harriet squeezed her eyes shut and pressed her hands to her stomach, her face blanching. "Oh God, I don't know what to do. Reid is gone and Mr. Elliot and the ranch hands have been looking for him all morning. He's nowhere to be found."

"When was the last time you saw him? Where was he heading?" Belle knelt beside Harriet, wrapping her arms around her friend's shoulders.

"He left the house at midnight, watching for the rustlers. I didn't think they'd strike a second time, but Gil said he sensed another attack." She sniffed back her tears.

"You've checked every acre of the ranch for him?" With a ranch that significant, one could easily get lost for days. *Which is unlikely for Gil.*

"As best as I could. I was hoping you saw him during the nightshift, or any shift, and that he had left a message for me."

Belle reached up her sleeve and retrieved her plain white handkerchief and pressed it in Harriet's trembling hand. "I'm afraid I haven't, Harriet."

"Then the Death Riders have him."

"The Riders wouldn't kill a chance at getting ransom money." Belle pulled Harriet to her feet. "It's common knowledge the Elliots are one of the wealthiest families around, so I am sure he's still alive and being held for ransom." Belle swallowed. "If they do have him, I might be able to help you get Gil back."

"What?" Harriet's head jerked up. "How could you possibly help?"

"There's no easy way to say this, so, I'm just going to say it." She closed her eyes. "Colt is part of the gang, and his brother is the leader of the Death Riders."

"Colt." Harriet's jaw went slack before her eyes sparked. "You knew? You knew and didn't tell anyone? You could've prevented this."

She grasped Harriet's hands. "Believe me. I wanted to tell

someone the moment I found out, but Grant threatened that if I didn't keep quiet, he would murder Reid and then come back for me," Belle explained in a rush. "I was waiting until Reid returned to say something, but it's been so long, and we haven't heard a word from him regarding the date of his return. I wanted to tell him and not just anyone in town in order to warn him that they would be coming after him. If Colt's brother is gone and he's alone, maybe I can ask Colt to intervene." She headed for the stables.

Harriet scrambled after her. "It's too dangerous, Belle. As much as I hate to say it, we need to wait for Reid to return. You can't just ride in there and demand for Colt to capture Grant to release Gil. If Colt is a part of the Death Riders, he is more dangerous than we imagine. We can't underestimate what he might do."

"But if we wait, it might be too late." She trotted into the stables, calling for Jimmy, but he was nowhere in sight. "Harriet, help me saddle Rogue."

Harriet grabbed the tackle from the hooks on the wall as Belle tugged open the stall door and gently rubbed the horse on the nose, hoping her anxiety would not spook him as she slipped on his bridle. Harriet swung up the saddle blanket and saddle onto his back. Then, the women set to work on tightening the girth and adjusting the stirrups together.

"You don't have to do this." Harriet finished the last buckle. "I can send someone else."

"You and I both know that Colt is Gil's best chance." Belle scooted an upside-down crate beside the horse. "Colt won't let anyone hurt me."

"If I thought there was any other way—" Harriet pulled Belle into a fierce embrace. "Be careful."

"I will." She stared up at the horse. She was raised around the beasts, and she would do this—no matter her lack of training. Not caring that she wasn't wearing a split skirt. Belle stepped onto the crate and climbed into the saddle, her skirts hiking up to her shins and revealing her black stockings and sensible white cotton petticoat. "If I am not back in two hours, send a telegram to Reid to the town where he was last to warn him, and then tell everyone in town who the Death Riders really are and send help."

"God speed, my sweet friend." Harriet slapped the horse on its rump.

The moment she was out of town, Belle whipped the reins and sent Rogue into a gallop towards the Lawson ranch. The speed nearly jostled her out of the saddle, but she did not allow herself to panic. Instead, she focused on the horse's stride, allowing herself to feel each movement as Reid had taught her. The wind thrashed her hair loose from its tight coiffure. The gait of the horse hiked her skirts up to her knees, but she paid no heed to it. She pressed onward, focusing all of her strength on not falling off Rogue. She knew from Colt's letters where his ranch was located. He even had written about what natural markers she could follow. She passed under the arch to the ranch and kicked Rogue to an even faster pace.

When the ranchero came into sight, Belle slowed her mount to a trot and then a walk to get as close as she could without detection. She secured Rogue to a cedar branch and crept toward the house, praying she might find Colt alone, but two yards from the door, the low rumble of masculine voices stopped her in her tracks. She fell to her knees and crawled under an open window at the front of the house, straining to hear what was going on inside.

"And when the train stops at the station, Jesse and Russ will board and get control of the engine room," Colt instructed.

Jesse. Jesse is in on this too? Disappointment flooded her. She had served him a handful of times, ate with him at the box social, and even danced with him. She had thought he was an upstanding young man, seeking an honest living. *How many more men will I misjudge?* Belle wrapped her arms around herself to keep warm as a breeze swept through the valley, sending the fallen cedar leaves around her twirling.

"Good. Now, where did you hide the stagecoach robbery loot?" Asked a deep voice, which could only belong to Grant. Belle pressed herself against the wall, shivering as she remembered the darkness in his eyes when he warned her that he would kill her if she did not remain silent.

"It's in here," Colt replied. "There's a loose floorboard under the rug."

"It's beyond time to divide up the loot," Jesse whined. "I've been needing it. I've got a load of debts at the saloon and about town. Grant, tell him to divvy it up."

"Yeah," Russ seconded.

Belle started at the sound of smashing glass.

"This may just be the place for you to hide out, Russ, but this is my home," Colt growled. "Save your empty whiskey bottle rage for the saloon, or I'll take a cut out of your stake to pay for the damages *with* interest."

Please Lord, don't let Joshua be in the Death Riders as well. Belle crouched on her feet and very slowly, raised herself up until she could just barely peek over the windowsill. Scanning the room, she spied Colt, Grant, Jesse, a man she didn't recognize, and that horrid drunk Russ, but no Joshua or Gil. She barely refrained from sighing in relief. *Thank you. Fannie would have been crushed.* But just because Gil wasn't in the room didn't mean he wasn't in another room tied up.

Moving the table aside, Colt pulled back the braided rug, yanked out his knife and stuck it in the floorboard. With a crack and pop, he jerked up the plank before reaching inside and removing two small burlap sacks.

How evil is Grant and the rest of the Death Riders that they would shoot two men for so little? The men knelt in a circle and dumped their loot into the center, hooting with glee as they ran their fingers through the coins. With the gang occupied, Belle crawled around the ranchero looking for a window that led to a bedroom, or a room where they could be keeping Gil.

"See? That's how it's done, Colt," Belle heard Grant's booming voice. "When I received your last letter about *another* cattle drive, I packed up everything I had in the canyon. Don't you disappoint me by not taking to heart all of my tips. Ma wouldn't like it for you not to learn the family trade."

Belle heard footsteps and to her horror, Colt had led Grant away from the group and into the bedroom, which was much too close to Belle's new hiding place outside the window.

"I'll still need the gang to respect me whenever you are away, so don't make me sound like your kid brother," Colt growled, closing the door behind them.

"Didn't you hear me? You don't need their respect as a leader. I'm planning on staying. I packed up everything when I read that you wanted to spend more time with your precious cows. Didn't take much time, but I won't let you mess up what we've got going," Grant corrected him. "You've been sounding a little too much like Abel these days."

Belle's heart dropped at the name. Surely Colt had not gotten careless in his façade. *Lord, protect him. Let him get free from Grant.*

"I don't see what the big deal is. You asked me to start poaching the Elliot's cattle and I have been. Then, you pressured me to hit them again too soon. We barely got away last night because of your so-called leadership," Colt fired back.

"Yeah, well we only escaped because I shot that Elliot in the leg. I would've killed him if you hadn't tripped and grabbed my arm." Grant spat a wad of tobacco on the floor. "That's the second time you've caused someone to miss killing a witness."

Belle slapped her hand over her mouth to keep from gasping out loud again. *They don't have him.* She had to get back and tell Harriet that Gil was somewhere out on the ranch and injured.

"What a joke of an outlaw you've turned out to be, Colt. If you weren't so good with a whip and gun, you'd be a complete disgrace after taking that bullet to your backside when you got in the line of fire of that ranger."

Colt waved his hand dismissively. "We got away without being recognized, and that's all that matters. By you asking the gang to rob more stagecoaches without even telling me, you've put more pressure on our group to be found by that ranger. Reid won't let up until we are all hung."

At the mention of the ranger, Belle paused. She was afraid to wait to hear more, but more afraid if she didn't hear their plans. Colt may not be able to warn anyone but she could.

"Which is why you need me here to push you to make the tough decisions." Grant mumbled around his wad of tobacco. "If you had your way, you would only rob if the opportunity threw itself into your lap, and even then, I don't think you would try very hard. You don't take the initiative enough and you don't have the guts to do what needs to be done."

"Like how you instructed the men to shoot those two stagecoach drivers to avoid being identified while I was in town?"

"Exactly." Grant slapped his little brother on the back.

"It could've been avoided, Grant."

"Yes, but now we have something more important than gold." Grant chuckled. "Fear. It's time we took care of that Ranger Reid before he gets any closer."

At those words, Belle drew a deep breath. She had to warn the town of their plans. She took a step back. Her foot landed on a branch, snapping it in half. Colt's head whipped up. His gaze found hers, sheer panic flashing across his features.

Belle stumbled backwards, falling to the ground. Grant's shouts filled the air. She clawed at the earth, lifting herself and bolted for her horse. In one desperate, miraculous leap, she was in the saddle. She kicked Rogue into a gallop as the front door of the ranchero burst open and Grant stormed out with the rest of his riders following close behind. She could hear them yelling as they clambered to get their horses, but she didn't dare look back. She pressed her horse faster than she had ever ridden before in her life.

The road bends too much with the river. If I just can make it to the other side of the river, I can make it to town in half the time. Frantic to put more distance between herself and the Death Riders, she turned her horse off the road and plunged into the river. Her horse lurched and to her terror, her hold faltered, and she tumbled headlong into the river.

CHAPTER 18

Grant aimed his revolver at Belle who was scrambling onto the bank, her soaked skirts making escape impossible.

"No!" Colt shouted. He released his whip, snapping the gun downward, the bullet spraying the dirt and sand beside Belle. "Leave her to me, Grant."

"You capture her now, or I'll shoot her dead in her tracks." Grant yelled.

Colt kicked his horse, forging the river. "Stop, Belle! Stop before Grant kills you."

She kept climbing the bank.

"Colt. Stop her, or I'll kill her now." The click of the hammer sent Colt's heart skittering.

"Belle!" He cried and threw himself from his horse, the water splashing to his thighs as he charged after her. Colt dove for her, wrapping his arms about her waist and jerking her to the ground as a shot rent the air.

She screamed—perhaps in pain, or from fear of the bullets. She attempted to crawl away again and before Grant could take another shot, Colt wrapped her in his arms again, despite her kicking and screaming.

"I'm so sorry. I didn't mean to hurt you. Grant was about to shoot you," he whispered. "Please, trust me. Stop fighting and trust me."

"It's Grant I don't trust." She ground out, kicking him in the shins.

He swallowed back a wince. "You were going to marry me once. There's a reason why you trusted me enough to say yes. Follow my lead and I will get you out of this." He scooped her into his arms and lifted her onto his saddle.

"Thought you'd go running off to tell that Texas Ranger that you'd figured out who the whole group of outlaws were, did you?" Grant hissed as he holstered his gun. "Well, I think you might not have thought this one out too much. If it weren't for Colt here, you'd be dead."

"I-I won't tell anyone, Grant." She swayed as Colt hoisted himself into the saddle behind her, caging her in between his arms. "I was only looking for Gil."

Grant rolled his eyes. "Like I could trust your *word* after I caught you spying on me not once, but twice now." He pulled out his bowie knife and turned it in the sun, allowing the glint to hit her eyes. "You've heard too much."

"Grant. I am warning you. You leave her to me." Colt growled, turning his horse to keep the shine of the blade from Belle's eyes.

A flicker passed through Grant's eyes, his hand twitching. He wanted to throw that blade, but Colt kept his gaze steady on him, his hand hovering over his revolver.

"What you going to do with the girl?" Russ spat a stream of tobacco.

"What I should've done with her the minute I found out she made a fool of my brother by spitting in the face of the

Lawson name. We need to get her a little further out of town, so no one will find her body. Sure beats killing her now and hauling her around as dead weight."

"No." Colt's grip tightened on her trembling arms, desperately trying to convey that she was safe with him.

"You got a better plan?" Grant narrowed his gaze, flipping the blade in his palm.

"What if we just set a ransom for her instead?"

Grant stroked his beard, considering Colt's suggestion. "Who will pay a ransom for her? I thought you said she came from a poor family?"

"The Elliots," Colt replied. His hand covered Belle's and he discreetly squeezed it. "Bet Gil's new bride would give up the entire ranch just for this girl."

"It's true," Jesse interjected. "I've seen the way Harriet treats Belle. She thinks of her as a sister, and she would do anything for her."

Grant gave a short nod. "Okay. We'll send Clyde with a note to that Jimmy kid in town to deliver that says if they don't send us money in five days, we'll deliver her tied on the back of her horse—dead." Grant dug through his saddlebag, found a pencil and piece of crumpled paper and jotted down his ransom note. "Colt, bind her hands and keep her in front of your saddle," he said, handing Clyde the note.

"No tie is stronger than I am." Colt stared at Grant, unwavering. He would not bind her.

Grant rolled his eyes. "Fine. Clyde, get this to the stable boy tonight and find us at the canyon. We need to put some distance between us and this town."

Colt secured her mount, following as the gang whirled their horses about and with a whoop, charged across the prairie, the mountains to their right growing smaller.

Colt pressed his chest to her back. "I've got you, Belle."

"You can let me go. Please. I don't believe Grant. He won't release me unless I'm dead."

"If I do that now, he'll kill me. I would trade my life for yours in an instant, but it wouldn't do you any good. If I'm gone, he'll get the ransom money and might even hurt you." Feeling her tensing, he added, "But I won't let that happen."

"What are we going to do?"

"We have to wait for just the right moment. Until then, try not to worry. I'll keep you safe. I promise I'll get you out of this. If you ever doubt me because of the part I have to play, remember that everything isn't as it seems." He swallowed, wishing he could say more to put her mind at ease. "I won't let them hurt you."

THE GANG at last reached a large single oak in the prairie where a woman awaited with fresh horses, including Colt's usual mount, a lovely bay mare.

"Who is that?" Belle whispered as Colt dismounted.

"Grant's wife, Jill." He reached up for her. "Take my advice and don't talk to her if you can help it. She is more slippery than Grant."

Belle slid off the horse and would have crumpled to the ground if Colt's hands didn't tighten on her waist. "Are you unwell?" He asked, his voice low so the others wouldn't hear his concern.

She leaned heavily on his arms, her legs feeling completely useless. "Of course I am unwell. I've been chased and set in a saddle for six hours. I've never ridden that long before," she whispered, aching to rub her lower back, but not daring to for fear the men would see. "Are we stopping for the night?" She looked out onto the long, rolling prairie with the sun kissing the tip of each grassy hill. Under normal circumstances, she would have relished its wild, untamed beauty, but in the company of the outlaws, the beauty had turned into something to be feared, for out here, the outlaws were the rulers of this wild land, and she was at their mercy.

The horse shifted from hoof to hoof, shaking his blond mane as Colt turned his back to her and pulled on a buckle and loosened the girth. "Just changing horses. We can't risk staying too long."

"You going to share?" Russ slurred suggestively as he reached out and gave Belle's curl a tug.

"Oh!" Her hand flew to her head and her eyes smarted with pain. In one fluid motion, Colt uncoiled his whip, lashed the tail around the fiend's hand and jerked him away from Belle, yanking him down to his knees.

Jesse guffawed as Russ howled in pain and Colt shouted, "You lay one finger on her again, and I'll have your eye, Russ." He loosed his whip before turning and pointing to the rest of them. "That goes for everyone." He stared at Grant, daring him to disagree. "I mean to wed her at the next town." Colt turned so that only Belle could see the true meaning in his eyes before he grabbed her by the waist and lifted her into the saddle of the fresh horse.

Her heart thudded with relief at Colt's brief reassuring tilt of his lips. *He's bluffing.*

Grant grinned. He slapped Colt on the back. "Finally showing some gumption. About time you shed them gentlemanly ways of yours."

Colt placed his foot in the stirrup and pulled himself up behind her and directed his horse onward as the Death Riders mounted their horses and passed them, tearing down the road. Colt kicked his mare into a trot. "No one in this group will be touching you tonight, or any night," Colt said in her ear.

She turned to him, her chest tightening, but seeing the sincerity in his eyes she believed he would take care of her. "I know you aren't like them."

Colt lowered his voice, "I wasn't able to explain all in front of my brother, and he hasn't let me this far out of his earshot since he arrived home, but like I said before, I've been colluding with the Texas Rangers and have been working very closely with them to capture my brother and the rest of the Death Riders. When Clyde brought that ransom letter, I was able to send a message to Reid instead."

Belle's heart soared. "What? how?"

"I gave him a bottle for the ride and while he was packing it up, I switched out the notes. Lucky for us, Clyde can't read."

"Then, there's a chance Reid can capture the gang at last?"

"And with capturing Grant in the act, Reid will get the proof he needs in order to have a judge grant immunity from the crimes I committed when I was young. This will not only give me protection from my brother, but more importantly, Grant won't be able to kill anyone else."

"How long have you been trying to get away from Grant?"

"About four years. It took a while for me to save up enough to buy the land in Las Vegas and when I did, Grant left me alone for three years as he 'worked' in San Antonio, and I thought that I had finally escaped him. But ten months ago Grant came to the ranch and demanded I start robbing with him again, or he would end me. It was then I realized that Grant would never willingly allow me to leave the Death Riders . . . just like how he wouldn't allow Abel to leave. In order to be truly left alone, I had to turn him in, so I contacted Reid, and we've been working together since late last winter to imprison him. During that time, I came to know the Lord, and I experienced forgiveness that I never thought possible." He shook his head. "I'd hoped for change for so long, I was surprised when it actually happened in my heart."

"It's taken this long for Reid to capture him?"

"Grant is very good at covering his tracks and having an alibi handy, so we've been trying to catch him in the act, but Grant hasn't let me in on the details of the robberies for years. He springs them on me at the last minute. I try to stop the raids before they happen by telling Reid when to expect them, but lately, Grant has been sending the men without me. At first, I thought he was suspicious of me, but he hasn't killed me yet, so I suppose I'm safe. This is the first theft that we've planned together in years, and I alerted the authorities. The train will be filled with armed lawmen, ready to take Grant to prison, but now, there are complications to that plan." He grimaced.

She swallowed. "Meaning me."

"Yes. So much can go wrong. But we can't afford to linger any longer. My brother will get suspicious if we fall too far behind." He kicked his horse into a gallop.

"So, marriage. When were you going to tell me about this wild last resort plan?" Belle asked, her heart unable to comprehend what Colt's confession could mean.

A hint of a smile crept onto his lips. "At the last resort. But don't worry. It likely won't come to us marrying for me to protect you."

But what if it does? Would it be all that bad to marry the real man she had fallen in love with through their letters?

CHAPTER 19

When the Death Riders at last decided to set up camp, Belle was unable to put off her need any longer. She glanced around for any bit of privacy. *There are no trees to be seen for miles. Of course, they had to pick a place without a lick of shelter.* She swallowed back her embarrassment and rose on her tiptoes, whispering into Colt's ear, "I need to use the necessary."

His eyes widened, and he gnawed the inside of his mouth. "Oh, um," he scanned the area and realized her dilemma. He scratched his forehead. "I'll watch the men and make sure that no one follows us, but Grant isn't going to allow you to go without me."

Belle felt her face heat. She crossed her arms. "Well, that certainly is *not* going to work."

"We'll walk down the hill a bit, so the men can't see, and I'll keep my back turned." He gave her an apologetic shrug. "It's the best I can do."

"It's not like I can run away," she mumbled to herself, but seeing as he had no other choice and that she was almost to the point of hopping back and forth, she sighed, resigned to the fact that she couldn't even have a moment to herself. She closed her eyes against Colt's telling Grant, but she could hear his chortle.

"Let's go." Colt said, touching her elbow and helping her down the hill. "Sorry, but I have to comply with Grant, or else he will put an end to our little charade." When they were out of sight of the camp, he immediately released her arm. "Stay here, would you?" He strode out about thirty more yards, kicking around the grass and swatting his hat back and forth on the tops of the weeds.

"What are you doing?" Belle asked to distract herself from her growing discomfort.

"If I'm going to turn my back on you, I want to make sure there aren't any rattlers in the grass waiting to sink their teeth in your calf." He returned and plunked his hat back on. "I'll wait right here, but if you don't come back in five minutes, I'll have to turn around." At her look of horror, he continued, "It's either that or Grant will come running over the hill to look for you, and we both don't want that."

She nodded and hurried away as Colt whistled a tune. *I could run. I'd have five minutes . . . before they'd get the horses and come charging after me and then I am sure I would lose even the privilege of having Colt's back turned . . . it would be Grant, staring at me.* When she had finished readjusting her underdrawers, she patted her wild curls back before securing them with her white hair ribbon, which was the best she could do without a comb or pins, which had long since fallen out and hastened back to Colt.

"May I turn around?"

Taking a deep breath to still her rattled nerves, she smoothed her skirts. "Yes." In the setting sun, Belle could make out a faint redness creeping up his ears and neck. *At least he's as embarrassed about this as I am.*

He wiped his beading forehead with his sleeve. "When we get back to camp, don't leave my side for an instant. I trust a nest of cottonmouths better than those outlaws to keep their distance from you." When they reached the top of the hill, he grasped her elbow once more. Nearing the horses, he guided her to his bay mare, removing the saddle and tossing it to the ground away from the others. He pointed at the saddle. "It makes a mite better seat than the ground."

Grateful not to be sitting directly on the soil, Belle sank onto the hard leather and wrapped her arms around her knees, resting her head atop them. *I'll have to send Mr. Harvey a thank you note for making these dresses with high collars and long sleeves . . . if I live that long that is.* She ran her fingers over the hem of her black skirt, saddened to see tears in the hem and long streaks of dirt on the skirt. Not even the best of washings could bring it back to Mr. Harvey's high standards. A plate of beans was thrust under her nose.

"Time to eat up, Miss Parish." He squatted down next to her with two plates.

Hesitantly, she reached out and accepted her plate. Colt shoveled the beans into his mouth, not even bothering to cool them with his breath. Belle took a small spoonful and sniffed them, their pungent aroma making her gag. "They smell like I'd rather starve."

"You'll need your strength," Colt whispered and unscrewed his canteen, taking a swig of water before passing it to her. "Drink."

At the thought of water, her throat burned. She grasped the canteen and drank until the water dripped down her neck. With water in her belly, the beans didn't look quite so terrible. She blew on them and stuffed a spoonful into her mouth. The beans were so overly salted she almost choked on them. Colt shoved the canteen into her hands again and between the two, she managed to eat half her plate.

Relieving her of the plate, Colt nodded towards two bedrolls at the edge of the camp, near the horses. "I grabbed an extra bedroll before we left the ranch."

"I didn't even stand a chance of getting away, did I?" Belle crossed her arms. "My bedroll is entirely too close to your bedroll. It's improper."

He lowered his voice. "If you are too far away, I won't be able to help you if you should need it."

Belle felt weak as his meaning lingered in the air. "Can't you stay awake and watch over me?"

Colt reached out as if to touch her flushed cheek, but stopped midair and dropped his hand. "I'd try, but what's going to happen when I fall asleep tomorrow night even harder than ever? It's better I sleep lightly and try to keep an eye on you as much as I can," he responded. "I don't think it's wise for me not to sleep at all when we will need all the strength we can muster in the days to come." He shook out her bedroll for any creatures, which may have made themselves at home, before motioning that it was safe for her to crawl inside. "Go ahead."

She scooted inside the blanket, grateful for the warmth and protection as she lifted the blanket over head and closed her eyes. *God, let me wake up and find that all of this has been a terrible nightmare.* She paused. *Minus the part about Colt being a good man after all . . . that isn't a nightmare. Let Reid find us quickly, Lord. Amen.*

The rustling of cicadas woke her. Her eyes snapping open. Her situation washed over her anew, nearly drowning her. She twisted and spied Colt with his hat over his eyes in his bedroll, his revolver and whip beside him.

She pulled the lace ribbon out from her high collar and traced the gold ring with her fingertips, seeking comfort. In the firelight, she saw a faint shimmer on the inside of the ring. She rolled over onto her stomach, slipped the ring from the ribbon and squinting, held the ring closer to the firelight. *What in the world? Is that an inscription?* She tilted it in the light and read, *Psalm 91.* She searched for a memory of what the chapter said, but she couldn't recall it. *I wish I had memorized more verses in Sunday school.* She sighed and rethreaded the ring, tying it around her neck once more, turning over to find Colt studying her.

"Go back to sleep. I'm watching out for you."

And with those words, her fear of beasts faded—knowing that she was safe under Colt's watchful eye.

THEY REACHED San Antonio in the late afternoon, coming to a halt in a violent, swirling cloud of dust. Colt followed suit of the other men, tying his horse to the hitching post in front of a hotel that was run down from years of dust storms. He lifted a weary Belle from the saddle, but crossing the threshold, the hotel looked moderately clean on the inside. Grant ordered three rooms and as soon as Colt had his key, he gently grasped Belle's hand and led her straight up the stairs, pausing at the door with a six painted on it.

Her gaze darted from him to the open door and with a fatigued sigh, she crossed the room to the window. She pushed back the calico curtains and glanced down onto the busy city.

"Grant expects me to tie you up while we go to the saloon." He raked his hand through his blond hair. "It's not safe for you to run yet. We need to come up with a good plan that Grant won't be able to predict. I was thinking that tomorrow, when we rob the train, it might be a good time for you to make a break for it. Grant will be distracted and won't realize you're gone until it's too late and Reid apprehends him."

Belle scrunched her brow. "But, if there are going to be rangers on the train, wouldn't they arrest Grant and we would be free anyway? Why risk trying to escape?"

"Grant has fooled me before, and he might do it again. I need to make a second plan in case this one doesn't work. I don't want you anywhere near the train when the bullets start to fly."

"But I'm sure Grant will want to leave me tied up at the campsite all day." She leaned against the windowsill, crossing her arms.

"We will be gone for the better part of five hours and Grant won't want to back track to pick you up. He'll more than likely find a place for you to wait near enough to the ambush for you to be shot by him if things should go wrong. He wouldn't want you alive to risk you testifying against him. I'll make sure that I fall from my horse, so my mare can get away from me and that your hands are tied loosely enough for you to catch her. Then, I want you to ride back into San Antonio and go to the stables and leave her there for me to fetch." He reached into his back pocket and planted the money in her palm. "This should be more than enough to get a fresh horse and tack. If I am not back in two hours, I'll need you to send a telegram to Las Vegas, warning them about Grant and then, you're to head back to the Harvey House on the next train."

She blinked back tears.

"Don't be scared, Belle. I know it's my fault—"

She swatted her hand under her damp lashes, sniffing

back her tears. "It's not that. I-I just can't believe you would risk so much for me."

He grasped her hands in his. "I wasn't lying. I would die for you, Belle."

"I pray it doesn't come to that," she whispered.

"I do too. When it comes time for you to run, make it look like it takes effort to loose yourself from the ropes in case anyone sees you, but don't make a *noisy* show of it because I don't want you to draw fire unnecessarily." He reached into his belt and withdrew a bowie knife, setting it on the washstand by the door. "I would say that you should run tonight, but Grant is only more dangerous when drunk. I have to meet with him now, so keep the door locked and try to get some rest." He tugged his Stetson and shut the door.

CHAPTER 20

The doorknob jiggled, sending her scrambling for something to throw, but all she could find was her heeled shoe. She seized one from the floor beside the bed and raised it over her head with both arms. "Belle." Colt's voice came through the door. "Let me in?"

"Oh, thank God." She lowered her arms and drew back the chair she had pushed under the doorknob, barely keeping herself from throwing her arms around Colt's neck in sheer relief that it was him at the door and not some crazed, drunk cowboy.

Colt whipped off his hat. "You okay?" Seeing her shoe in her hand, he raised an eyebrow. "You didn't want to wield the knife I left you?"

"I forgot."

Colt plucked it from the table and returned it to his belt. "I overheard Grant saying that he's planning on killing you before the raid tomorrow because you know too much."

Her stomach revolted. She inhaled sharply, bending over double.

"The only possible way to keep that from happening is to do one thing." He captured her fingertips, lacing his fingers through hers. "You and I need to marry at once. Grant wouldn't hurt you if you were my wife, and the gang wouldn't dare touch you without Grant being on their side because they know he would plant a bullet between their eyes if they went against a Lawson. While Grant may seem without morals, the one law he would honor is that of the sanctity of his brother's marriage."

Belle dropped her shoe to the floor with a little laugh. "Really? I can't believe we are even discussing this, but does this town even have a preacher?"

"He's in the parlor downstairs. I told him to bring his wife as a witness. We have to move fast, but I, of course, won't act without your consent. My only thought is that of protection for you. Our marriage would be in name only, but it would be enough to keep you from being Grant's next victim." He held his hat over his heart. "Please, believe me. I *am* the man in those letters."

She stared at the man. Even though he wasn't exactly as she had imagined, he did possess the character she required in a husband. He was indeed a God-fearing man, brave, a protector, and he loved her. *What more could I ever ask for in a husband?* "I believe you." Belle pushed her shoulders back and slipped her hand around his arm and allowed him to lead her downstairs to the parlor, her heart pounding with every step. Colt pushed open the parlor door to a small room with worn furnishings, which might have once been elegant a long, long time ago.

The short, thin preacher and his robust wife stood at the window, their smiles faltering at the sight of Belle. "I-is this the lovely bride? My, aren't you a blessed man." The preacher shook Colt's hand as he gave Belle a nod as his wife met his gaze, something silently passing between them.

She ran her fingers over her hair, wishing she would have taken a moment to brush and braid her wild hair. She nearly giggled at how shambolic she must appear to the prim and proper couple.

"Indeed, sir." Colt squeezed Belle's hand, the pressure stilling her racing heart. "We're ready when you are." He turned to the preacher's wife, "Ma'am, do you have that bouquet?"

She drew an enormous bouquet of wildflowers from behind her back and handed them to Belle. "You're a mighty lucky girl, honey. This man found us and then went and picked this bunch of wildflowers. He said it wasn't a proper wedding unless his girl had a field of wildflowers."

He remembered from my letters. Belle accepted them, her heart warming as she gazed up into Colt's deep brown eyes. "Thank you," she whispered as the preacher motioned them to stand before him. Even though the circumstances were quite different than she would've imagined them for her wedding, she had her bouquet of wildflowers and a good man. *Surely, he will look after me kindly all of his days if he does such sweet, simple things only to please me.*

She tried to focus on the preacher's words, binding her to this handsome and confusing rancher, but all she could think about was Colt's ardent promise of protection—and with that promise, she felt something flutter to life, which she thought had faded into nothing more than a withered dream.

The preacher lifted a piece of paper from his Bible and set it on the table. "Please sign the wedding certificate, which my wife will act as witness to, and you're officially married."

Colt dipped the pen into the inkwell and, without hesitation, signed his name and handed the pen to Belle. With shaking hands, she signed. *It's done. I'm married to Colt Lawson.* She straightened and met Colt's concerned eyes, giving him a tiny smile.

He slid his hand around her waist, drawing her to his side, already protecting her. Was he going to kiss her? Should she kiss him? And to her surprise, the thought was not frightening . . . it sent her heart to racing for an entirely different reason. *It's tradition after all.* At his stiffening, she at once saw the reason why.

"What's going on?" Grant staggered into the parlor.

"I've just made Belle my bride." Colt kept his arm about her and stared unflinchingly at his brother. "She's officially a Lawson now."

"Don't let me interrupt," Grant lifted his glass bottle, the contents sloshing inside and tipped his hat, swaying unsteadily. "I've got some more liquor to drink. Have a good evening, Mr. and Mrs. Lawson."

Colt reached inside of his pocket and handed a crisp bill to the preacher. "Thank you, sir."

"My pleasure." The preacher exchanged confused glances with his wife and departed as quickly as they had come.

Her heart lodged itself into her throat as Colt led her up the creaky stairs to room number six and quietly closed the door behind him. "Now what?" Belle asked, barely keeping her voice from shaking.

Colt ran his finger along the perimeter of his Stetson. "Now, we have to stay inside here for the rest of the evening. I'm sorry it had to come to this, but I wouldn't have married you if there wasn't any other way."

"I know." Belle moved to the window. She gazed up to the moon, thinking of how simple her life had been only a few short weeks ago before she discovered who had robbed her at gunpoint . . . when Colt was nothing but a cad in her eyes.

Now, there was so much more to him than that first impression.

Colt proffered a pillow from the bed and tossed it by the door. "I'll sleep on the floor, and you take the bed."

She perched on the edge of the bed. "I was never able to thank you for all of your help before. There was always someone too near."

He shrugged and sat on the floor, leaning his pillow against the dresser and spreading his long coat over his legs that were sprawled before the door, acting as a barrier between her and danger. "No need."

"Yes, there is a need. You're taking a great risk by protecting me."

"Any man would've been happy to marry you even if it only means being near enough to guard you and never actually being near."

How can he be so kind to me after I humiliated him by leaving him at the altar? After snubbing him in town?

"I'm only sorry I messed up your plans with your ranger." He undid the top button of his shirt, pulling at the collar.

She shot to her feet and promptly began fluffing the remaining pillow. "He's not *my* ranger and we never made any plans beyond that of dancing."

"Oh?" His eyes flickered for a brief moment before he snuffed it out along with his smile.

"I had thought he'd never married simply because he hadn't found the right woman yet, but the man is conceited as a peacock." Her cheeks burned, remembering their last conversation. She laid down on the bed without even bothering taking off her shoes and sighed. "What are we going to do when this is all over, Colt?"

He tucked his hands behind his head and closed his eyes. "I suppose we'll just have to wait and see how everything ends up. I may not be alive for you to worry about anyway."

"Colt Lawson." She sat up, her feet swinging to the floor. "Don't ever say such things."

He met her gaze. "Sounds like you almost care."

"Of course I do," she whispered. "We are friends after all."

"Friends?" He chuckled. "I guess that is better than being branded a liar in your eyes. What I meant was that Grant is a dangerous man, and he might overpower me. You shouldn't underestimate him. Ever."

"What made him so dangerous? Was he always this way?"

"Ever since he was a young man, his solution to our money problems was to rob people. At first, he only worked by himself, but then, as he became more daring in his robberies, he pulled in Abel and me." He leaned back and picked at the faded, worn wallpaper at the door frame. "But then, he met a girl named Alice Walker and she changed everything for him."

Belle remembered the ring Reid had that day at the lunch counter so long ago. *A.W. is Alice Walker? If so, Grant must still care for her if he's been wearing that ring.* "How so?"

"She was the youngest daughter of the mayor. No one thought us Lawsons were worth anything and everyone knew Grant was trouble, except for Alice. Her golden curls and bright cornflower blue eyes entranced Grant and he fell madly in love with her. For a while, he stopped robbing stagecoaches because of her." He paused. "But then, Mayor Walker found out about Grant's courtship, and he forced her to marry the banker's son, and when Alice died in childbirth, Grant donned his mask and courted her elder sister Jill just to spite the father. Jill had been labeled a spinster by the town, but she had always been infatuated with Grant, so she jumped at the chance to be with him. After their elopement, he forced us brothers to rob Alice's husband's bank, using Jill as a distraction."

"Oh my." She pressed her hand to her chest.

"Abel tried to convince him otherwise and wanted out before we robbed the bank and that's when Grant killed him . . . and I knew if I didn't help in the robbery, I'd be next."

"I had at least thought we were dealing with a man who might be reasoned with, but this is madness."

His lips pressed into a grim line. "All this to say that you should not worry about how this whole marriage is going to work out just yet. We need to rest up before tomorrow."

"Where's the robbery taking place?" Belle rested her head on the musty pillow again.

"It will be just outside of San Antonio." He yawned. "Well, we better try to sleep."

She shook out the thin blanket, wishing there was another blanket in the room she could give to Colt.

"Goodnight, Belle." He crossed his arms for warmth.

Even if I offered, he would never accept the blanket. Belle curled under the thin quilt. "Goodnight, Colt." Long into the night, she lay wide-awake, wondering, hoping, and praying.

COLT CHECKED Abel's pocket watch again. Five minutes before midnight, Colt slipped on his overcoat and stood over Belle. In the moonlight streaming through the hotel's window, she looked so young—so innocent. He brushed back a curl from her forehead. She moaned and stirred in her sleep. He smiled, his gut twisting. Despite all she had been through, she trusted him enough to allow herself such a deep sleep. He rested his hand on her shoulder, grazing her arm with his thumb. "Belle? It's time."

She jerked up, rubbing her fists over her eyes. "Already?"

"Grant made a new plan at the saloon." He knelt before her and grasped her hands in his. It was imperative that she understood the importance of tonight. "Remember our plan. Pay attention to the route, so you can retrace your steps."

It took only a few moments for them to slip out into the hallway to meet the others. No one spoke so as to keep the hotel clerk from waking. The group crept downstairs. Grant snatched the hotel's cashbox, stealing outside where Jesse stood with the readied mounts.

Colt wrapped his hands around her waist and lifted her into his saddle. At her shiver, Colt slipped off his long coat and wrapped it about her shoulders. His compassion sent the men into jokes about Colt's new husbandly duties and how she had him wrapped around her little finger already. Jill merely frowned—a flicker of jealousy in her eyes.

Colt glared at them. "We here to jeer, or get rich?"

Grant nodded his approval and motioned the group forward. They rode out of town at a walk to keep from gaining notice until they reached the edge of town, where they broke into a gallop.

They rode hard for three hours until they reached a creek burrowed in a grove of trees near the railroad tracks and well hidden from view. Colt hopped down and reached up for Belle. She put her hands on his shoulders and allowed him to lift her from the saddle. He kept his arms around her for a second or two longer in case she fell, but she seemed stronger today. She stretched her back and rubbed her right shoulder blade.

Colt grasped her hand and led her around a boulder. "No matter what happens, or what you hear during the robbery, I still want you to ride back to town. However, if Grant is too close behind you, duck into that cave I pointed out to you on the way here, and stay there until I come and get you. Supplies are in my saddlebags. If I'm not there in three days, you should be safe to make it back to town. You paid attention to the route, yes?"

Her wide eyes filled with concern. "But what about you? If something goes wrong, how will you get away?"

"You let me worry about that." He glanced behind them. "Now, let's get back before Grant comes looking."

She grabbed his sleeve, stopping him. "You'll try to be careful, won't you, Colt?"

He gave her a sad smile, her concern touching. "I wish I could say I will be, but—" He drew her around the boulder.

"Get some shut eye, men. The train will be passing by in the morning," Grant ordered, taking another long swig of whiskey.

Like the other night under the stars, Colt laid their bedrolls at the edge of camp, but this time, the bedrolls were touching each other. He caught Belle biting her lip, but she swallowed back her discomfort and slipped under her blanket.

"Colt, take the first watch." Grant sank down onto his bedroll with his bottle. He motioned up the tree, making the drink slosh inside the colored glass. "Sit up there and call out if you see anything on two legs."

Belle dared to peek at where he was sending Colt, her fear mirroring his own.

All the way up in that oak? She won't be able to see me. I won't be able to see her. What if one of the men tries something? His pulse pounded, but he could not disobey a direct order. He squeezed her hand, discreetly transferring his knife into her palm and climbed up the tree. For an hour, Colt perched in the branches, praying and waiting as the faint howl of a single coyote was answered by the pack. Even though it appeared all were resting, Colt couldn't shake the feeling that Grant was up to something.

He heard the faintest click of a revolver. "Belle!" He shouted and dropped from the branches on the tips of his toes, crouching down to roll and broke into a run as Belle shrieked at Grant hovering over her with his gun aimed directly at her.

She slashed her knife just above Grant's knee. He knocked the knife from her grip as the other outlaws scrambled to their feet, stumbling in their drunken stupor for their weapons to come to the aid of their leader. Colt's hand found his whip and with a yell, he snapped the leather around Grant's shooting hand and steered the bullet to rent the sky. Colt launched himself at his brother. He threw a single punch, knocking him out cold.

Belle ran to Colt as Russ stumbled toward her and caught her by the skirt, but she jerked away, leaving him holding a tattered piece of black cotton as she fell to the ground.

"Get away from her, Russ!" Colt shouted, ducking Jesse's fists before landing one of his own that stunned the young man.

Belle slammed her heel into Russ's nose and scrambled to her feet, running for Colt. He threw her onto the bare back of his mare and snatched his saddle pack, swinging himself up behind her and kicking his mount into a dead run.

CHAPTER 21

They charged through the cedar and oak trees, hurtling down hills. The darkness enveloped her as everything blurred in the pounding of the horse's hooves. Colt gasped, changing the direction of the flight, stones skittering over a steep cliff that he had narrowly avoided.

Belle clutched the horse's mane and pressed her back against Colt's chest, trying not to scream. As if sensing her fear, his arm tightened reassuringly around her waist, letting her know that, like always, he would protect her.

They rode for what seemed like hours until they came upon the cave nestled deep in the hill country as dawn began to break. Colt halted the horse and quickly slipped from the steed's back before reaching for her. Shivering, Belle stared at the mouth of the cave and beyond into the darkness. Her entire body began to tremble at the thought of hiding in the dark for so long. "Can't we keep riding?" She asked, even as the horse's labored breathing brought a regretful ache to her heart.

Colt's broad shoulders sagged as he gestured to the

mare's chest that was white and foaming from their flight. "The horse is exhausted and with the day beginning, I'm concerned that if we pressed onward on a spent horse, my brother will catch us. At least here, we have the chance that he might miss us. He doesn't know this area as well as I do, and I'm the best tracker in the Death Riders, so we should be safe to rest here. Grant might even let us go in favor of claiming the gold on that train."

High-pitched howls sounded nearby. Her head snapped up, and she bit back a scream as she kept herself from flying into Colt's arms as she had the night her horse ran away ages ago. *If I go too far into the cave, I might not make it back, but if I ask that we stay near the mouth of the cave . . . the Death Riders might find us and kill us anyway.* She wrestled with her fear. *God, help me. I can't do this on my own.*

As if reading her thoughts, he continued, "If we only move around the first few corners of the cave, we can be hidden from view, but can still have a hint of daylight to see, which will allow us to build a small fire that won't be easily spotted, and we can get you warmed up."

Colt wrapped his strong, warm hand around hers and gently guided her and the horse into the cold, damp cave. Dried branches crunched underfoot as the leaves parted from the brush of her skirts. When they reached a corner of the cave, Colt handed her the reins.

"You and Pepper wait here. I'll gather a stack of wood for a fire before I bring you both any further into the cave."

Belle clutched the horse's reins. The horse nudged her shoulder as if to remind her she wasn't alone. "Pepper, huh? Nice to meet you." She reached out and stroked her nose, finding comfort in her company and secretly happy that Colt was the type of man who would name his horse. Suzanne wouldn't even allow her to name the kitchen cat because she didn't want Belle to think of it as a pet. She said that it was there to catch mice and nothing more. Belle shook her head, dismissing Suzanne once more from her head. *Even in the darkness of a cave hundreds of miles away, she still haunts me . . . because I let her.*

"This should hold us for a bit. I'll have it blazing in a moment." Colt passed her with an armful of dried cedar and oak limbs.

Hearing him arrange the wood, Belle waited until she heard the flare of a match. She led the mare around the corner to find Colt bent down on his knees, gently blowing on the fire, coaxing it into a hearty flame. He leaned back on his heels. "You can just drop the reins if you want. Pepper is too tired to bolt."

Belle let the reins slip from her grasp and kicked away some dried leaves that had been blown deep into the cave and sank down on the stone floor, tucking her skirts tight about her legs. The cave held a wretched chill. She shivered and a lock of hair fell over her cheek.

Colt gently stroked back her hair, his fingertips lingering for a moment on her cheek. At his touch, her defenses lowered, the strain of the day easing. Shocked by the strength of her feelings, she drew away and ran her fingers through her locks, feeling something coarse brush against her fingertips. She removed a twig with a single leaf attached from her tangled mane and tossed it into the fire. "Not sure how that got in there, but at least I can say I helped with the fire now," she chuckled. "I must be a sight."

"A sight for sore eyes." His gaze held her own with such intensity that she thought he might kiss her.

She regarded his full lips and wondered what it would be like to be kissed by him. She leaned forward as Pepper chomped down on a curl, yanking her to the cavern floor.

"Ow." She scrambled away from the horse and rubbed the side of her head. "What on earth got into you?"

Colt snatched the horse's reins. "Sorry. I should've mentioned that Pepper sometimes bites. Bad girl." He grunted and led the horse a safe distance from Belle's curls and secured the reins to a stone jutting up from the cave floors.

I hope he didn't notice that I wanted to kiss him. Clearing her throat, she put away all thoughts of Colt Lawson's full lips. *But would it be so bad if he did notice? He did say he loved me . . .* Before she could start blushing again at how quickly the thought of kissing returned, she shook out her skirts and sat by the fire once more. "So, what did you manage to bring in your saddle pack?"

"Mostly bullets, a matchbox, some money, a little food, and a knife." He retrieved a loaf of bread and handed it to her. "I'm sorry it isn't more. I only packed what I thought could last you three nights."

"Then we must do our best to make it last." She tore off half the loaf and then tore that piece in two, handing him the largest.

The crack of lightening made Pepper dance and Belle jump as a storm rolled through the hills, the cave dropping in temperature. "Uh, is it normal in these parts for it to get this cold so fast?"

"No." Colt hopped up to inspect the sky from the mouth of the cave. "Belle, come see."

Belle set aside her bread and scrambled to her feet and followed him. The sky churned, turning black as the wind bent the trees. She clutched his arm.

He smiled up at the swirling cloud. "Looks like the sky is brewing our escape. If a tornado touches down, all tracks will be obliviated."

"Do you think we'll be safe enough here?" Belle shouted as the wind picked up and the howling grew louder, whipping her skirts taut against her legs. The leaves ripped from the trees and a nearby branch cracked free.

Colt seized her hand and guided her back to the fire. "If we stay in the back of the cave, we should be fine. Even without a tornado, the heavy rains should throw Grant off our trail long enough for us to get away." He gently rubbed Pepper's nose and whispered into her ear as the thunder made the horse skitter.

Belle dusted her fingers free from the bread. "What are you telling her?"

Colt gave her his crooked smile. "That she's safe and she should rest while she gets the chance and not to bite the pretty lady's hair."

Belle laughed, rubbing the sore spot. "I forgive her. She was only jealous."

"Jealous?" Colt's brows shot up as he rubbed Pepper's neck, leaning against the wall. "So, does that mean you were flirting with me?"

"She certainly seemed to think so. She doesn't want to share her best friend." Belle giggled and shifted to stretch her legs out in front of her. "Well, I better take the advice you gave to Pepper and sleep while I still can."

"We all should." Slipping out of his long coat, he handed it to her and slid down the wall until he was seated and lifted his hat to cover his eyes, crossing his arms.

Belle was cold when she awoke. She stirred, looking over her shoulder to find that the fire had died out. She sat up, intending to use the moment alone for her needs when she heard murmuring. She stiffened. They were not alone. She crawled over to Colt and placed her hand over his full lips. He started.

"Shh," she whispered, leaving a finger on his lips. "I-I think Grant is here."

Crouching on his hands and the tip of his boots, Colt silently crept to the corner of the cave and keeping low, peered around to the mouth of the cave. He scrambled back and whispered, "I can't believe it, but you're right. Grant and the rest of the Death Riders are here, seeking shelter from the storm."

"Where's your gun? We have the element of surprise. I'm sure you could get us out of here." Belle's heart caught in her throat at the thought of what she was suggesting. *But it's either them or us.*

"In the skirmish earlier, my gun came out of the holster." Colt smothered the fire, minus one large limb.

"No." Belle raked her fingers down her cheeks, trying to keep her panic from erupting. "What are we going to do? We can't stay here. He'll find us the moment Pepper makes a sound."

Colt pressed his lips into a grim line and exhaled. "We don't have much of a choice. We're going to have to go deeper into the cave."

Her stomach twisted. She pressed her hands to her stomach to stay the tremors in her arms. "What if we get lost? I've heard how people die in caves from only one wrong turn. Millie, my Harvey Sister, told me about her second cousin who went into the caves as a child and *never* came home. We'll get lost for sure." Lightening cracked, filling the cave with light for a split second, enough for Colt to spot the fear painted on her face.

"Come here." He wrapped her in his arms, the weight of his muscle slowing her rapid breathing as she focused on the steady beat of his heart and his scent of leather and woodsmoke. "If we stay here, he'll kill us both. If we at least attempt to find another way out of here, or hide deeper in the cave until he leaves, we have a chance at surviving this ordeal."

She lifted her chin, drinking in his reassuring smile. If she had to be trapped with anyone in a cave, Colt Lawson was the one she would have picked. She nodded, and his arms slowly eased away as he snatched up the saddlebags and quietly slung them over his shoulder.

Belle glanced at the horse. "What about Pepper?"

His strong façade faltered as he clenched his jaw and sighed. "We'll have to leave her." He slipped the bridle off of Pepper, affectionately rubbing the horse's nose. "Hopefully, Grant will think Pepper got loose and is just seeking shelter like him."

Belle detected doubt in his voice, but she gritted her teeth, knowing that it was their only chance. *Lord, give us strength.*

Colt hefted the four limbs he must have prepared while she was sleeping and carried them in his left arm while he lit the torch of the fifth, holding it low to the ground in his right hand, motioning her to take his arm with the torch. She wrapped her hand about his elbow loose enough for Colt to be able to move freely.

With each bend of the cave, she could feel Colt's tension lessening. "You aren't nervous?"

He shrugged. "Only because of Grant. When I was boy, my father used to tell us of his adventures exploring caves and how he survived when he became lost, so I know a little bit about caves if that makes you feel any better?"

She rolled her eyes, giggling softly. "You probably should have led with being a cave expert in your argument to get me to follow you. It would have helped ease my worries."

Smiling, he continued as if they were merely strolling in

the cedar grove beyond the church. "I'm scanning the path for any sudden drops, so I'll need you to discreetly mark the walls of the cave or the floor to help us find our way back." He paused, studying her hair. "Would you mind using pieces of your white hair ribbon?"

Belle tugged free the large Harvey House bow from her hair, allowing her curls to spill wildly over her shoulders. "I'm not certain how discreet this would be. It's Harvey House white."

Colt rubbed the ribbon between two fingers and handed it back to her. "Hmm. I had hoped it was dirtier from our travel. What about lighting a match, blowing it out, and using the burnt end to mark a little 'x' on the wall every turn?"

"Perfect. Where are the matches?" Belle tied her hair back with the ribbon, impressed with his ingenuity.

He nodded toward the saddlebag lying on his chest. "Would you mind getting it? With the torch and the wood, it's difficult to reach."

Belle moved closer to him, his natural musk weakening her knees. *This is no time for such thoughts, Belle Parish . . .* She paused. *Belle Lawson.* That correction did little to stay the wobble in her knees, but she reached into the bag and felt the leftover bread, a canteen, and a book. She lifted it out, finding the leather worn. "You carry a Bible?"

"Where I go, it goes."

She flipped it open, fanning the leaves to find them wrinkled with little pencil marks in the margins and verses underlined. It looked like her own. It looked like a Bible the man in her letters would have owned.

"We best hurry. I don't want them catching up with us," he whispered.

She returned the Bible, her fingers brushing over a small

box. She retrieved a match and with a shaking hand, ignited it with his torch and at once waved it to extinguish the flame, marking the nearest wall.

He sucked in his breath through his teeth at the faint mark. "I sure hope my Pa was telling the truth about the ease of walking around in caves. Let's keep going."

With those words, her muscles tensed, aching to sprint for the sun, but having no other course, she clenched her fists and plunged into the unknown.

CHAPTER 22

The darkness was unlike anything Colt had ever experienced before. Even with the faint glow of the torch, he had to be careful not to stumble on the uneven rock underfoot. He glanced at Belle and caught her drawing in deep gulping breaths and slowly releasing them, her eyes wide.

"You doing okay over there?" Colt's question sent her jumping.

"Sorry." She flushed. "I was only remembering another time I was locked away in the dark as a child."

He raised his torch, the light exposing a tear trickling down her cheek. He wished he could retrace his steps and see them out in the sunshine, away from ill memories.

She swayed. She focused on the ground before her, putting one foot in front of the other in a fashion that made him wish to drop the torches and comfort her in his arms.

"I've never told this to anyone because I knew that I would only be ridiculed for exposing my fear, but I'm deathly afraid of the dark."

"I wish there was another way out of this situation. If I had known—" *If I had known, what? I had no other choice but to take to the caves with her.* He bowed his head. "Lord, guide us to an escape. Comfort us in our fear and embolden our spirits."

"Amen." She whispered, smiling up at him. "That's the first time I've heard you pray."

"If you stay with me, it won't be the last."

"Your Bible is pretty worn."

"I-I got it during a raid."

"What?"

"During one of the raids directly before I went to Reid, Grant robbed a preacher man. Grant took everything the man had of value, save for that Bible. When he went to shoot him, I stood between them and managed to talk Grant down. The preacher gave me his Bible and told me to read it. And I did. Twice so far. That day changed my life."

A muffled cry echoed through the cavern walls. Belle and Colt halted and listened as the shouts grew louder.

"They must have found Pepper. We need to make a run for it." Colt handed her the torch and grabbed her free hand, running with his armload of torches.

The deep, rumbling voices of the outlaws seemed to gain on them with every second. The path curved to the right and then left until it split.

"Oh, God." Belle whimpered. "What are we going to do?"

"Left, or right?" Colt whispered. He whipped about, desperately trying to make out which was the better path, but the light only extended a few yards each way. "Please, let this be the correct path, Lord." Colt ran headlong down the right passageway for what seemed like an hour until the voices faded to nothing, and Colt at last halted, panting as Belle sank in a cloud of skirts on the cavern floor.

"I think." His breath came in short gasps. "W-we've lost them."

Peeling off the long coat, Belle lifted her damp curls from her neck and unbuttoned the top three buttons of her collar, allowing the cool air to kiss her lovely neck.

"Don't leave it unbuttoned." Colt sank beside her, handing her the canteen before rolling up the coat and shoving it in one of his saddle bags.

She lifted her brows in question as she took a gulp of the water.

"You'll get sick. You're hot now, but when your body temperature goes down, you'll get cold from your sweat." He accepted the water and took a swig himself.

"How long do we need to wait before heading back?" She panted.

"At least a few hours. Grant won't want to stay for too long because he knows the rangers will be coming for him." He leaned his head back on the cave wall and closed his eyes, exhaling.

The stillness of the cave enveloped them, giving him an odd sense of peace.

"Colt, why didn't you just tell me the truth? Why did you keep it a secret? I know Reid made you promise, but it could have saved us so much pain."

Colt removed his Stetson and placed it on his knee. "I regret having to keep it from you, but I did what I could to ensure our future." He sighed. "But when Reid used my silence to his advantage, I started to pursue you and wanted to tell you despite Reid's warnings. However, he brought our plans to the attention of the head of the rangers, and he made it clear that my arrangement with the Texas Rangers would be at risk if I told you. I didn't want to chance not being granted a pardon because if I didn't have my freedom,

I could never marry you. I pleaded with the official to change his mind, but he said they didn't want to risk Grant finding out when we were so close, so I pushed for Grant to arrange his most daring raid yet to catch him in the act. I figured the sooner I was free from Grant, the sooner I would be free to win your heart. But I think I know the real reason Reid held my freedom hostage."

"Me?" She shook her head. "I don't know why he would when he obviously didn't wish to marry me. But, speaking of marriage, there's been a question burning in the front of my mind since the moment I laid eyes on you. Why haven't you married? There are plenty of girls to choose from, so why not just marry, I don't know, maybe Dolly? She would be more than happy to oblige. You didn't have to settle on Grant's mail-order bride prank."

He grinned. "There is no such thing as settling when it comes to you, Belle. But, to answer your question, you see how Dolly acts around me now? Well, for three years, she only thought of me as a handsome enough cowboy to entertain her until she found a husband, but three months ago when she heard about how my ranch was becoming more and more successful, she started parading herself in front of me. She didn't care what others thought as she only wanted my money. The townspeople thought I was no good because they were suspicious of Grant, so they kept their daughters away, and besides, I didn't want them. I wanted a girl who liked me for me and not my ranch." He fiddled with the brim of his hat. "And when I met you, I knew there wouldn't ever be another girl for me." He grasped her hand. "Not ever."

AFTER A FEW HOURS OF REST, Colt stood and offered her his hand. "I think we can make our way back now. Either they are lost, or they left us for dead."

She accepted his hand and stretched her back as Colt gathered the remaining unlit torches and one that was currently halfway burnt. She shook her skirts, hating the feeling of being grimy all the time. Belle followed closely behind Colt, her eyes searching for a glimpse of the small "x" that marked their path, but she couldn't spy anything. Not one single "x." "Colt? I don't see any of the marks."

He lifted the torch, scouring the walls on either side of them. "How often did you mark the way?"

She furrowed her brow. "At every turn . . . but we were running so fast at the end that I missed a time, or two," she admitted, waiting for him to take back all the kind things he had said to her. "I'm so sorry." Tears filled her eyes.

"It's not your fault. *I* should've paid better attention as to what we were running past and made mental notes on unique rock formations." Colt scowled and lifted the torch to the wall again. "Nonetheless, we have to keep searching for those marks." He grunted and rubbed his forehead. "I should've used pieces of my shirt to mark the way. Soot is just too easy to miss." He sighed and continued winding with the path until they came to a narrow opening. He dropped the unlit torches. "Blast. I don't remember this at all. Do you?"

"I would've remembered squeezing through that." Belle shivered. "We must've made a wrong turn." She rubbed her arms up and down. "It's so cold. Do you think it's possible that we went further down into the cave?"

"Unfortunately, there's a very good chance that we did." He unfurled his long coat and draped it on her shoulders, his expression grim in the waning torchlight as he gathered the wood once more. "Let's retrace our steps and try again."

Time blurred as they walked, save for the changing of the torches. They only had one remaining after this one died. She swallowed, not wanting to even contemplate how it would feel to be in such utter darkness.

Colt thrust his arm before her, blocking her way. He lifted his torch. There was no ceiling or sides to guide them. The cavern was colossal. He groaned. "Oh Lord. We're completely lost."

Her legs wobbled, and she collapsed onto the cave floor, her chest heaving, each breath labored.

"Belle!" He knelt beside her, setting the torch on the ground and gathering her hands in his and rubbing his warmth into them. "I'm so sorry. So very sorry."

Her teeth chattered. "Y-you are sorry? Why aren't you b-blaming me? It was *my* job to mark the trail and all I did was get us hopelessly turned around because I was so frightened and desperate to escape Grant that I neglected to mark the last few turns. Grant isn't the enemy. I-I am."

"Nonsense." He gathered the torch, sat beside her, crossing his legs as he wrapped his arm around her shoulders and bowed his head, his nearness slowing her breathing. "Lord Jesus, guide us out of this mess. Protect us and give us strength and courage to face what is ahead. Amen." He cleared his throat. "I suggest we keep moving while we still have the strength of the bread in our bodies. There's bound to be a second entrance to this cave. How hard could it be to find it?"

With his torch nearly spent, he handed the six-inch stump to Belle before lighting the last tree limb and as her eyes met his, neither of them spoke their fear of what would happen when they ran out of wood. Belle slipped her hand through Colt's arm and took a deep breath, trying to assuage her fears of confined areas. The faint dripping of water and the echo of their steps was deafening in the silence as they shuffled down the winding passage that grew more and more narrow until the ceiling was so low that even Belle had to crouch down.

"Are you certain we should keep going this way?" She asked, almost grateful for the growing pit of hunger churning in her stomach for it meant less food she would have to hold down.

"I don't know where else to go but forward. If it gets too narrow, we can head back, but honestly, I'm afraid of retracing our steps because we already know that it won't lead us out and we are quickly running out of time." He squeezed her hand. "Stay close to me?"

"Always."

Colt gripped the torch and sank to his knees, crawling forward through the crevice on his belly.

Belle held her breath and followed suit, crawling behind Colt. A sharp rock bit under her fingernail and she hissed, pulling her hand back.

"You hurt?" Colt twisted his head to glance over his shoulder back at her, the ceiling grazing his shoulder blades.

She gritted her teeth against the pain and kept crawling. "I will be when we can stand again." *God, please don't let there be any slimy cave creatures slithering next to me.* She shivered, remembering Millie's tale of cave salamanders that her second cousin collected before he had disappeared. *I wonder if some kind of cave creature ate him?* She crawled faster.

Another minute on her belly saw the ceiling vanishing and they once again were in a cavern so large that Belle couldn't even see the top of it. *Well, I suppose, I might be able to see the top of it if I could see anything at all beyond the yard of light.* She scrambled to her feet and viciously brushed her skirt free from the memory of the narrow passageway. She shuffled forward, her foot feeling naught but air. She gasped and fell to her backside, shuffling backwards. "Don't move, Colt! Hold your torch towards the floor."

Colt lowered his torch and inhaled sharply through his teeth at the chasm below. "It looks like we may have to go back after all."

"I can't go back through there. I can't." Belle's hands trembled so violently that she stuffed them under her arms to keep Colt from noticing as he squatted down beside her.

He wrapped his arm around her and helped her to stand. "We'll find a way around. Just stay close to me and only step where I step." He walked in front of her, methodically waving the torch back and forth, checking to ensure the path was wide enough for them.

Belle wished she could close her eyes and open them only to find this was a nightmare, but it wasn't a nightmare from which she could wake and the path before them was shrinking. "Colt," she whimpered.

"It's okay, I see the other side. Can you keep going?"

She nodded, though she was certain he couldn't see as she concentrated on her next step and the step after, anything to keep her mind from looking to the left and seeing nothing below. Her foot sent a loose spray of gravel to the left and scattering down the side of the cliff. She didn't hear it land. She swallowed and closed her eyes for a second. Her foot landed on another patch of loose gravel and her body shifted not of her will.

"Colt!" She screamed. Her legs draped over the edge as Colt leapt toward her and grabbed her forearm, dropping his torch.

He yanked her onto solid ground and into his arms as she sobbed into his shoulders. He rocked back and forth.

"I-I almost fell." She sobbed, clinging to his vest as he stroked her hair. "W-we aren't going to make it out of here alive, are we?"

He gently grasped her head between his hands and gazed into her eyes by the flickering light of the torch. "I'll get you out of here alive. Do you hear me? I never make a promise I don't intend to keep."

She drew a jagged breath and wiped her eyes with the torn cuff of her once impeccable uniform. The torch sputtering.

Colt snatched the torch, holding it up to encourage the flame as he squinted to see what lay ahead. "We are almost to the other side, but there's a small catch."

"Besides our light dying?" She trailed her fingers down her throat, her voice strained from screaming.

"We'll have to jump about three feet to reach the other side. I'll jump first and then, I'll be ready to catch hold of you."

Belle pressed her back to the wall as Colt released her hand and leapt, her heart thudding with relief as he landed safely on the other side.

"It's not bad at all. Imagine you're jumping over a creek, and you don't want your skirts to get wet."

Belle laughed, her voice echoing off the walls. "Playing like the ground is burning hot coals might be a better idea. As children, Miss Fairfield and I would crawl over everything in the lawn if it meant that we didn't have to touch the fiery grass." She imagined herself a girl again, sucked in her breath and sprang. The moment her foot touched the other side, his arms wrapped around her waist and pulled her against his chest.

Belle gripped his shirt, panting until she felt a gentle press of lips atop her hair. Her breathing evened as she lifted her face to him. What would it be like for him to kiss her in earnest?

"I hate to keep pushing you, but we must keep going. We only have hours left of light."

"Dear heavenly Father, get us out of here." Belle grasped his hand and they hurried away from the chasm. They turned left, right, straight, and then traveled in what seemed like circles. Belle's feet grew sore, but she knew that if she didn't keep going, she would die in the dark with the last thing she ever saw being Colt's face. *But I suppose that Colt's face would be the last thing I would ever want to see.* The thought gave her pause, and she shifted her gaze to her husband. "Colt, do you regret marrying me to keep me safe? If it weren't for me, you wouldn't be in this situation now."

His brows shot up at her question. "I know that you may have thought I only wanted a bride because I was desperate or lonely, but I felt something as I read your letters. I felt hope for a future with a strong woman who wanted a better life, a better life that I could offer her as an honorable man. However, I didn't want to marry you like I did."

Her stomach twisted. "Oh."

"I never wished to make you feel like you didn't have a choice. I wanted you to choose to be with me because you loved me, not because you feared for your safety and your life." His thumb stroked the back of her hand. "Do you think there's still hope for us even though it is a little late to be asking?"

He loves me yet. Belle's heart fluttered. "I never thought of being a mail-order bride, or even wanted to be a bride until Angelique presented me with your letter. After I sent my answering letter, doubts began to creep into my heart, and I was dead set on sending you a rejection, but your second letter, your *real* letter, made me pause long enough to consider marriage as a viable option. I saw something in you in that letter, which grew with every letter afterward. I saw that you had something in your heart, which I had always wanted in a husband—kindness." She shook her head. "When we met, I was so surprised to find you in a lie that I discounted everything you wrote as false because that was how I was raised. But I know now that you *truly* are a kind person. You only lied because the truth wasn't yours to tell yet."

He turned to her, lifting the torch high, "Belle," he whispered, bending to her, his lips seeking hers when his eyes grew wide. "Duck!" He tugged her to the floor as the cavern filled with high-pitched screeches.

CHAPTER 23

*B*elle screamed as the sound of hundreds of tiny flapping wings flashed by their heads. Colt threw his arms around her shoulders, shielding her head as he cradled her against his body, the creatures brushing against them as they flew from the cavern.

Belle shuddered and slowly released her vice grip on Colt's plaid shirt, her fingers stiff after her fright. "What were *those*?"

"Bats." He beat his Stetson against his leg. "Nasty bloodsucking death birds." His eye twitched. "Let's get away from here . . . I don't want to risk them coming back." He picked up his torch, grabbed her hand, and hurried them along the damp path.

Belle nodded grimly before marching forward and straight into a puddle, the freezing water soaking her stocking. "What in the world?"

"My Pa used to tell me about an underground lake he discovered once on his explorations. I never really believed him though." He lifted his torch, the light reflecting off the water. "Always thought it was a tall tale." Colt hiked around the edge, Belle following closely behind. He stretched out his arm to see as far as his torch would allow to find an alternative way around. He groaned. "This is the narrowest point of the water. We only have to swim across about four yards to reach the other side. You *can* swim, right?"

"Of course. I'm from Charleston. Miss Fairfield used to take me with her for her swims in the river as a child and then every trip to the sea."

"A trip to the sea? That's a sight I think might unsettle me —no land beyond the beach." He handed her the torch and began unbuttoning his worn plaid shirt.

Belle felt her jaw dropping at his muscled chest. "Um. Why, may I ask, are you undressing?" She quickly averted her eyes as he stripped himself of his shirt. *Oh. Wait. I'm married to him.* She tentatively glanced at her husband's bronzed, toned torso. He turned and caught her gaze and grinned at her as if he knew she was admiring him.

Her cheeks blazed.

"It's too cold down here to walk around in a wet shirt the whole time." He explained, removing his chaps and rolled them up in his shirt and stuck the bundle into one of his saddlebags before pulling off his boots. "I'll have to hold the torch and the saddlebags above my head to keep them dry. I'll deposit them on the other side and then come back for you."

"Oh, of course." Belle switched her gaze to her hands when she realized that she would be walking around in drenched clothes for hours if she didn't follow suit. "Actually, I think I can swim across myself, but I'll need you to take my dress and, um, underskirts over with you," Belle mumbled, avoiding his gaze. "Mind you keep your back to me the entire time."

"Absolutely," he agreed and faced the lake as Belle quickly unlaced her shoes, peeled off her stockings and stuffed them into her shoes before unfastening the buttons on her uniform and petticoats. Standing only in her chemise, corset, corset cover and drawers, she bundled her petticoats inside her uniform and tossed the pile along with her shoes in front of Colt. "I'll be right behind you. Do *not* turn around unless I say I am dying."

"Yes, ma'am." He chuckled and with her dress and things rolled up in a bundle with his own clothes and boots in his right hand and her shoes dangling by their laces and torch in his left, he slowly lowered himself into the water and gasped. "Man alive that is cold." Within moments, he was to the other side, hauling his dripping, muscled torso out of the water by his taut arms. He scraped the droplets from his skin with his hand, keeping the torch upright, the light flickering against his glistening chest.

Belle was so distracted that she forgot to test the water. She lowered herself to her shoulders and gasped from the cold. "It feels like a pond about to ice over."

"Told you it was cold!" Colt called, laughing at her squeals.

Feeling something brush against her leg, her heart dropped into her stomach as she gasped again. "Colt! There's something in the water." She felt it brush against her leg again and screamed, kicking away at the creature and screaming again and again.

She heard a splash and felt Colt's arm wrap around her waist as he hauled her onto the cavern floor, dripping.

He scanned her arms and legs for bites as she whimpered.

"No marks. I think whatever it was down there was just curious."

Realizing that her legs were bare from the knees down, she hugged her knees to her chest, glancing at Colt. *I probably should be blushing, but my body is too cold.*

He swiveled on his knees and faced the opposite wall. "I'm sorry. I thought screaming like a banshee qualified as you sounding like you were dying."

"I would have to agree," Belle said through chattering teeth as she wrung out the hems of her under drawers. Seeing it was the best she could manage for now, she reached for her pile of clothes and made herself decent. "Well, that was miserable."

"Do you want my long coat?" He slipped on his boots, finishing his dressing.

"Thank you, but you wear it since your pants are soaked." She tied her shoelace and pulled her skirt over her ankle. "You can turn around now."

He sank down beside her and sighed. "I need a break after all that." He pointed to her lace necklace. "Is that your mother's?"

She slipped it from her neck and handed it to him. "Yes. I usually wear it under my uniform as jewelry and lace is against the Harvey House rules."

He held it in the flickering torchlight. "'Psalm 91.' Huh, that's an odd selection to have inscribed in a wedding band."

"You know it?"

He grinned, handing back the necklace. "Don't look so surprised. Just because I don't attend church regularly doesn't mean that I don't read my Bible every day. I enjoy memorizing as it helps me go to sleep at night. They are verses about trusting the Lord. I memorized these after Grant killed our brother."

"Can you recite them?"

"It may not be perfect, but if you want to read them—" He reached for his saddle bags, but she stayed his hand.

"I want to hear your recitation."

He closed his eyes and drew in a breath. "'He that dwelleth in the secret place of the most High shall abide under the shadow of the Almighty. . . He is my refuge and my fortress: my God; in Him will I trust. Surely He shall deliver thee from the snare of the fowler, and from the noisome pestilence. He shall cover thee with His feathers, and under His wings shalt thou trust . . . thou shalt not be afraid for the terror by night; nor for the arrow that flieth by day; nor for the pestilence that walketh in darkness; nor for the destruction that wasteth at noonday . . . For He shall give His angels charge over thee . . . they shall bear thee up in their hands, lest thou dash thy foot against a stone. Thou shalt tread upon the lion and adder . . . because he hath set his love upon Me, therefore will I deliver him: I will set him on high, because he hath known My name. He shall call upon Me, and I will answer him: I will be with him in trouble; I will deliver him . . .'"

"I can see why you memorized that chapter." Belle tucked a damp curl behind her ear as she leaned back on her hands. "I had forgotten until now, but I vaguely remember as a very small child, seeing mother cross-stitching those verses, but she was never able to finish it. When I asked her about it, she said it was a reminder . . . but I never knew for what." She shrugged. "I may never know, but if those verses were so important to my parents, I should study them once we are out of here." She swallowed. "If we get out of here. I am so sorry I didn't give you a chance to explain before. I knew God was calling me out West, but when I caught you in that first lie, I ran. I didn't wait for God to answer me. I merely acted. If I had waited for an answer, maybe we wouldn't have ended up in this cave."

"Or maybe it could have ended up much worse with Grant's return and your arriving early." Colt's hand covered hers. "I don't blame you for running from me. I didn't give you any reason to trust me."

"I do now," she whispered.

His eyes sparked in the torchlight. "You do?"

"Of course. You have proven again and again that I had misjudged you."

His fingers found the ribbon in her hand and lifted the precious silver wedding band. "Belle, you don't know what it means to me. My entire life, almost no one has ever trusted me with anything. To know that you trust me with your life—your heart." He swallowed. "Would you do me the honor of wearing this as a symbol of my love for you and my promise that I will always be truthful to you and will strive all of my days to make you the happiest woman alive?"

Belle's eyes filled with tears. "Is that what you truly want?"

"Nothing would make me happier."

"Not even making it out of this cave alive would make you happier?" She teased.

"Nothing would make me happier to have you accept this ring *and* get out of this alive so I can spend the rest of my life with you." He twisted the ring in his fingers. "Will you?"

"Yes," she whispered, and he gently slipped the ring onto her finger on her left hand. The torch flickered and both of them stared at the shrinking tree limb. "Our time is almost up."

He held his arm out to her, and she tucked herself beside

him, enjoying these last moments together in the light. With every step, Belle prayed for deliverance and at the torch's sputtering, she turned to face him, urgently memorizing Colt's features.

He gently brushed away her tear with his thumb. "If you are the last thing I see before I die, I will die a happy man."

Her eyes fell on his strong jaw and full lips. She felt a rush to kiss him. He leaned forward, but he only stroked back a lock of her hair. The torch began to dance until it twirled upwards and whipped downwards so wildly that it extinguished itself. Belle grabbed hold of Colt's hand, expecting to be enfolded in a blanket of darkness, but a faint stream of light to the right of the cave caught their attention. "Colt!"

"I see it. Please Lord, let it be a way out." Colt wrapped his hand about her waist and inched towards the light. The closer they approached, the more Belle could see. They were surrounded by overgrown vegetation spilling inward from a fifteen-foot-wide hole in the ceiling above, allowing the moonlight to flow into the darkness.

Colt hooted with delight and swept Belle off her feet, twirling her around. Without setting her feet to the ground, he halted and looked deeply into her eyes. He lowered his lips to hers in a tender kiss that stole her breath. Her hands wove from his shoulders to about his neck as she drew him to her. Her heart hammered at her forwardness. She kissed him back as he lowered her to her feet and wove his fingers in her hair—his kiss reflecting the urgency of her own to convey all that was in his heart. His kiss held promise, hope, and an ardency she had never before known.

With a jagged breath, he untwined his fingers from her locks and took a step back. "I'd like to revisit this kiss once I get us out of this cave, Mrs. Lawson."

She giggled, her cheeks heating. "I nearly forgot we were in here."

"Me too." Colt grinned and studied the distance between cavern floor to the hole in the ceiling and pulled out his whip. He pointed to what looked like a fallen log, which was covering a quarter of the exit hole. "If it's sturdy, it's our ticket out of here." He let loose his whip and with a mighty crack, it wrapped itself around the limb. He tested the braided leather and hand over hand climbed up a few feet before dropping to the ground. "This will work just fine. We will be out of here in no time, Mrs. Lawson."

She touched the rotating handle of the whip. "I am not certain my arms are strong enough to climb so high."

He kissed her on the forehead. "I'll climb up first and then lower the whip. With my arms adding length, you should easily be able to secure it around your waist and I'll lift you up." He smiled down at her. "I'm almost sad to leave."

"This cave of terrors?" She laughed, even though she felt it herself. The moment they left, they would be in a world that would question their hasty marriage and judge Colt for his past, despite his helping the law capture the Death Riders.

"Because this is where we will always remember that I first kissed you." He wrapped his arms around her. "And maybe, one day, you might say this is where you felt a little more than a friendship towards me."

Her lips parted. She was already in love with him and wished to tell him so, but the words were so much more difficult to say than write.

"You don't have to reciprocate my love right away. I only want you to know where I stand. I love you, Belle, and I want you to be my wife because you *wish* to be with me and not because you were forced to out of necessity, or because you thought you were going to die in a cave with me." He turned and leapt, grabbing hold of the rope and climbed hand over hand toward the moonlight and freedom.

He scrambled through the top and laughed with relief. His laughter died and Belle watched in horror as the mirth faded from his face as he caught sight of something . . . someone? With his gaze locked, he moved his finger a hairsbreadth back and forth, warning her to remain silent.

CHAPTER 24

Colt's fingers itched for a weapon as the Death Riders surrounded him, but his gun was long gone and his whip impossible to retrieve. Jill and Clyde were missing, but that didn't mean they weren't hiding in the trees, ready to take him down should he run. He slowly lifted his hands. "Grant. I would have thought you had your mind on that train robbery."

"Didn't go as planned." Grant rolled the wad of tobacco from one cheek to the other, releasing a stream of spit. "Where's your woman? The one that you would choose to abandon your own brother for rather than forsake?"

"You mean the one you were going to kill for no good reason?"

"She was turning you soft and I didn't rightly want to end another brother if I could help it. Now, where is she?"

Colt allowed his shoulders to hunch. "She slipped and fell into a chasm."

"Well, ain't that too bad." Grant snorted. "Russ, take a look around."

Russ slid from his saddle, his hand on his holster as he kicked about the bushes. "Come out, little missy."

He prayed she stayed hidden as Russ peered into the hole that opened into the cavern.

"See anything?" Grant called.

Russ sauntered back to the horses. "Nah, she's not down there."

"She could easily be hiding down there. The way my brother was protecting that girl, he'd sooner die than let her fall. When I said, 'take a look around,' I meant for you to climb down there and check it out."

Colt kept his expression blank. If they found her . . . Grant was right. He'd die before any of them laid a hand on her.

Russ found the log with Colt's whip. "Didn't pull it up yet, huh? She must still be down there."

"I didn't have a chance to retrieve it yet. How did y'all find me?"

Grant smirked. "I knew about this cave exit from Pa's journals. He had a map of this place. He wasn't too great of an explorer though as he missed that mammoth of an entrance on the other side." Grant chuckled, spitting again.

Russ disappeared in the mouth, lowering himself on the bullwhip until Colt heard him drop to his feet.

Cover and hide her in the shadow of Your wings, Lord.

"Don't see nothin' down here. I'm coming up." Russ pulled himself out of the cave, leaving Colt rattled, but grateful for the man's laziness as he left the braided leather whip dangling.

Grant lifted his revolver, pulled back the hammer, and aimed at Colt. "I told you to never lie to me, brother."

"What are you talking about? You knew I had feelings for Belle and yet, you tried to take her from me."

"At first, I thought the girl had addled your brain, but everything became clear when the train robbery went wrong. Jill got arrested after a good fight with the Texas Rangers. She even tried to warn us that *you* betrayed me."

"Grant, that's absurd. Why would I betray you—" A shot echoed through the grove of trees and Colt gasped. He sank to his knees, clutching his upper chest.

"You were working with them Texas Rangers." Grant holstered his gun, shaking his head. "My own brother deceiving me. First, Abel betrays me, and now you. Seems that I am the only Lawson worthy of preserving the family name."

"Grant . . ." Colt groaned, reaching out to him across the mouth of the cave with fingers dripping in blood.

"I shot you above the kill spot, so you'd have time to consider your ways before you died from blood loss, or infection." Grant turned his horse. "Only a brother would get a privilege like that from me. I'm sorry you made such a poor choice. Goodbye, brother. Use your last hours wisely before you bleed out." He motioned to his men and yelled, "Let's ride."

With the hoofbeats waning in the distance, Colt dared to whisper, "Belle?"

"Colt!" She called, voice jagged. "Colt, are you hurt badly?"

He grunted. *Have to get her out.* He crawled to the opening and grabbed hold of the leather. "Wrap around your waist." His forehead beading with sweat, he released his hold on the wound and drew her up, hand over hand until her arm wrapped about the fallen log. Upon seeing him, her face contorted.

He fell to his side with a groan, pressing his palm to the

wound, the pain radiating through his body. He reached out to her. "Y-you are safe now."

"Colt! What did he do to you?" Tears spilled onto her lovely cheeks.

He hated that he would never hold her in his arms again or kiss her until she blushed. "G-Grant was feeling generous. Shot me in the sh-shoulder. L-left me alive."

Belle ripped off the ruffle from her petticoat and pressed it against his wound to staunch the bleeding. "I don't know what else to do. How can I help you?"

He grunted. "Stop the bleeding if you can and then we can worry about getting the bullet out if I don't lose too much blood and die first." His torso convulsed. "S-so cold."

Belle paled as she unbuttoned the top of his shirt and managed to get the clothing off the wound. She pressed her hands firm on the exposed wound, praying for healing. "Jesus, help us. Please stop the bleeding. If his life is in my hands, he's a dead man, but in Your hands, he can be healed."

His breaths came in shallow gasps. "Y-you need to work on your bedside manner, wife."

She ripped a few more strips from her petticoat and turned him over. "There's an exit wound. Praise God." She pressed cloth against both sides and wrapped a long strip around his shoulder and across his chest, tying it as tightly as possible. "I have to run for the doctor. Surely, we aren't so far away from civilization."

"You won't make it in time." He panted, licking his dry lips. "I-I won't—"

She pressed her lips against his, the warmth causing his heart to spark—willing him to live.

"I have to try." She pushed back a lock of his blond hair.

The lovely vision of his wife blurred. "I love you, Belle. Don't ever forget that."

Her lip trembled. "Oh Colt, I love you too."

He closed his eyes. "I've waited so long to hear those words from your lips. I'm only sad I may never hear them again."

She touched her finger to his lips. "Shh, you mustn't speak that way."

He brushed away her tears with his shaking thumb. "When I saw you that first day, you became a thief too, because you stole my heart. I only wish I could've convinced you sooner . . ." His words gave way to a rattling cough. "I'm so sorry I lied."

"I've already forgiven you." She gently stroked his cheek with the back of her hand. "Keep fighting while I run for help. Tell me where to go."

He slowly nodded, even that action causing pain to ripple through him. "I suppose that's our only course of action. Head right. Go over t-the—" He panted, his words becoming more labored. "The creek and take a left. The town, Boerne, is about an hour ride from here." He took her hand and kissed it before giving into the darkness.

THE CRICKETS SANG as the moonlight filtered through the trees, illuminating Colt's still form. Belle lowered her ear to his mouth and thanked God that he was still breathing. She gently kissed him on the forehead. "I love you with all of my heart and with every breath in my body, Colt Lawson, and when I get back, I'll tell you again and again and again." She pressed her lips to his, her heart aching, praying it wouldn't be their last kiss.

Glancing both ways as if she would see Grant hidden in the shadow of the cedars, waiting for her, she drew a deep breath and picked up her skirts and ran through the trees, dodging the branches until at last, she burst through them.

Her side burned. She pressed her hand against it and jogged through the ever-present pain. Her chest hitched, but the thought of Colt lying alone and possibly dying kept her running. She stumbled over a brush and sprawled on the ground. She rolled over onto her back, groaning. Catching her breath, she dragged herself to her feet, determined to keep going. Her skirts grew heavier and heavier, and the high collar of her uniform felt like it was strangling her as it became drenched in sweat.

At last, she came upon the creek. Belle collapsed onto her hands and knees on the creek bank, dipping her face into the cool water and gulped a mouthful. Water dripping from her chin, she looked up at the full moon. Only days ago, the thought of running in the dark would have paralyzed her with fear, but the night was nothing like the darkness she had experienced in the caves. To her light starved eyes, the moon was as bright as the noonday sun.

Pulling off her shoes and stockings, she lifted her skirts above her knees and crossed the stream, the water stinging her awake. She stuffed her feet back into her shoes and began trotting again for about ten minutes when she heard them.

Their eerie, infantile howl chilled her blood. With renewed vigor, she charged through the trees, but with every step, it seemed as if the howls were getting closer. *Lord! Save me. I need to get Colt help.* She pumped her arms at her sides, sprinting across the prairie. Frantic, Belle gasped in pain as her side stitch grew unbearable, and she slammed to the ground. She rolled to her back and inspected the palms of her hands. Her right hand throbbed. Turning it over, she found a three-inch slit pouring blood. She ripped another strip from her petticoat, wound it around her hand and scrambled to her feet to run again, but something was wrong. She paused and listened. The howling had stopped.

Belle's heart raced as she glanced to her left to find a pair of yellow eyes glinting in the moonlight. She looked to her right—another three pairs of yellow eyes. Bending down, she grasped the rock that had cut her and another by its side. Clutching the rocks, she stared back at the coyotes. *Help me!* They bared their teeth and Belle lifted her arms above her head, yelling as loud and rough as she could when a horse charged over the hill. The rider fired into the pack, taking down three coyotes before the pack dissipated.

"Reid!" She screamed, her voice cracking. "Over here."

"Belle? Thank God. Are you well?" He rode up to her, leaping from his saddle and wrapping her in an embrace.

"Yes, but Colt has been shot. I need to bring him help." She sobbed, nearing hysterics before she realized his arms were still around her. She pushed herself away from him, wiping her tears. "We need to fetch a doctor."

"Where is he?" He looked over her shoulder as if expecting to see Colt nearby.

"Not too far by horse." She pointed behind her, still panting.

He took in her disheveled state. "You were running to Boerne alone?"

"If I didn't, he would die for certain." She lifted her chin, pushing her curls from her face. "Can you help him or not? I've left him alone for almost an hour now."

"I can." He grasped her elbow. "But you need to rest."

She jerked her arm away from him. "He may die still if we don't hurry. Please, either come with me now, or go for the doctor."

"He stands a better chance if I go to him first." Reid lifted her up into the saddle. "I've mended quite a few bullet holes in my day and even one of my own. I'll stitch him up first and then bring him to town." He swung himself up behind her and kicked his horse into a gallop, following Belle's directions back to the cave where the man who held her heart lay dying.

While the run had been arduous, it wasn't long until they burst into the grove. Belle dropped from the saddle and ran towards where she had left Colt. His still form brought a whimper from her lips as she knelt beside her husband and pressed the back of her hand to his forehead. Feverish, but alive. *Thank You, Lord.*

With his pack slung over his shoulder, Reid knelt beside them and assessed the wound before he slowly turned Colt on his back. Colt groaned, but mercifully remained unconscious as Reid unwrapped the bandage.

"You did a commendable job with your bandaging. I couldn't have done better myself. If you hadn't been so meticulous and Grant so lenient with his revolver's target, he could have easily bled out. There's an exit hole, thank the Lord. Judging from his blood loss, I won't need to cauterize it now. The doctor may later, depending on infection." Reid removed a small kit from his saddle pack, then opened his canteen and poured water over his hands, giving them a little scrub before opening the kit atop his handkerchief. "Best I can do without soap."

"You are going to sew him back together?"

"Yup." He poured water over the wound. Colt's brow knit in pain, but he remained silent.

"How long until we can bring him to town to see the doctor?" She looked away from the needle gleaming in the moonlight. She nearly laughed at her squeamishness. She could be chased by outlaws, captured, left for dead in a cave, and tend to Colt's gunshot wound, but a needle made her queasy?

"About a half hour. I don't want to wait around for his brother to come back and make sure that he is dead. Find some dried limbs and leaves to build a fire. I can stitch him up better with a little light and clean the needle properly."

Belle scrambled to her feet and gathered the kindling as she prayed for Colt's safety and for Reid's ability to sew him up. With an armload gathered, she hurried back and carefully stacked the wood, stuffing enough dry leaves for the wood to easily catch against a match. In a matter of seconds, the fire flickered to life.

Reid stuck the needle into the flames, turning it so that it was licked evenly. After the tip glowed red, he pulled it away and threaded it. "You're going to need to hold down his arms while I do this." He rent his knife through what remained of Colt's shirt, revealing the full extent of the damage.

Seeing his bare torso again, her heart ached at the memory of the last time she saw his shirt off. She placed her hands over his forearms to hold him back as Reid went to work closing the wound. Colt's arms went taut as he groaned. Belle swallowed back her tears but held firm. Belle kept her gaze on his face, trying not to think about the needle and the pain it was causing Colt. "How will we get him to the doctor?"

"A travois." Reid gritted his teeth in concentration as sweat began to bead on his forehead.

She glanced down to gauge Colt's wound and at once spied the bloody thread retreating back under Colt's skin. She closed her eyes. *Don't get sick.* She gasped against the spots in her eyes. "A what?"

"It's what the Indians use for transporting their sick or

wounded." He finished tying off the thread. "Got any more of those rags?"

Belle turned her back to the men before lifting up her black skirt to rip off another strip from her petticoat, which was growing scandalously short, but what was modesty in such a situation? She turned around and handed the strip to Reid.

He wrapped it around the top of Colt's chest before turning him to stitch up his back. With the stitches complete, Reid wrapped Colt's shoulder and back, grunting as he gave the petticoat a final tug for security and gently laid Colt down on his back. "You stay here and watch him. I'm going to go chop down two saplings and make the travois before Grant comes back."

"What makes you so certain Grant will come back?"

He shrugged. "Grant is going to regret not finishing him off, or regret having shot him. One way or the other, Grant will be back tonight. I've been following the Death Riders for a long time with Colt. He's a good man. I'd hate to see him end like this."

She spread Colt's shirt over him and fetched Reid's bedroll to spread it over his body. She gently stroked his hair back, her limbs aching with exhaustion. She curled on her side next to him with her head resting in her arm as she gazed at him.

Hearing Reid clear his throat, Belle sat bolt upright and realized that she had fallen asleep. She tucked her hair behind her ears, stood, and shook out her skirts.

"I thought if I used my bedroll in the middle instead of just rope, it would be more comfortable for him." He finished securing the travois to his horse. "Only problem is that I hope the ride doesn't jostle him out of it."

He must have retrieved the bedroll while I slept. She gritted her teeth, realizing what he must have thought of her seemingly lack of propriety and what he would think after her suggestion. "There's room enough for two and I don't weigh that much, so I can ride back here with him and make sure he stays as still as possible."

Reid's ears tinted. "Well, to do that, you would have to lay down next to him and I don't think you would find that very appropriate."

Belle cleared her throat. "Um, I may be able to settle your mind on that score. Colt and I are married."

Reid almost dropped Colt into the travois. He stepped away, his jaw clenching. "What did you say?"

"We had to wed to keep me safe from Grant." She tucked Colt's bullet laced long coat about him.

"Uh huh. I'm sure that's what he told you." He plucked a rock from the ground and hummed it into the trees, the rock whacking against a trunk.

"It's not like that at all. I *want* to be married to Colt. He's kind, sweet, caring, and only wants to protect me." *He is acting like he didn't cast my feelings aside.*

"I don't understand. I thought you were falling in love with me." Reid slapped his Stetson against his leg as he turned away, muttering. "I don't get it."

Colt moaned, and Belle knelt beside him and gently wiped his forehead with her cuff, deciding to ignore Reid's last statement. What was important now was Colt's survival. "Does the town suspect he's part of the Death Riders?"

"No one knows yet. But now that Grant obviously knows Colt is on the right side of the law, I'll send a telegram when we reach Boerne and clear his name while alerting all to the identity of the Death Riders now that I have the proof and witnesses to arrest them."

Colt coughed, leading to a gasp of pain. Belle pressed her

hand to her new husband's cheek, silently begging him to hold on a little while longer.

Reid tugged back on his hat. "Don't worry. He'll be fine. You stay with him the whole way and I'm sure he'll make it to the doctor's office in Boerne."

"Thank you, Reid." She crawled into the small travois and laid down beside her husband, tucking his head into her shoulder and spreading her arms to grip either side of the travois to lock him in as Reid gently prodded his horse forward.

The jolt startled Colt awake. "Belle? Belle, where are you?" He mumbled, his eyes glazed over as he lolled his head, trying to find her.

"I'm here." She released the pole of the travois and lifted his chin so that he could find her.

"You came back for me," he whispered, his eyes rolling back as his head bobbed.

"Of course I did. You didn't leave me, and I won't ever be leaving you, my darling."

CHAPTER 25

The train screeched to a halt, jarring her awake from her pallet in the baggage car. She fumbled, reaching to straighten her hat. She grasped at the air above her head before remembering that of course she didn't have her hat. She rubbed her cheek and felt the indention of her skirt in her face from where she had been resting her cheek on her knees that were drawn under her chin.

Since they couldn't afford to put Colt in the first-class sleeper cars, they decided to ride in the baggage car, so he could lay flat. She glanced at Colt beside her on the stretcher, sleeping peacefully thankfully due to the doctor's final dose of morphine after a week being watched over in the doctor's recovery room. Once it wore off, though, she would need to begin administering the herbal treatments. *Chamomile tea to get him to sleep along with crushing lavender and rubbing it on his chest with a carrier oil.* She went over the doctor's instructions once more. "Lavender is for sleeping, but Sage and Oregano are to help fight infection."

Reid snorted awake, lifting his Stetson and stretching his arms. "Thank God we made it to Las Vegas."

She patted her hair, shook out her skirts and smoothed them as Reid swung open the car door and helped her to the ground.

"Belle!" Angelique cried out, running towards her with Harriet—a lantern held high by each.

"I thought I would never see you again. Thank God you're unhurt." Angelique pulled away and held her at arm's length. "I was worried sick. Sick! What were you thinking riding into a group of outlaws by yourself?"

Harriet wrapped her arms around Belle. "When I arrived home, there was Mr. Elliot with Gil on his back atop the table, blood caking his clothes. I cried my eyes out with relief that Gil was found alive *and* with horror that you had just ridden to your doom. Mr. Elliot raced into town to fetch the doctor for Gil and to send help when he ran into Reid." She glanced over Belle's shoulder, "Speaking of which, I need to thank him for saving your life."

"While Reid did manage to save Colt, Colt was the one who saved me." Belle felt her cheeks heat with her secret.

"But isn't Colt one of them?" Angelique looked to Harriet as if for confirmation. "I thought Reid brought him back, so he could get him well enough for questioning before sentencing him for his crimes."

"You didn't get Reid's telegram then from Boerne?"

"Reid didn't mention anything about Colt's innocence. He only said that he found you both and when he'd be back." Harriet's brow wrinkled. "There's more to the story?"

"There's so much that needs explaining, but Colt is a good man. He's been secretly helping Reid to thwart the Death Riders' raids. Colt was doing everything in his power to capture Grant in the act of the train robbery and get him arrested for his crimes. Reid told me that Grant's bandana was tugged free during the robbery and was witnessed, which is enough for him to be put away, along with his gang." She sighed. "I'm sure Reid will clear Colt's name, but right now, I need make sure Colt sees the doctor. He hasn't been awake for more than a few minutes since we left the last town and I'm worried about him."

"Rudy will see to it." Angelique nodded to her husband who was climbing into the train car with Reid. "I'm so glad you are well, and that Colt is innocent after all. Rudy was so concerned for his friend, and the whole town was shaken by your disappearance."

Harriet nodded. "Miss Trent was arranging a search party for you when Ranger Reid said he had it under control and set out after you."

Rudy and Reid paused with Colt in the stretcher between them. "Angel? Colt looks pretty bad off and will need a place to stay in town. Would it be too much to ask—"

She put her hand up to halt her husband's question. "No need to ask. He will stay with us."

Rudy directed Reid onward and the ladies followed.

"May I stay with you as well?" Belle inquired. "I don't want to leave Colt alone overnight."

"Are you nervous about the Death Riders returning for him? I would say yes, but we only have the one spare room, so you'd have to make do with a cot in the kitchen." She said, muttering through the possible sleeping arrangements. "No, that won't do. Rudy won't mind taking the cot. You sleep with me."

"There's no need to displace Rudy. I will share Colt's room. You see—"

The women gasped. Angelique, at a loss for words, gripped Belle by the shoulders. "I know you two have grown close, but you cannot possibly stay in the same room. Even in separate beds . . ."

Belle lifted her left hand, her mother's silver ring glinting in the lantern light. "That's one of the things that occurred while we were away. Colt and I were married."

"What?" The ladies exclaimed in unison, pausing before the general store.

"I'll explain everything, but I need to see to my husband right now. Maybe we can have tea after the doctor sees to Colt?" She suggested, craning her neck to catch a glimpse of Colt as Rudy and Reid carried him on the stretcher to the side entrance of Angelique's home.

"I didn't even know you were still interested in Colt, and as far as I remember, you turned him down on multiple occasions." Angelique held the side door that led into her small parlor that shared a wall with the store.

"Well, I didn't really have much choice in the matter." Belle followed the men.

"He *forced* you into marriage?" Harriet crossed her arms. "Doesn't really sound like he's a hero, Belle."

Belle held her hands up, trying to hold their judgments at bay. "It's not as unscrupulous as it sounds."

"It sounds pretty bad to me." Angelique planted her hands on her hips, scowling.

"I'll explain everything at tea, and then, I will need to attend to a few things at the Harvey House, but first, I need to hear what the doctor has to say about Colt."

Harriet assisted Angelique with the tea while Belle stood outside the spare bedroom door, waiting to hear the doctor's initial assessment of Colt's wounds. Belle leaned her head back against the wall and closed her eyes, praying.

"Mrs. Lawson?"

She jumped, startled more by the address than by his hand on her shoulder. "Yes, Doctor?"

"Mr. Lawson is still unconscious, but it's a miracle there hasn't been any infection. He is to stay here for a week. Nothing less. We cannot risk moving him again."

"Angelique has graciously opened her home to us, and I'll be sure that he stays put."

"Good. I've given him some medicine, so he's sleeping comfortably. Check on him every thirty minutes or so. Reid informed me of your ordeal as well. Are you injured?" The doctor set down his medicine bag and nodded to her bandaged hands. "Did the doctor in Boerne see to you and your hands?"

"He did and told me to use the same herbal treatment he prescribed my husband. They are almost all better."

The doctor gathered his things. "Very good. Ranger Reid mentioned the herbal treatment to me, and I quite agree. Keep applying the herbs and let me know right away if he gets a fever, or you require more herbs. As for you, keep your hands clean."

"I will," she replied, shutting the front door with a sigh of relief that Colt was, for the moment, safe and healing. She smiled as her friends rolled the tea service into the parlor, hinting at their eagerness to hear her tale.

She joined them and accepted the full cup from Harriet, taking a sip and closing her eyes to savor the sweetness along with the homey crackle of the fire before she filled them in on her being captured, Colt's gallant rescue, their wedding, being lost in the cavern, Colt being shot, and her run for help.

"And once we arrived to Boerne, we stayed there for a week before the doctor agreed that he could be moved." Belle finished.

"So, you two really are legally married?" Angelique finished off her blueberry scone.

Belle helped herself to another cup of Earl Grey. "Everything is legal. Colt Lawson is my husband."

"I take it that you didn't manage to squeeze a honeymoon in between your adventures, so are you going to secure an annulment?" Harriet whispered. "I thought you were wanting to marry Reid?"

Belle's neck warmed. She plopped three lumps of sugar into her cup. "Our time has stitched us together, and whenever I am apart from him, I feel the threads pull."

"So, you love him then?" Angelique grasped Belle's hand.

Belle dipped her head. "I'm very fond of him."

"That's not what she asked," Harriet retorted, mirth making her eyes dance in the candlelight. "Fond of him? Really, Belle? Tell us."

She smiled down into her tea, watching the steam curl. "I love him, and he loves me."

The ladies squealed, which had Rudy opening the spare room door and raising his finger to his lips before closing the door again.

"But the thing is," Belle worried her bottom lip, "we were married under such unexpected circumstances that I think we both will need time to adjust to the idea of marriage. It's as if we are doing the courting after the wedding."

"With his injury, you will have plenty of time for talking." Angelique patted her hand and reached for a second scone.

"I hope so." Belle finished off her cup and sighed as she rested it in the saucer. "I suppose I should head over to the Harvey House for my official resignation and apologize to Miss Trent for letting her down after all."

"She'll understand that it was extreme circumstances which led you to breaking the contract by marrying Colt."

Harriet set aside her cup as well and rose. "Do you want me to come with you for emotional support?"

"Please. It helps having my friends about me after all that I've been through. Can you meet me first thing in the morning?"

"Are you sure you don't want to rest for the remainder of the week before charging back into the Harvey House? I'm certain they would understand," Harriet advised, concern in her voice.

"I had plenty of a respite in the baggage car. If I can get a few hours of sleep before the morning, I should be fine, and besides, I need to collect my things from the dormitory and change into something decent. But I have to admit that I'm rather dreading letting the Harvey House know that they will need a replacement. I'll sorely miss bringing in my own paycheck."

Harriet worried her bottom lip. "You may be able to have the fee waved, but I don't know. Only in the rarest of circumstances do girls get to break the contract without a penalty."

"I'd say this is a pretty rare situation," Belle laughed.

"Speaking of changing your clothes, I will draw you a bath now, if you'd like? Rudy had a bath installed this spring, so it is no trouble at all." Angelique slipped her hand into her apron pocket and held out a wrapped bar of lavender soap and a small tube of liquid Castile soap. "I laid out a fresh change of clothes for you that Harriet brought over from your room." Her cheeks tinted. "I figured you would not want to wear a nightgown just yet?"

"That would be heavenly," Belle sighed and bid the ladies goodnight, delighting in washing off the dust of travel before dressing in the simple shirtwaist and navy skirt Angelique set aside for her.

Belle stepped into the spare room. Colt's heavy breathing assured her that he was asleep. Spying the wooden rocking chair in the corner, she pulled it beside his bed, trying to be quiet, but accidentally scraped the hardwood floor in the process, jarring Colt awake.

"Belle? Belle?" He cried out, his head coming off his pillow. "Are you safe?"

"I'm here," she whispered, taking his hand.

"Belle?" He called again, not seeing her from her seat in the low rocker.

She perched on the edge of the bed and gently grasped his chin, drawing his eyes to her. "Shh, I'm here."

"I didn't . . ." He opened and closed his mouth as if the words were hard to release. "Didn't see you and I thought Grant—"

"All is well. The doctor gave you some medicine that is clouding your memories." She fetched the glass of water from the side table and placing her hand against the back of his neck, she lifted his head allowing him to quench his thirst.

He gasped for air between gulps until he nodded, and Belle adjusted the pillow and moved to return to the rocking chair, but his hand caught her wrist, staying her.

"Don't l-leave me."

"I won't. It's my turn to take care of you." She sank on the edge of the bed. "I'll be right here."

He closed his eyes, giving into sleep. Belle studied his strong jawline and his lashes that did little to soften the hard lines left by life. As the minutes ticked away, her back ached from holding her position, but not wishing to awake him by pulling away from his vice grip, she lowered herself onto the pillow only inches from his face. Her fingers itched to rake through his thick golden locks that were usually hidden under his hat. She traced his chin with her fingertip.

Colt mumbled in his sleep and wrapped his good arm around her waist, his body relaxing as if he was protecting her even in his sleep.

She swallowed—uncertain what to do. *If I move his arm, he'll jolt awake again, and I can't risk him busting his stitches.* She rolled her eyes at her reasoning. *Admit it. You want his arm around you.* Belle sighed as the weight of his arm seemed to push aside the fears of the past few days, and with it, her eyelids felt impossibly heavy. *I'll close my eyes for a second and move when it's time to apply his treatment again.*

COLT STIRRED, his shoulder flaring at the movement when he heard a faint snore. He glanced down and started at the sight of Belle curled up beside him, fully clothed with her head resting on his bicep. Had she been there all night? She groaned at his movement, stretching with her eyes closed, her fist meeting his nose. He chuckled. "Good morning."

"Oh!" Belle scrambled off the bed, tumbling back in her slumber and catching herself on the rocking chair. "I'm so sorry. Did I hurt you? You had called out last night, and I was trying to calm you. I didn't want your stitches to bust." Her face engulfed in flames.

"You didn't hurt me." He grinned. "It was a bit of a shock waking up with you on my good arm, but it was a good shock."

She glanced to the door. "I'll see if Angelique has breakfast ready and bring you some. You want breakfast? You probably want breakfast and some chamomile tea." Without waiting for an answer, she dashed for the door.

"Mrs. Lawson?"

Her hand paused on the door at his use of her new name. "Yes?"

"What do you want to do about us? I know that in the cave, you said you would give me a second chance, but now that we are out of danger. . ." His gaze rested on the ring.

She crossed the room and slowly sank beside him. "If you haven't changed your mind, I have not either."

Belle would be his bride in earnest? His chest expanded with hope and disbelief all at once. "Well, I suppose that settles it, because I still want our second chance too." He lifted her hand to his lips, wishing he were strong enough to wrap his arms about her and pull her onto his lap. "When I am well enough to be moved, we can go back to my ranch, but uh, it only has one bedroom, so I can sleep in the kitchen if you'd like."

"Oh?" Her brows raised. "And why would you do that?"

"To give you as much time as you need. I'd offer to sleep in the barn if that made you more comfortable, but I don't want to risk being so far away from you in case of—" He halted, not wishing to bring up *his* name.

"In case Grant comes home," Belle finished. She cleared her throat. "Before anything else, I need to call upon the Harvey House to speak with them about my contract."

So, he would be sleeping in the kitchen.

She paused at the door, smiling over her shoulder. "And a one bedroom sounds quite cozy to me."

CHAPTER 26

*B*elle smiled at her throng of Harvey Girl sisters in the dormitory parlor. *Who knew I could have so many friends?* "I'm so glad to see you all again," Belle grasped Harriet's hand as Fannie brought in a tray of baked goods for the girls to nibble on. Belle spied a piece of chocolate cake and reached for the slice, vividly recalling Colt's recommendation of it that first day. Taking a bite, her eyes widened. "This is divine. How could you all not have *made* me eat a piece of this before?"

"You shall have an entire cake for yourself if you'd like," Miss Trent said as she joined the group and hugged Belle. "Thank goodness you are unharmed, my dear girl. To think, our sweet little Harvey Girl taken by those horrid, dangerous men."

"It was terribly frightening," Belle speared another fluffy bite, sighing. "But thanks to a certain gentleman cowboy, I'm well."

Harriet's eyes sparkled as she added, "You'll never guess who it was."

"Who?" The ladies clamored. "Who!"

"My husband." Belle giggled at the earsplitting squeals, clapping her hands over her ears.

"You're married?" Fannie exclaimed.

"I've lost you already?" Miss Trent sighed. "Well, I knew it was going to happen eventually, but I didn't expect you to break contract after you were so adamant about remaining single. But how did it all happen? Weren't you opposed to marrying Colt?"

Belle set aside her plate and quickly attested to Colt's innocence and his using a marriage certificate to protect her from the malevolent hands of the Death Riders. The girls shivered at her account, and Miss Trent's face turned so white that Belle feared she would faint.

"You were so brave," Millie whispered. "If I had gotten lost in that cave, I would've died from fear."

"I would've died from the bats." Harriet hugged her arms.

"The cliff!" Miss Trent murmured.

"The underground lake," Fannie shuddered. "I can't believe you had to cross an underground lake with who knows what kind of monsters lurking in the water."

Belle shuddered. "At times, I thought I would perish from fear and exhaustion, but Colt was always there, reassuring me that it would be okay."

The girls sighed collectively at the thought of being rescued so romantically, despite the horrible shock that Jesse was a part of the Death Riders.

Miss Trent cleared her throat. "Well, I hate to mention this after all you've been through, but can you at least work for another week or two while we try to get a few more girls reallocated here? Las Vegas is always short staffed. If you do, I'm certain I can waive the contract fee as I did for Harriet."

Colt can't be traveling for two weeks anyway, so I might as well avoid the fee even if it means I must be away from him. She nodded and reached for her tea as the gong sounded from across the street and the girls jumped up from their chairs, scrambling out the door and to their stations in the dining room.

Miss Trent fetched her notebook, flipping to the week's shifts. "Will you be able to work nights? Or is that too much to ask of a newlywed?"

Belle ignored the heat in her cheeks and happily accepted Miss Trent's terms. For the next two weeks, Belle worked hard to please Miss Trent until replacements finally arrived and Dolly was more than happy to inform Belle that she needn't bother coming in anymore, but the rest of the ladies took the news with tears and cries of congratulations.

Even though Colt would never admit it, so as not to seem overbearing, she knew he missed her during her long hours at work. He would be relieved to hear that her days of being a Harvey Girl were at an end, and, to her absolute surprise, she found she was excited to begin this new chapter in her life—working alongside her husband on their ranch.

Belle hung up her uniform in the closet for the last time and donned her pretty bright red skirt, cream shirtwaist and red blazer and pinned on her chapeau. Her carpet bag was packed and waiting on the bed. The only thing remained was her treasure box. She lifted out her mother's handkerchief and gently wrapped her father's watch inside before tying it with a pretty blue ribbon, intending on giving it to Colt as a wedding present on their first day in their new home as he had lost Abel's in the cave.

Tucking her treasures inside her bag, she reached for Miss Sophia Fairfield's—*Mrs. Ashton's* letter and read it again, soaking in the delight that Sophia was happy and promised to come visit Belle next summer. Belle tucked the letter into her reticule, picked up her carpetbag, and left the Harvey House as quietly as she had come. Except, this time, she was a bride running to her groom and not away.

She climbed into the phaeton that the stable boy Jimmy had brought around to the dormitory for her and lifted the reins.

"Belle." Reid called from the sidewalk across the street. He trotted over to her. "Harriet just informed me that you were finished at the Harvey House." He swiped off his Stetson, running his fingers around the brim. Something on his vest caught in the evening light.

"Reid, did they make you sheriff?"

"After we got Grant in custody, I felt like my last mission was finally complete." He swallowed. "I'm tired of riding across the states and think it's time to settle down. As the town's sheriff was arrested himself for the kidnapping of Miss Fairfield, they were going to hire someone anyway, so I threw my hat into the list of names."

"Lorna will be thrilled." Belle smiled. "And so will a lot of the single Harvey Girls."

"Good. Good." He shoved his hands in his pockets, and, for the first time, the confident Ranger seemed ill at ease. "And you were right before . . . I was arrogant in assuming that you cared for me more than a friend." He cleared his throat. "I also wanted to let you know that I respect Colt for his correcting actions—for taking care of you. I received word from the ranger headquarters, and with the capture of all the remaining Death Riders, Colt has officially been granted a pardon, so you don't have to worry about your husband being carted off to jail. Have a good evening." Before Belle could respond, he trotted across the street and up into the sheriff's office.

Heart soaring at the good news, she directed Rogue down

the main street toward the ranchero where Colt was supervising his ranch hands. She grinned as she snapped the reins, anticipating Colt's surprise that she was at last coming home to him with the good news of his being pardoned.

The horse seemed eager to stretch his legs after being boarded for so long and soon, the town was far behind them, and she was nearing the ranchero's threshold. She pulled back the reins, craning her neck to look up at the fresh sign. *Belle Ranch.* She pressed her hand to her chest and snapped the reins, eager to kiss her handsome cowboy.

The last time she was here, she saw it as a prison that held Gil, but now, she looked at the ranchero with new eyes. It was set in a field of wildflowers with a cedar tree gently caressing the corner of the rooftop. *What a lovely view I will have from my kitchen window.* Belle smiled as she caught sight of the flowers blossoming as if to welcome her home.

Colt rose from his rocking chair, flicking back the brim of his hat, concern in his eyes until she lifted her hand in greeting. He trotted down the steps to her phaeton.

"Welcome home, Mrs. Lawson." Colt held his hand up for her.

Not wanting to injure him, she lightly placed her fingertips in his hand, but leaned more on the side of the phaeton to bear her weight as she hopped to the ground.

"Did your shift end early?" Colt kept his hands on her waist.

"Sure did." She giggled, darting away from him and retrieving her carpetbag.

His eyes widened. "You planning on staying?"

She felt her cheeks bloom, but she kept her smile in place and walked backwards to the house. "Would it be all right with you if I did?"

Colt caught her hand. "Look here, little missy. I know this

was a rather unconventional marriage, but I cannot allow my bride to cross the threshold like that."

She looked down at her red dress, worried that she had stained it. "Like what?"

He closed the distance between them and swept her up into his arms.

"Colt! Your wound." She protested, dropping her carpetbag in her concern that he would bust his stitches.

"Will be fine. You weigh next to nothing, and if you stop arguing, I can put you down once you are safely on the other side." He crossed the threshold in two strides and carefully set her on the pine-planked floor. "I know it isn't as large as the Elliot ranchero, but it's comfortable and I built it with my own two hands." He studied her face, trying to gauge her reaction to her new home.

She ran her fingers over the framed picture that she had sent Colt so long ago and took in the beautiful beams on the ceiling and the hardwood floors. The room was bare besides the braided rug with a solid rectangle table atop. "Such a large table for one man," she commented and ran her hand across the smooth surface.

He stuck his hands in his pockets and shrugged. "I built it when I wrote to you asking you to be my wife the first time. I figured we'd need a good size table for our family one day."

She blinked her tears away. She ached to reach for his hand. In the cave, touching had been so easy, but after two weeks apart with her living at the Harvey House, she felt shy, and Colt seemed to sense it as he grasped her hand in his. "It's lovely, Colt."

"I'm glad you like it." He squeezed her hand and slowly released it with a sigh, "Well, I wish I would have known you were coming, or I would have seen to this sooner instead of taking a rest on the porch, but I need to check and see how the new ranch hands are getting along." He set her carpetbag on the table, tugged on his Stetson and headed for the door. "Make yourself at home and I'll be back as soon as I can, darling."

Belle crossed the pine floors, admiring the craftsmanship of each room. It wasn't as sprawling as the Elliots' ranchero, but the care with which Colt built this home for them was hewn in every beam, painted across every wall. She found Colt's bedroom—their bedroom. To her shock, every piece was store bought and as fine as any in the Fairfield's home in Charleston. She unpacked her carpetbag, hung her dresses, and set out his present atop the dresser. The four-poster bed with a mosquito net called to her weary bones. *Maybe a quick nap would be best before attempting to make dinner.* Slipping off her shoes and jacket, she crawled atop the quilt and fell fast asleep.

Belle tossed and turned as the memory of the darkness suffocated her. She was back in the cave, scaling the wall, but this time, she missed her step on the ledge, and Colt wasn't there to catch her. Instead, Grant was there. He grasped her by her neck, and she tried to scream, but she had no air in her lungs. She whimpered and moaned, crying for Colt to save her.

The door to the bedroom burst open, and she was suddenly very aware of Colt standing next to her with his shirt unbuttoned, his blond hair standing up every which way. "Belle? What's wrong?"

She sat up, finding a blanket spread over her. How long had Colt been home? "I'm sorry. It was only a nightmare. I think the coyotes outside made their way into my dreams." She crossed her arms over her chest, shivering. "How long have I been asleep?"

He sat down on the edge of the bed. "Not sure, but its nearing midnight now."

"What? No." She shoved aside the blanket, even as she shivered. "I meant to make you dinner for our first night home.

He rested his hands on her shoulders. "You've been working night shifts for too long and needed your rest. Do you need me to find another blanket?"

She shook her head, her dark curls spilling over her shoulders. "It's just my nerves."

He stood, concern lingering in his eyes. "Well, if you need me, I'll be right around the corner in the kitchen."

She grabbed his hand and gently pulled him back towards her. "Would you mind staying with me?"

He looked unsure. "Uh . . . in here?"

"Please? Just lay next to me," she whispered, her heart beating faster at the thought of him so close to her, but her fear rose at the thought of him being so far away. She had gotten used to having him near in the dark after the cave.

"If you are sure," he said as Belle scooted over and made room for him.

"There's been a lot in my life I haven't been certain of, but you, Colt Lawson, are not one of them."

Colt lowered himself beside Belle, gently placed his arm around her waist and stroked her hair as if to protect her from bad dreams. She smiled and drifted off to sleep, knowing she was safe and loved at last.

Author's Note

Dear Reader, thank you so much for reading Book Two in the Aprons & Veils series! If this is your first time reading about the Harvey Girls, know that they did indeed exist. In the 1890s, there were not many respectable jobs for women, so when Englishman Fred Harvey created his chain of fine dining restaurants along the Atchison, Topeka, and Santa Fe railroads, single women without an education, or in need of earning their own way, were given a chance to earn an honest wage without the speculation that they offered anything else but food as a service.

With Mr. Harvey's strict rules about the waitress's code of conduct, the women were given their independence while still maintaining their good name and place in society under the protective, fatherly arm of Fred Harvey. These extraordinary, brave women became known as the Harvey Girls, the ladies who tamed the Wild West with fine china, good pie, and exceptional service with complete propriety.

For the purpose of my story, I did take some small liberties with the Hotel Castañeda, but I did attempt to stay as close as possible with the historical pictures and references available. This Harvey House is one of the few still standing and has been fully restored to operate once more.

If you enjoyed the story, I would love if you could please take a moment and leave a review or rating. Happy reading, friends!

Grace Hitchcock is the award-winning author of multiple historical novels and novellas. She holds a master's degree in creative writing and a Bachelor of Arts in English with a minor in history. Grace lives in the New Orleans area with her husband, Dakota, and their sons and daughter. Join her at GraceHitchcock.com

Sign Up for Grace's Newsletter!

Keep up to date with Grace's news on book releases and giveaways by signing up for her email list at GraceHitchcock.com

More from Grace Hitchcock

Forced into a betrothal with a widower twice her age, Charleston socialite, Sophia Fairfield is desperate for an escape. But, while her fiancé is away on business, he assigns his handsome stepson, Carver, the task of looking after his bride-to-be. Much to her dismay, Sophia finds herself falling in love with the wrong gentleman —a man society would never allow her to marry, given Sophia was supposed to be his new stepmother. The only way to save Carver from scandal and financial ruin is to run away, leaving him and all else behind to become a Harvey Girl waitress at the Castañeda Hotel in New Mexico.

The Finding of Miss Fairfield by Grace Hitchcock
APRONS & VEILS #1
GraceHitchcock.com

You May Also Like...

Upon her father's unexpected retirement, his shareholders refuse to allow Willow Dupré to take over the company without a man at her side. Presented with thirty potential suitors from New York society's elite, she has six months to choose which she will marry. But when one captures her heart, she must discover for herself if his motives are truly pure.

My Dear Miss Dupré by Grace Hitchcock
AMERICAN ROYALTY #1
GraceHitchcock.com

A very public jilting has Theodore Day fleeing the ballrooms of New York to focus on building his family's luxury steamboat business in New Orleans and beating out his brother to be next in charge. But he can't escape the Southern belles' notice, nor Flora Wingfield, who is determined to win his attention.

Her Darling Mr. Day by Grace Hitchcock
AMERICAN ROYALTY #2
GraceHitchcock.com

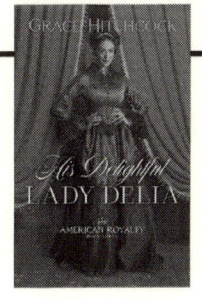

After years of being her diva mother's understudy, it's time for Delia Vittoria to take her place on stage. Attempting to make amends for a grave mistake, Kit Quincy is suddenly pulled into Delia's plot to win the great opera war and act as her patron and an enigmatic phantom. But when a second phantom appears, more than Delia's career is threatened.

His Delightful Lady Delia by Grace Hitchcock
AMERICAN ROYALTY #3
GraceHitchcock.com

Praise for Grace Hitchcock's Novels:

"Sparkling with vivacious energy, this romance launches Hitchcock's American Royalty series.... Fans of the TV's *The Bachelorette* will adore this historical spin on competitive courtship that features all of the glitz, glamour, and drama that the Gilded Age brought to New York City's elite."

Booklist on *My Dear Miss Dupré*

"To the modern reader, the plot of this book is reminiscent of the popular reality show, The Bachelorette. In what is a unique take, author Grace Hitchcock has combined the modern with the old fashioned by setting her book at the height of America's Gilded Age. . . .Overall, the book is amusing and entertaining, a relatively quick read. The characters are interesting and possess great depth."

Historical Novels Review on *My Dear Miss Dupré*

"In 1893 Chicago, the World's Fair brings excitement to residents and visitors, and danger to a group of young ladies in this rousing solo debut novel [. . .] Hitchcock keeps the pace quick and tension high as the characters face dangers both physical and emotional. Readers will enjoy the snappy dialogue, vivid depictions of the famous World's Fair, and the surprising historical details."

Publishers Weekly on *The White City*

"A delightful romp! *His Delightful Lady Delia* is full of yearning and humor and just the right touch of old-fash-

PRAISE FOR GRACE HITCHCOCK'S NOVELS:

ioned Victorian melodrama. Delia's upstanding character and her quest for acceptance make her an endearing heroine, and Kit offers dash and integrity and a trace of vulnerability. Enjoy!"

Sarah Sundin, bestselling author of Until Leaves Fall in Paris

"*Her Darling Mr. Day* is a delightful and charming romantic romp. Grace Hitchcock has created wonderful characters who face mystery and adventure while falling in love. I know my readers will find this novel as endearing as I did and highly recommend it."

Tracie Peterson, Bestselling Author

"Grace Hitchcock does an excellent job of weaving history of the era and Louisiana region into the romance with well-drawn characters, who came alive in their first scene and stole their way into this reader's heart. A gutsy heroine with determination to spare, trapped in society's rules of the day, had me cheering for her from the beginning. *Her Darling Mr. Day* kept me reading when other things needed doing."

Lauraine Snelling, Bestselling Author

"Delightfully original! Set during the glittering Gilded Age, *My Dear Miss Dupré* is a captivating story that will charm readers from the first page until the last. Grace Hitchcock is a writer to watch!"

Jen Turano, *USA Today* Bestselling Author

Made in the USA
Columbia, SC
21 March 2024